Sherlock
Holmes
Consulting Detective

Volume Ten

AIRSHIP 27 PRODUCTIONS

™

Sherlock Holmes: Consulting Detective, Vol. 10

"The Affair of the Norwegian Sigerson" © 2017 I.A. Watson
"The Problem of the Unearned Beard" © 2017 Aaron Smith
"The Adventure of the Irregular's Innocence" © 2017 Greg Hatcher
"The Problem of the Theatrical Thefts" © 2017 Aaron Smith

Cover illustration © 2017 Graham Hill
Interior illustrations © 2017 Rob Davis

Editor: Ron Fortier
Associate Editor: Fred Adams Jr.
Production and design by Rob Davis
Promotion and marketing by Michael Vance

Published by
Airship 27 Productions
www.airship27.com
www.airship27hangar.com

ISBN-13: 978-1-946183-28-6
ISBN-10: 1-946183-28-8

Printed in the United States of America

10 9 8 7 6 5 4 3 2 1

Sherlock Holmes
Consulting Detective
Volume X

TABLE OF CONTENTS

Sherlock Holmes

in

"The Affair of the Norwegian Sigerson"

(A Novella)

By

I.A. Watson

"You can file it in our archives, Watson. Some day the true story may be told."

Mr Sherlock Holmes' last published words,
from "The Adventure of the Retired Colourman"
in *The Case-Book of Sherlock Holmes*

The account of Dr John Watson, 25th June 1891:

olmes was dead.

The reality of it crept in slowly as we stood in Highgate Cemetery beside a grave that contained no corpse. Holmes was lost, fallen into the Reichenbach torrent in final struggle with the deadly Professor Moriarty. Neither body had been recovered from that terrible cataract. The locals of Meiringen were unsurprised; other men fallen to the cascade had been swept into hidden underwater channels and swallowed forever.

The vicar droned on, promising resurrection and eternal life. I was reminded of all too many military padres repeating the same words over all too many comrades lost to battle. Surely Sherlock Holmes had fallen nobly, to a struggle just a fierce and no less important than theirs?

Mary sensed my bleak mood. Her grip tightened on my arm in sympathetic support. She has as much to be grateful to Sherlock Holmes for as any person present; Holmes had recovered for her an inheritance of Agra treasure and saved her life. If not for Holmes I would never have met Mary. She would never have become my wife.[1]

I controlled my emotions. My grief was too great to unleash, too vast to chronicle.

I was far from alone at the memorial ceremony. Three or four hundred mourners crowded the wet turf to offer their respects. Holmes' friends, allies, and clients gathered around the empty grave to pay tribute to that remarkable man. On my other side stood Mrs Hudson, stiff and pale, unwavering in her devotion to Holmes even after his death. She had already confided that because of the bequest he had left her in his will she had no need to let his rooms again. They would remain as he had quit them, a memorial to the great detective.

---

1 Governess Mary Morstan engaged Holmes' services to investigate *The Sign of the Four*, the second full-length Holmes novel, later often published as just *The Sign of Four*.

Beyond our bombazine-swathed housekeeper stood a long line of policemen, some uniformed, others in the strange cheap suits and long-coats that pass for plain clothes amongst the detective branch of Scotland Yard. Gruff Tobias Gregson stood soberly shoulder to shoulder with his long-time rival Lestrade. Behind them gathered Bradstreet, Hopkins, Barton, Forrester, Brown, Forbes, Hill, MacDonald, Patterson and the rest, a contentious honour guard for a man who had variously helped and confounded them on countless cases.

Many of our clients were present. I had exchanged a brief word with Musgrave before the service and traded nods with Baskerville, Trevor, Phelps, Miss Violet Hunter, and a dozen other men and women who owed their safety, reputation, or sanity to my fallen friend.

I recognised many academics and professional men in the crowd, scholars who had exchanged correspondence on Holmes' many monographs, specialists to whom he had referred enquiries, allies in his investigations. My friend Lomax of the London Library was amongst those come to pay his respects.

Across the turf on the humbler side of the assembly a great press of cabbies, runner-boys, flower-girls and street toughs kept vigil in uncharacteristic silence, hats held between their fingers. Wiggins, erstwhile leader of that scrub of street-arabs that Holmes had dubbed his Baker Street Irregulars, attended with his new fiancée, failing to hold back tears for the man who had given him his chances in life. A girl I knew only as Martha, whom Holmes had employed as an undercover informant, looked as if she might faint. Cartwright of the Express Office had his eyes screwed shut. Even the scent-hound Toby sensed the sombreness of the occasion, crouched to the floor beside his master Sherman, his expression mournful.

Of all those gathered, only Holmes' family were conspicuous by their absence. Even Mycroft, Holmes' sedentary elder brother, had felt unable to bear attending the service. Surely the great press of mourners and their profound and earnest sorrow would have comforted him had he been able to come?

The vicar pronounced the benediction. Mary and Mrs Hudson laid flowers upon the grave. Holmes has always been fond of honeysuckle. A great swell of well-wishers filed past the memorial, which gave Holmes' name and dates and was subscribed, "The best and wisest of men".

I tried to avoid the crowd but it was natural that those who had known of my close friendship with Holmes would wish to seek me out and offer what solace they could. I nodded and muttered platitudes back at a multitude of kindly remarks, little heeding from whom they came. Mary held my sleeve close and supported me as I struggled to survive.

"Is it certain that he is dead?" That was asked of me time and again. It was a question I had wracked myself with night after night, awake in my bed.

Yes, it was certain. Holmes had met James Moriarty on the narrow unguarded path atop the deadly falls at Reichenbach. The great detective had finally broken that old schemer's empire. On 27th April a dozen trusted confidantes received sealed instructions and evidence to bring down Moriarty's forces in Britain and Europe. Within twenty four hours police on four continents had sprung into action, galvanised at last by the careful deductions and detailed plans my friend had dispatched.

Holmes had calculated that the destruction of the Professor's organisation would require a week. If Moriarty could eliminate Holmes within that time then that pervasive web of criminal endeavour might be saved, restored in time as great or better than before by the brooding black spider who dwelled at its centre. If Holmes retained his freedom for a mere seven days then no genius however dark might restore the painstaking felonious work of a decade.

We had fled, Holmes and I, scarcely ahead of the best assassins that the most dangerous man in the world could command. Moriarty's hellhounds pursued us without let from Victoria Station to Canterbury, cross-country to Newhaven, across the Channel to Dieppe. We avoided them for a while by flight to Brussels and Strasbourg, but there a telegram awaited us with news that Moriarty himself had avoided capture, had eluded Lestrade, Gregson, and the entire force of British law.

I see in retrospect that Holmes knew a final encounter with the escaped Professor was inevitable.

Our flight took us up the Rhône valley, then up the Leuk, over the snow-choked Gemmi Pass down to Interlaken, and thence to the village of Meiringen with its neat proper Englischer Hof. It was from there that we diverted to view the famous waterfall, and on that precarious ledge that the urgent note came, supposedly from the innkeeper summoning me to assist an English lady who had fallen seriously ill.

Holmes knew when I parted from him to hasten to her assistance that his enemies had closed upon us. Holmes sent me away to spare my life from Moriarty and his marksman.

Such a meeting it must have been, those dreadful implacable intelligences clashing in close proximity for only the second time. Moriarty allowed Holmes a short time to leave a farewell account for me of what had happened. I wonder if the Professor availed himself of the opportunity to leave a similar message for his second? And then, thwarted by each other's intellects, finally matched in schemes and insight, that awful rivalry had culminated in physical action, grappling atop that precarious ledge above the devastating drop.

I have previously diaried, though I doubt I shall ever publish, my account of those terrible hours; my discovery of the ruse that had been perpetrated to separate me from my friend, my hastened journey with heaving chest and heavy heart back to Reichenbach; my discovery of Holmes' note weighted beneath his cigarette case. So passed Mr Sherlock Holmes in service of humanity, in ending the greatest evil of our modern age.

Of course I made sure he was gone.

I was there a week, assisting the police and representatives of the British Embassy dispatched by Mycroft. I watched as dragnets were cast across the basin pool and as hunters trekked along the river banks searching for the lost men. Hundreds of searchers, known and unknown, joined together to seek those fallen foes. All to no avail.

By the end, every expert on the scene was prepared to swear that no man who had plummeted from that height into the cauldron below the falls could have survived. A drowned man or one broken to destruction by such a terrible fall might be carried away through the uncharted underwater channels that drained Reichenbach. His corpse might never be found.

With a heavy heart I braced myself to return to England with the worst of news for Holmes' friends and supporters.

All that remained was Highgate and a last farewell.

The sun was shadowed behind clouds as the funeral party dispersed. Many people did not depart immediately, as if retreating from the graveside would be an acceptance that Sherlock Holmes was truly gone.

Lestrade edged up to me whilst Mary was talking with Miss Hunter. "A private word?" he murmured.

I stepped aside with him. Stanley Hopkins followed us, evidently by arrangement.

"What is it?" I asked, keeping my voice low.

"We've acted on all Mr Holmes' instructions now," Lestrade reported to me, in the manner of a soldier reporting to a deputy commander when his superior officer was lost in the field. "We've taken almost all of them, those that survived to be taken. Only three or four of the top men have slipped the net for now."

"Three or four might still cause problems," I judged. "Moriarty chose his lieutenants well. How did they elude you?"

"There was a bungled arrest in Liverpool, a case of mistaken identity in Cardiff. At least one of the targets was out of Britain when we swooped on the rest: the Professor's assassin gunman."

"Ah, yes. Makes sense that he would have been on the Continent with his master in those final days of the hunt. Perhaps he was even close by at Meiringen, waiting for his chance?"

Lestrade grunted acknowledgement. He and Scotland Yard had failed to detain Moriarty. I knew that the Inspector somewhat blamed himself for Holmes' loss, although no man might have taken the Napoleon of Crime with any certainty of success save Holmes himself. "From what we can gather, operations in Europe, America, India, and Africa have met with success," the Inspector advised. "I've heard from Dubugue in Paris and Leverton of the Pinkertons, and I received a brief cable from Von Waldbaum in Danzig proclaiming victory. Others will follow."

"Then Holmes would adjudge his sacrifice well spent," I admitted.

The Scotland Yard men frowned. "There's something else," Hopkins confessed. "Have you heard anything, doctor, about new men entering the underworld?"

I had not. "There will inevitably be some changes in the hierarchies of the criminal classes," I considered. "Moriarty's entire command structure has been apprehended or set to flight, along with many of the malefactors who consulted him for aid in committing their misdeeds. Nature abhors a vacuum. I suppose that is true of felonious society too."

Lestrade nodded soberly. "That's true, Dr Watson. And I'll shed no tears over the throat-cuttings and back-stabbings amongst thieves and murderers that followed on from our Moriarty investigation. But Hopkins here believes there might be a new attempt to organise, someone seeking to capitalise on Moriarty's downfall. I am tending to agree with him. We had hoped…"

"I am not Sherlock Holmes, gentlemen," I had to remind them.

"None of us is," sighed Hopkins. Of all the Scotland Yard men he was the one who most tried to emulate the great detective's methods, albeit with limited success. "Still…"

I beckoned across for Wiggins and Billy to come and join us. They trotted over, the Diogenes Club's newest steward and the likely young lad who had once been our house-page.

"Have either of you heard about some new criminal taking hold where

Moriarty's men have so lately been uprooted?" I asked them.

Billy's irreverent grin flashed briefly across his face. "So we're *not* giving up! I knew we wouldn't, sir. 'E wouldn't want us to!"

Wiggins rolled his eyes at his eager fellow. "I can ask around for you, Dr Watson. There's a few whispers, that maybe not all the disappearances an' odd things were just score-settling or local disputes once Moriarty's restraining 'and was gone. There's an awful lot of Krauts in London all of a sudden, and none of 'em making 'emselves popular down the docks."

"The blokes what sorted out the Keeling Crew?" Billy speculated. "And come to think of it, there was that barney at Madge Cotter's Cockfight Pit."

"Where would that be, my lad?" Lestrade asked, reaching for his notebook.

"No clue, guv'ner," Billy answered. He somehow managed to keep his face straight.

"It's no matter what's already 'appened," Wiggins suggested. "It's what 'appens next, innit?" It occurred to me that in his new role as a liveried messenger to the reclusive members of the powerful and influential Diogenes Club, young Wiggins was in a position to hear everything, and to report what mattered to that institution's most prominent member, civil servant Mr Mycroft Holmes. "I'll ask the lads to keep an ear out."

"I'll see what can be done as well," Billy promised. I wasn't clear what our ex-page was doing these days. I determined to ask Mrs Hudson when opportunity allowed.

Lestrade addressed me, not the cheeky commoners who were denying him information. "If you happen to learn anything, doctor, it would very much appreciated."

"And if you have time," chimed in Hopkins, "feel free to help us sort through the notes that Mr Holmes left us. There are crates of them, dossiers on hundreds of criminals great and small. If we can't assemble prosecutions from some of the material that Mr Holmes left us then I'll eat my hat."

I made vague promises to look over the files. The Scotland Yard men departed to their duties. The Baker Street boys shuffled away to cause trouble and hear secrets.

At last only Mary and I remained. "I'll take a short stroll," my wife told me. "Show Sherlock what you brought for him."

I felt ridiculous addressing a dead man at a grave he wasn't even in. Even so, I reached into my coat pocket and pulled out the flimsy magazine I had folded there.

"This came out today," I told the headstone. I held out the new edition of *The Strand Magazine*. "I have placed an account of you in here, Holmes. A memorial. Not a full book this time, just a short piece describing a case which seemed to especially affect you. I changed some names to protect illustrious identities, but it felt right to describe your encounter with Miss Adler."[2]

A photograph of the opera singer, given to her lover and claimed from him by Holmes, was ever present on my friend's desk. Irene Adler was, to Holmes, the epitome of her sex, and when he spoke of her he never felt the need to qualify her as anything other than The Woman.

"Anyway, I have released a number of stories for Doyle to print, couched as fiction," I went on. "I hope that is all right. I want the world to know who and what you were. You will not be forgotten. Never."

I turned away and returned to Mary, forced at last to believe that my dearest friend was gone and that our adventure was over.

A Private Memoir of Madame Irene Adler, 25th June 1891:

It was Thursday, which management assured me was always the quietest house of the week. Box office would improve on Friday, be substantial for Saturday's matinee, and all seats would be sold for that evening's grand finale. I had been told privately that Prince Nicolas would be in the royal box and that he had expressed a fervent desire to meet me.

A decade ago I would have been thrilled. A Trenton girl on an adven-

---

2 This would be "A Scandal in Bohemia", the first published Holmes short story and one of literary agent Arthur Conan Doyle's favourites. Originally released in *The Strand Magazine* dated July 1891 but circulated in late June, then collected in 1982 in *The Adventures of Sherlock Holmes*, the account of Holmes' brief encounter with and response to the American adventuress has elevated Miss Adler's significance in the Canon above any other female character. Like Moriarty, she shared only two brief scenes with the great detective in the accounts published by Doyle, and like him she has made her way into other media as an essential Holmesian cast member.

As early as William Gillette's 1899 stage adaptation *Sherlock Holmes*—the one that first established Holmes with hooked pipe and deerstalker hat—Irene Adler appeared as the detective's romantic interest, albeit under the pseudonym Alice Faulkner. That production ended with her marriage to Sherlock Holmes.

Mme. Adler is discussed further in the afterword to this story, "The Apocryphal Holmes".

ture across Europe, new to the operatic stage and just building a following, I was then still dazzled by the glitter from royal crowns. I no longer have any interest in dalliances with men of noble line. I thought I was done with matters of the heart.

That afternoon had been rehearsal. I insisted upon it. The orchestra at the Zetski Dom theatre-cum-opera house was enthusiastic but not entirely as versed in supporting vocal music as I might have wished. Our opening performance had been reasonable but lacking in true professionalism. *Rigoletto* requires precision. We would practice until we had it right. Cettigne[3] in Montenegro might be as provincial a national capital as was possible in Europe but music and art must never be compromised.

I returned to my dressing room to rest my voice for a while and to catch up on my reading. I settled in a comfortable armchair away from my make-up desk and business escritoire and kicked off my shoes. I allowed myself a dip into a sinfully luxurious box of Swiss chocolates that I had bought for myself (not one from the pile of gifts from admirers that was stacked up by the door for other members of the company to help themselves) and allowed the heady liqueur to melt upon my tongue for the sheer sensual pleasure of it.

Well why not? It was the anniversary of my not-divorce.

Godfrey Norton and I exchanged our wedding vows under extraordinary circumstances on 21st May 1887, at St Monica's on Edgeware Road, London, England. The notorious consulting detective Sherlock Holmes was present as our principal witness, albeit he was disguised as some kind of mendicant. Even then I was aware of certain irregularities in the ceremony but cared little about them. If I had been a woman to value the customs of society I would not have become mistress of the royal scion who styled himself 'the Prince of Bohemia', nor made Godfrey's acquaintance as my legal representative when that affair had reached its inevitable close.

I am not a fool. I knew that English marriage ceremonies no longer had to be performed before noon to be legal; that two witnesses are required to sign the parish register, not one disguised sleuth; that special licenses for marriage without banns require a bishop's signature. Since Godfrey did not insist upon those things I deemed it our nuptial vows that mattered and went ahead with a union joined by love and our oaths, not by the law.

Godfrey had other ideas, I discovered. When he learned that I no longer retained material which might blackmail a future monarch for a literal king's ransom he was furious in his disdain. His suggestions for the

---

3 This city is called Cetinje in the present day.

means of our future prosperity were vile. He had mistaken an adventurous spirit for a calculating courtesan. When I resisted his proposals things
deteriorated between us. When evidence absolute was presented to annul
our union I was pleased to escape and devote myself to restoring my interrupted operatic career.

Technically I was not divorced since technically I was never wed. I
still allowed myself the liqueur to celebrate the anniversary of our parting.

When my luxury was consumed I reached for the newspaper that awaited my attention. *The Times* and *The New York Herald* are hard to get in a
postage-stamp European country surrounded by peaks as yet unassailed
by railway lines or decent roads. I had sailed in from Bari, Italy to the
tiny port of Antivari, practically the only way to reach the Montevidean
capital without hitching oneself to mountain goats. The London paper
awaiting me had arrived that day, although its publication date was June
6th, more than two and a half weeks earlier.

I unfolded the broadsheet and froze as I saw the first item: MR
SHERLOCK HOLMES BELIEVED DROWNED AT INTERLAKEN,
SWITZERLAND.

I saw him so keenly then, that gaunt haunted face with those piercing
eyes, those long sensitive hands that betrayed him as he spoke, the restless
procession of expressions that played across his features as that unparal-
leled brain flitted from deduction to deduction. I had met him only thrice,
passed less than two hours in his company, but I had not forgotten him.

There in my reading pile, confessing my interest, was a much-thumbed
edition of his great friend's account, *A Study in Scarlet*.

And was he gone now, that massive personality, that endless intellect
who had crossed me so briefly and haunted me so long? My hands shook
on the paper.

It was as well that Thursday's house was only half full. I did not render
my best performance.

The account of Dr John Watson, 26th June 1891:

oughs, aches, and summer breathing difficulties, those were the
bulk of my problems the day after Holmes' memorial. I might
not have wished to carry on with the mundane business of my
medical practice but I had patients depending upon me.

"It will be good for you, James," Mary told me; she often called me

James, since to her John was a name with mournful associations.[4] "You are always at your best when you are helping other people. Do what you can for them. Besides, it will be your first chance to update your notes on some of your old patients."

Just one week previously I had sold my busy Paddington practice to return to my former Kensington surgery.[5] I wanted more time away from a queue of invalids to concentrate on writing up my accounts of my extraordinary investigations with Holmes; reverting to a smaller practice would enable me to cut my medical workload by almost half.

Holmes' death had kicked the stuffing out of me. I admit it. Besides, Mary's assistance in building up our Paddington patient list had been invaluable. I should never have managed it without her diligent organisation, but now her declining health diminished her capacity to be involved and I had no wish to wear her out.

We had then been married for a little over two years, and she was my only solace in those weeks after Holmes' loss.[6]

I smiled as she tapped on the door of my consulting room and brought life and warmth to it. "You have a visitor," she announced, and stepped aside to allow Billy to slink in.

Mrs Hudson claims that Billy has elevated the slouch to an art form.

Our irascible former page grinned at me, touched finger to forehead in salute to Mary, and revealed his news. "I've found 'em!"

"I'll leave you to your consultation," my wife told us, retreating so Billy could impart his news in confidence.

---

4 Watson's Christian name is only mentioned on four occasions in-canon, three times as John and once in dialogue from Mary as James (in "The Man With the Twisted Lip" from *The Adventures of Sherlock Holmes*). His middle name is never recorded save as the initial H., perhaps inheriting it from his father whose initials appear on a fifty guinea watch that Holmes examined in *A Study in Scarlet* No less a Sherlockian than Dorothy L. Sayers wrote a speculative article suggesting that Mary disliked the name 'John' and therefore used 'James', the anglicised version of Watson's posited middle name Hamish.

5 The location of Watson's medical practice is somewhat erratic in the Canon, shifting between Kensington and Paddington then back again. Fans playing "the great game" of reconciling apparent anomalies into a coherent continuity have long concluded that Watson must have exchanged his quiet Kensington surgery for a busier Paddington one but then retreated to his former practice during "the hiatus" when Holmes was considered dead. Shortly after Holmes reappeared in England in April 1894, Watson records selling his residential Kensington practice to a Dr Verner, whom he later learned was a distant relative of Sherlock Holmes, and returned to live at 221B Baker Street for another eight years.

6 This account is set less than a year before Mrs Mary Watson's untimely passing, well before Holmes reappearance in England in April 1894. No cause of death is recorded in the canon. T.S. Blakely noted that there were two occasion in *The Sign of Four* where she 'turned faint', suggesting that she may have inherited a heart condition from her father.

"Found what?" I asked, although I thought I might guess from my young visitor's expression.

"The Krauts!" he exclaimed. "Them blokes what—'oo—is shouldering in on the docks."

"Splendid. Let's contact Lestrade."

Billy shook his head. "Bit too early, sir. All I 'eard was there's a parley going on down Southwark,[7] on St Katherine's Dock. Some o' the lads 'oo run the rackets down there 'ave been told to come along or else. But if there's a whiff of copper[8] then the whole meet will vanish."

"What do you propose?"

Another Billy grin. "Why, I was thinking of strolling along and taking a look-see for meself, Dr Watson. One fellow might sneak in there where an army of bluebottles could not."

"Or two?" I suggested.

"Two might manage." The lad looked relieved. I imagine he'd been hoping to rope me in all along.

"When is it?"

"Tonight, sir, around nine. The wharves will be quiet then. I'll find out which warehouse they'll use. If we gets there early we can take cover somewhere and 'ear what's said."

It's what Holmes would have done, assuming he hadn't disguised himself as some disreputable salt and limped in amongst them. For those of us lacking his thespian abilities early concealment seemed like the best plan.

There was still one problem though: I was not Sherlock Holmes.

"We will need Lestrade," I decided. "I'm sorry, Billy, but he is the professional. Just him, not a string of uniformed sergeants and constables."

"Mr 'Olmes reckoned that Inspector Lestrade wasn't the sharpest tool in the shed," Billy reminded me.

I felt another pang of loss. "Holmes isn't available. Lestrade is reliable. Besides, if we hear anything actionable we'll need a police witness."

Billy was reluctant. On how many occasions had he listened at the door while Holmes lectured Lestrade on the shortcomings of Scotland Yard investigations? But I knew the inspector to be honest and dependable in a pinch.

---

7 Pronounced "Suth-huck" with a soft "th" as in "with".

8 Many sources credit the slang term 'copper' for a police officer to the metal of the badge of authority or to the metal helmet used by early officers. However, *cop* is an Anglo-Saxon word first recorded in the 18th century, meaning 'to catch', possibly derived from the Latin *capere*, by which etymology the term means 'catcher'. Early versions of handcuffs were referred to as 'handcops'.

"Bring 'im, then," Billy conceded with a sigh. "We'll meet on Little Terrence Street, say ten to eight. Wear something dark. Bring a weapon. I'll be off to get the detail of the meet."

"Be careful, then," I cautioned the headstrong youngster. He was not Sherlock Holmes either.

Billy hastened away to follow his enquiries. I unlocked the drawer where I kept my service revolver and began to field-strip it so as to be ready for action.

✱✱✱

A Private Memoir of Madame Irene Adler, 26th June 1891:

The world was smaller without Sherlock Holmes. Though I had never looked to see him again, an existence where that possibility was denied me seemed stifling and bleak.

I roused myself for our rehearsal. Whatever odd sentiment one may feel for the loss of a dear opponent does not excuse letting down the company, nor offering less than one's best in the performance of one's art. Still, troupe, conductor, and orchestra all seemed relieved when I finally called a halt. I retreated to my room to brood alone.

After a while Cosi tapped on my door. Her knock was tentative since she knew I was retreating from world. When I bade her enter she came timidly, bearing a plain sealed envelope.

"From a gentleman," I recognised. Cosi is a dear girl, but much given to accepting tips from my would-be admirers to deliver me a succession of fervent *billet-doux*. A generous romantic nature inclines her to hope that some liaison she might arrange for me could lead to my intimate happiness. Was I ever so simple and trusting a creature? I think not.

I held out my hand. Cosi blushed, bobbed her knees, and passed me the letter. "It *is* from a gentleman," she confessed. "Him that was in box three both nights, watching so close."

I knew whom she meant. He had given my performance his full attention, not as a critic would to judge, but rather in the form of a communicant receiving final unguent upon his deathbed.

I opened the missive fiercely, contemptuously, ready to dismiss another clumsy invitation to some fumbled attempt at seduction.

I unlocked the drawer where I kept my service revolver.

The note said:

'An old acquaintance would be given great pleasure if Miss Adler would consent to sup with him after the opera. Miss Adler will perhaps recall this acquaintance if he mentions that she once in 1887 wished him a good night in Baker Street in London, adding his name. In Montenegro, however, he prefers simply to sign himself
'I.M. Sigerson'[9]

My hands trembled on the paper. I well remembered the words I had spoken that evening four years before.

I had said, "Good night, Mr Sherlock Holmes."[10]

I looked at myself in the long mirror atop my dresser. The professional mask of poise and control had slipped for a moment, revealing the remnant of that naïf who had blushed at the attentions of a prince. My face was pale, except for cheeks that flushed like a schoolgirl with a guilty secret.

Memories cascaded past, of those heady terrifying days in London, avoiding the malice of my royal lover's trusted retainers who sought back from me those tokens he had once given me to demonstrate his love. They were cunning and cruel men but I was clever. They hunted letters and pictures that would implicate their master in a scandal. I hid those things away as protection against more violent action.

Of course I will not name my lover. I understood our implicit contract when I became his mistress, and discretion was a part of it. He has not, and never has had, any reason to fear I will break my word. He knows that now and is satisfied.

I have wondered since whether Godfrey had been so honourable. Knowing as he did of my past—I would never lie to a man I loved, for what kind of love is that?—was he perhaps tempted to use that information against the prince? If so, my royal ex-swain's reactions might make more sense.

Anyhow, those times were sharp in my memory; fear of those imperial agents, passion with Godfrey, excitement at thwarting those who plotted against me; a sense of everything coming to an end. And Mr Holmes.

And now a dead man was here in Montenegro, hearing my Gilda each

---

9 I.A. Watson is indebted to W.S. Baring-Gould, whose excellent biography *Sherlock Holmes* first unearthed this remarkable correspondence.

10 As recounted in "A Scandal in Bohemia".

night, and my world had changed again.

I rang for Cosi. "I will meet this gentleman," I told her, to her delight. "Arrange a light cold supper and give us some privacy."

I sharpened my wits and prepared to give the performance of a lifetime.

The account of Dr John Watson, 26th June 1891:

Londan Basin is the busiest harbour in the world. That curving, tidal reach of Thames is thick with tall ships, lined with wharves and warehouses. By day it is a chaotic, bustling throng of men lading and unlading, of merchant wagons and shunting engines, teeming with stevedores and stockmen conducting the commerce that makes London the Empire's commercial heart.

By night much of the waterfront is unlit and abandoned, left to drunken staggering sailors and alley prostitutes and to the footpads who prey on both.

Billy met us outside the Lamb and Lion, one of the many drinking establishments that ring the perimeter of the south bank docks. It was a shabby four-ale bar whose saloon was little better than its tap room,[11] filled with mid-week drinkers spending their day-rates as quick as the barmaid could pour.

I was dismayed that our former page emerged inebriated from the throng.

"Billy..."

"S'all right," he told me, swaying a little as he wiggled a finger in my face. "Jus' 'elp me down that alley there."

Lestrade looked at me in dismay. I suppose he wondered what sort of wild venture I had dragged him into with a drunken informant in the worst part of the southern docklands.

I caught the staggering youth and steadied him in the direction he indicated.

"Watson," Lestrade hissed in my ear. "That fellow is..."

Then my years of experience with Holmes clicked in. Billy smelled

---

11 The traditional British public house was divided into two separate areas, the tap-room for serious cheap drinking and the saloon lounge for a better class of patron. The tap room often had little furniture and sawdust-covered floors. The saloon might include live entertainment and a piano.

of beer and lurched unevenly but the stench came from his overcoat not from his lips. His grip on my arm was firm and unwavering.

"I see you are getting into the spirit of the thing," I murmured to him as he steered me into the shadows. "You can rest easy, Inspector. Billy here is playacting for effect, I believe."

The young rogue snickered. "I've spent the last hour an' a half pouring stout down one of the muscle-boys going with One-Ear Henson to tonight's get-together, sir. And losing to 'im at darts, as if 'e stood a chance if I weren't winkling information out of 'im. I 'ad to know exactly where it's occurring, see?"

In the safety of the covered passageway that ran behind the Lamb, Billy abandoned his drunk act and stood up properly. He doffed the alcohol-soaked jacket and discarded it amongst the detritus that choked the cobbles.

"You have the information, then?" Lestrade interrogated him.

"I got it, officer," the irrepressible page agreed. "But we 'ave to be moving quick!"

I checked my pocketwatch. It was close to eight.

"It's to be the Murcheson Warehouse," Billy reported. "That's the big 'un behind the end crane, where they bring in the tea and cotton from Bombay and China. Problem is, it'll already be guarded."

"The men ordering the meeting will have anticipated early arrivals," I understood. "So what...?"

"We go another way," Billy told me with a cheeky wink. "There's always another way, Dr Watson. Come on."

Lestrade and I followed the youngster through a tight maze of connecting back alleys no wider than a man's shoulders. A doleful siren boomed in the distance where some ferry passed too close to one of the four-masters that had braved the evening gloom for a late docking. We splashed across the cart-ruts outside the official gates of St Katherine's shipyard and took worn steps down to the side of the lapping Thames.

Lestrade almost slipped into the embankment mud. "Where on earth are you taking us?" he demanded

"Where they won't be looking," Billy replied. "We're going under the wharves now. Don't be looking too closely yourselves."

He led us under the lattice framework of thick timbers and girders that supported the dock. Lestrade made to uncover a dark lantern but Billy stopped him. We groped by touch in the dim slippery spaces, ignoring the scuttling rats. There was other movement too, and the sounds of cheap rented passion. Lestrade furled his coat tighter around him as if to avoid contamination.

It took us the best part of twenty minutes to navigate the murky underdrawings. Twice we stopped at ladders leading to trapdoors above, and Billy then called on Lestrade to uncover his lantern long enough to check scratched markings on the lintels. Evidently neither exit was what we sought.

A little further on the pungent river-slime below the boards on which we balanced became turgid waters. We picked our way over crossbeams that scarcely rose above the rancid foam and collected sewage of the tidal basin. We had to navigate carefully around old chains hung from the boards above so that sounds of them rattling would not warn of our passage.

Billy found another ladder, as rotted and rickety as the others. This time Lestrade's lantern-beam picked out a grubby rag pinned to one corner of the trapdoor.

"Hold that light steady," Billy ordered. He produced a bayonet-knife and ran it through the crack between frame and door, managing with difficulty to push aside the swivel-bolt that held it shut.

Lestrade stowed his lantern again so that no illumination betrayed us as we climbed up into the Murchison Warehouse.

We froze as voices spoke near to us. "Seal the doors now. Nobody in or out."

"*Wie Ihr befelt,*"

"English! We are in England now."

"As you command, then."

"Check the galleries above. Even the rafters. No errors."

"Very well."

"Make sure our own sharp-shooters are ready, in case they are needed."

"I will."

Billy tapped Lestrade and I on the shoulder and gestured that we should move to better cover behind the crates that lined the walls. I paused only to ease the trapdoor back into position then scuttled after the others.

We took refuge amongst a jumbled pile of broken and open tea chests. Each box stood four feet high so we could make a hide behind them with a reasonable view of the main warehouse floor.

Concealed as best we could, we hunkered down to see what happened next. I drew out my field glasses and surveyed the scene.

Braziers had been set out in an approximate circle in the centre of the floor. Some twenty or so rough men were moving round, openly carrying firearms, clearly acting as guards.

Lestrade took his turn with the binoculars and hissed. "I recognise some of those men. I could take half of them in right now on outstanding warrants."

"Not without getting shot and dumped in the river," Billy warned. "Besides, the night's only just beginning."

Our young friend was correct. At the dot of nine a collection of no less than fifty thugs were shepherded into the brazier ring. Amongst them was the fixer that Billy called One-Ear Henson and the hulking brute body-guard with whom our guide had been drinking.

Lestrade commandeered the field glasses again. "Gaxton the Enforcer. Thayer the Fence. Willie Bruce and his lad; they're smugglers if we could but prove it. Bromsgrove the brothel-keeper. Not the big names—we took them with Moriarty. The next tier down."

"Some very nasty fellows there, Doctor Watson," Billy agreed.

"A few I'd have expected who aren't out there," Lestrade observed. "No Lonnie Dyson. No Firth the Lifter. Nobody from the Tongs. Nobody from the Irish."

The criminals were herded together by the armed guards. It seemed strange to watch such tough types be bullied by others. Some fear seemed to mesmerise them from fighting back.

When the visitors were assembled and quietened another cadre of thugs appeared from the far end of the warehouse. They flanked two men, a larger, younger shaven-headed fellow who must have stood six-feet four and who moved like a boxer, and a smallish figure in an old-fashioned carriage cloak whose full hood obscured his features.

Black Cloak moved to stand beside a brazier where the flames uplit a face that had previously been concealed by the shadows of his cowl.

"You were wise to come," he told his audience. "Those who did not will rue it."

"So we came," snarled One-Ear. "Don't mean we like it. Who the devil are you to call us like this, eh?"

The hooded stranger transfixed Henson with a stare. "Who am I? I am Professor James Moriarty."

A Private Memoir of Madame Irene Adler, 26th June 1891:

He had not changed much, this man who travelled under the name Sigerson. Too tall for his width, with features too angular to be called handsome, and long, delicate hands accomplished in the violin that nevertheless betrayed the calluses of an habitual boxer. His suit was in the European fashion rather than a London cut, and by his boots he had come to Cettigne by the mountain passes rather than by ferry.

I took in a thousand details without even thinking about it. He had a new pipe and was not yet accustomed to it or the tobacco he had purchased. His shirt and cuff-studs were new also; a dead man does not take his luggage with him. He had lost a little weight since I saw him last, perhaps from recent vigorous exercise.

There were slight traces of faded bruising on one wrist and under his jaw; he had struggled with someone strong, who had come close to overpowering him.

I saw him regard me too as he stood at the door of my dressing room, his piercing gaze flicking over my private chamber then focusing upon its only occupant. I raised my chin defiantly as he appraised me. I would not betray any fear to my opponent. Let him discern what he would.

"Madam Adler," he began, "I apologise for the unusual manner of my calling."

"When the gentleman who names himself Sigerson is present, one must prepare oneself for mysteries," I accepted. I showed him the paper announcing his death. "Do you not think it impertinent to undermine the integrity of so respected an organ of record?"

I was surprised to see a flash of uncertainty cross his countenance. "I deeply regret that belief of my passing must pain those who count themselves my friends."

"Perhaps you should come in. Have some canapé de anchois? Or the green turtle soup is excellent."

My puzzling visitor seemed to make a decision. He entered my dressing room like Caesar crossing the Rubicon, with as much deliberation. He closed the door, shutting out Cosi's wild curiosity.

"Will you drink some wine?" I asked him, gesturing him to the basket chair opposite my divan sofa.

He assented, folding down onto the wicker, long legs bending with an almost audible creak. I concluded that he had travelled far and fast in the days since his apparent demise.

"We have never had occasion to converse, madam," he mentioned.

"Not as ourselves," I agreed. "One of us was always a groom or clergyman, a street-boy or a bride. Indeed, even now it appears that one of us is a Norwegian."

Sherlock Holmes allowed himself a small snort. "A necessary imposture. You may have heard news of the death of Professor James Moriarty, a man of considerable ingenuity and influence, who..."

I held up a hand to caution him to silence. "Cosi," I called, "if you do not cease to listen at my door I shall become irritable. Go away now and do not disturb us again."

There was no sound outside my chamber. Cosi can be very quiet; but the minor shadow beneath the crack at the bottom of the door flitted away and did not return.

"I know of Moriarty," I assured my guest. "I was in London for some time after I retired from the opera. It is impossible to move in the circles I then frequented and not hear of the master-criminal who tugged the strings of every great planned crime in England. His name might not then have been commonly known but he cast a dark, long shadow. When news came of dozens of arrests by Scotland Yard and by police across the world it was obvious what had happened."

I judged that my guest was pleased I was able to keep up with him. So few men are comfortable with a woman whose mind paces or out-paces theirs.

"Then you will understand that my plans against him required careful timing and absolute precision. Most of all, it required my survival during the critical days when Moriarty's organisation was dismantled."

"You did not, then, tumble off a cliff into a waterfall."

"Almost, but not quite. It was a desperate little struggle there for a while. Moriarty and I were matched in intellect and strategy. The problem was not in overcoming him, but in doing so in such a way as to preserve my own life. At the end he was quite prepared to see us both topple and end our existences together."

"The sign of a bad loser," I judged. "Many men of genius are."

"Not all?"

"Some restrain their selfish narcissism for the common good."

Holmes tentatively tried the consommé á la Victoria. "As I have mentioned on occasion to my sedentary brother, taking an active approach to problem-solving and developing practical as well as theoretical experience can make a vital difference. For all his brilliance, Moriarty was accustomed to sitting at the centre of his web and drawing its strands around those who opposed him. He had not made a study of fighting arts such as *baritsu*."

"I am not familiar with the technique.[12] I assume it allowed you to overcome your adversary at the cliff's edge?"

"Just so. At the last I was able to trip Moriarty to plummet into the cataract, while barely managing to retain a handhold that allowed me to scale back to the path."

I nibbled a canapé, although my appetite seemed absent. Men have told me many remarkable stories to impress me. Sherlock Holmes was speaking only the absolute truth. "And then you departed, leaving your friend Dr Watson to assume your demise."

"As I scrambled away I was almost hit by a falling rock. Others followed it, some coming within a foot of my head. Someone was above, dropping an avalanche upon me. Moriarty had not come alone, but had brought with him the deadliest killer in Europe."

"Ah. And so you realised that though the snake's head was severed, the body would continue to thrash for a while. The man sought to complete the work his master had begun. You had to vanish."

"If I retreated to London, those about me might have been used as hostages against me. Had I returned to Watson, my friend would have been dead before day's end."

"Only, if you were dead such leverage would be unnecessary," I understood.

My visitor bowed his head in assent. "From Interlaken I made cross-country for Locarno, shedding as I went my identity as an English detective. I thought I had cast off my pursuer, but at the Milano Centrale railway station a bullet passed within an inch and shattered a plate glass window behind me. The round was discharged from a rather unique air rifle designed by blind gunsmith von Herder, a weapon that is property of Moriarty's right hand agent. I slipped away in the guise of a patisserie deliverer and began a dangerous game of hide-and-seek through Tyrolean

---

12 Actually, nobody is familiar with *baritsu*. There is no martial art of this name. Commentators have speculated that Doyle may have meant *bartitsu*, a fighting style pioneered by fellow *Pearson's Magazine* contributor E.W. Barton-Wright in 1899, four years before the published account of Holmes' survival in "The Adventure of the Empty House" mentions the use of *baritsu* on Moriarty. If so then not only is the martial art misprinted but also an anachronism.

In the years since Holmes' demonstration of his mastery of *baritsu*, however, pulp heroes Doc Savage and the Shadow have also been revealed as adepts of the art.

Innsbruck, across the Julian Alps, through Croatian Agram and Bosnian Saraiyevo, then to Belgrade and Sofia."

"Quite the Grand Tour," I admired. "Your hunter evidently did not catch his prey."

"His name is Moran, a former Colonel of the 1st Bengalore Pioneers. He is a noted big game hunter, an old *shikari*. Indeed, his *Heavy Game of the Western Himalayas* is a most informative manual. His later work *Three Months in the Jungle* is somewhat self-congratulatory for my taste, and clearly expurgated for a civilised readership.[13] Still, both volumes were useful insights into the mind of the man, helpful in predicting his search pattern and techniques."

I poured Holmes a very respectable Merlot. "You are not easy game to corner, Mr Sigerson."

"I hope not. Moran sought to hunt me as he would one of his tigers, utilising the remnants of Moriarty's European minions as beaters to startle me from concealment. He hoped that I might snap at the small fry and so allow him a clear shot. I shall not bore you with details of our skirmishes in Nish and on the Danube."

"I doubt that I would be bored."

"Suffice to say, Miss Adler, that his plans fell apart at the Iron Gate into Romania, where the border guard who watch the pass across the Transylvanian Alps were shocked to discover concealed weapons and a set of planted correspondence containing orders to assassinate their ruler King Carol I. Moran was deemed in the pay of the remnants of the Ottoman Empire and had to flee for his life down the Borgo Pass."[14]

"He was not executed, then?"

"Moran is too clever to be caught by mere watchmen. He abandoned his mercenaries and escaped alone."

I considered what that meant. "You cannot return home while he is loose. Your trail is cold but he will continue to search for your spoor."

"Yes. And there are three other villains who slipped the police net that are also unaccounted for. I will need to completely demolish every vestige of Moriarty's empire before Sherlock Holmes can live again—if ever I have the chance to go back to my former life." My guest paused, recog-

---

13 Moran's published works, released in 1881 and 1884 respectively, are mentioned in "The Adventure of the Empty House".

14 In 1866, Prince Karl of Hohenzollern-Sigmaringen came to power as Dominator of Rumania through a palace coup. He led his people to victory in the 1878 Russo-Turkish War against the Ottoman Empire that held Rumania as vassal and was proclaimed King Carol I in 1881.

nising the cost of his final clash with his greatest rival.

"Credit for your victory over Moriarty and his network is going to Inspector Lestrade and the agents of Scotland Yard," I ventured. "But then, that is not the first time that Lestrade has been awarded laurels that should properly go to you."

Holmes' intense gaze sharpened yet more.

"Yes," I told him, "I saw your hand in my husband's downfall. Geoffrey Norton proved not to be the man I had hoped him to be. You knew it, and Lestrade's dispatch of information to the Warsaw police might as well have had your signature on it."

Holmes was unabashed. "It seemed best to keep my part in the matter anonymous. I did not wish you to, to…"

"To feel that I had incurred a debt to a man who spared my future?" I suggested. "Did you really expect I would not see your hand in Geoffrey's arrest? In the annulment of our union?"

"I conceded that there was a good chance," Holmes acknowledged. "My record of keeping you from discerning my involvement in your affairs is hardly a sterling one. I thought it worth the attempt, though I am hardly surprised that you saw through the charade."

"It is not coincidence that brought you to Cettigne. Your adventures across the Balkans have brought you ever nearer to Montenegro."

Sherlock Holmes paused. For one moment I saw that vast intellect confused, unsure about what to do or say.

"You thought perhaps to find refuge with a possible ally who might assist you when you could not turn to your usual methods?" I suggested. "You have clearly been keeping a watch upon my affairs."

Holmes indicated an empty spot on my side-table where I had previously laid the volume that recounted his first adventure with Dr Watson. "And you likewise."

Of course he had previously searched my dressing-room! He could not be sure whether his enemies had suborned me. I might even have been one of Professor Moriarty's legion of agents.

It would have been hard to safely refuse an offer to serve that dangerous organisation. I had made certain while in London to avoid any such attention.

"I trust you are now assured that I have no malevolent intent towards you, Mr Sigerson?"

"I am quite satisfied that you are not in league with my adversaries, Miss Adler."

"Then be so kind as to call me Irene."

My guest's mouth curved up into a thin pleased bow for a brief instant. "I shall be pleased to do so, Irene."

The account of Dr John Watson, 26th June 1891:

Lestrade turned to me. Even in the shadowed recesses behind the tea crates I could see the expression of horror on his face. "It can't be!" he whispered urgently. "You said…"

I fought past a wild surge of emotions: shock at the stranger's claim; horror at the possibility of the villain's survival; dismay that Holmes was not here to stop him; wild desperate hope that if Moriarty had survived the Falls then my friend might have too; then a crushing sense of reality as more likely possibilities flooded into my shocked mind.

"I have never seen Moriarty in person," I told the Inspector and Billy in a hushed undertone. "For all that Holmes chased him for so long, for all the damage that the Professor wrought in our lives, I never met him face-to-face. Even Holmes encountered him but twice, and their last meeting was fatal."

Billy gestured towards the thin black-clad speaker. "So is that him or not?"

I couldn't tell. The man who now commended the meeting of felons had a gaunt face with sunken eyes and a large, prominent forehead. His head swayed as he spoke, something akin to the sideways movements of a cobra. Whoever he was, his performance was enough to give the water-front thugs pause.

"Moriarty is dead," the man Lestrade had identified as Gaxton said at last. His voice sounded rough, uncertain.

Cold reptilian eyes flicked up at the enforcer. "Did you imagine I would have no precaution in place against the authorities moving against me? No warning mechanism? No safeguards? No plan to disappear, to simulate my demise, to vanish and regroup?"

Stated like that it was all too possible. I confess a moment's doubt, that Sherlock Holmes might somehow have been outmatched at the last; that Moriarty had taken the great detective's life yet preserved his own.

"Moriarty died in Switzerland," the elder Bruce objected. "Everyone knows it. The papers…"

The possible Moriarty snorted in amusement. "The broadsheets are written by men, and men have weaknesses. Fears and greeds that can be exploited. History is written by the conquerors."

Lestrade blasphemed under his breath. "What if it is him, doctor? What if we face Moriarty without Holmes? How can we?"

The weight of my service revolver was heavy in my jacket. It occurred to me that I might step out from cover and place five rounds of rapid fire into that smooth white forehead before anyone could react. I could end the scourge upon humanity that had taken my great friend and who menaced everything decent in our society.

Of course I would die then, under a hail of return shots. I would leave Mary alone and betray Billy and Lestrade to the surviving murderers. But there, in that dusty storage shed, I still considered it.

Lestrade must have read my face. He laid a cautioning hand on my sleeve and shook his head.

"If you're really him," Gaxton asked the stranger, "what about the Krauts? Why aren't you...?"

"The Bavarians work for me," came the reply. 'Moriarty' gestured to his tall, muscular shaven-headed escort. "When my previous staff failed me I summoned a reserve crew. Herr Falkenrath and his colleagues have previously attended to my affairs in Munich and Nuremberg. Now they serve me here."

"They been taking down our own!" Thayer the Fence objected. "They come to my shop, demanding money, threatening fires..."

"There is much to re-establish," Black Cloak replied as calmly as if he were a schoolteacher returning a poor student essay to be done again. "Much damage has been done. Many seek to take advantage of that harm to steal parts of my empire."

"If you are who you say," Gaxton sneered. He had recovered some of his bravado. "Nobody here saw Moriarty up close. Nobody I know did. Most players out there didn't even know his name. You could be anybody, just got up like the Professor."

"You are not the first to voice that concern." 'Moriarty' lifted a crooked finger at Falkenrath. "Bring him in."

There was a rumble as a large box was wheeled into the brazier-light. The packing case was much larger than a tea chest, a cube of six feet in each dimension. A pair of the armed sentries manhandled it before the assembled criminals and unlatched the front.

"Each of you was wise enough to heed my summons," Black Cloak declared. "Not all were."

The forward panel of the packing crate fell down with a crash, reveal-

"Fears and greeds that can be exploited. "

ing the interior of the box. Some of the hardened thugs jumped back.

Billy gagged beside me, clutching his hands to his mouth and trying not to choke on his vomit. Lestrade's hands trembled on his gun.

"Lonnie Dyson," the Inspector gasped. "What's left of him!"

Fully detailing the pegged-out ruin fastened to the crate's interior would require a degree of medical description that would unsettle and unnerve. Suffice to report that the remains of the man had been affixed to all five remaining sides of container by chains and wire which had then been used to draw parts of his internal organs through incisions in his flesh. The corpse was fresh and gory. Liquid blood trickled out to puddle at the feet of the assembled criminals.

"You will receive your orders shortly," 'Moriarty' announced impassively, as if he did not stand within three feet of those demolished remains. "You will obey Herr Falkenrath as you would me. Those of you who comply will retain your dominions under my instruction. Those who do not… there are more crates."

He had them. I could see that from the way they stood, strong rough men herded together like sheep surrounded by a new hungry wolf-pack. I knew even before they spoke that they would accept their place and pledge their fealty.

Lestrade, Billy, and I huddled in concealing shadows in fear of discovery for another two hours before the warehouse cleared, and waited an hour after that to be certain before we escaped the way we came.

✻ ✻ ✻

A Private Memoir of Madame Irene Adler, 27th June 1891:

r Sherlock Holmes is best known to the world as a detective, a scientist, and the author of copious monographs on an eclectic range of topics. Yet when I consider him my first thought is always for the music lover.

Holmes is a talented violinist who might easily have made a career from his skill. His understanding of musical theory is second to none, for he is adept in both the mathematical and aesthetic elements. His appreciation of vocal performance is immense and gratifying.

In all of my adventures, it is possible that singing for Sherlock Holmes is the most intimate thing that I have ever done.

"That… it was remarkable," my guest marvelled as I finished 'Il Dolce Suono' from *Lucia di Lammermoor*.[15] "To bring such range to madness…"

I was flattered. I was relieved. No bride disrobing for her husband on her wedding night could have been more nervous than I was in performing that piece for Sherlock Holmes.

Sherlock's sensitive fingertips arched together as he reflected upon what he had heard. "You sang in the original key of F major rather than the more popular translation to E-flat. Your performance was *come scritto*,[16] eschewing the usual trills and mordents. What needs perfection with variation or personal show? To convey the soul of the music, to capture Lucia, one must surrender a performer's vanity and commit all to the music! Irene… it was sublime."

I blinked away tears. "I am… glad you liked it," I stammered. "After you gave me Bach's *Ciaconna*[17] I had to… give you something back."

Where was the sharp clear-minded woman who has navigated the courts of Europe, who has manipulated crowned heads and laughed away millionaires? Lost somewhere, I suppose, in that long afternoon's discourse on consonance and harmony, on Lind and Patti,[18] on *sul ponticello* and *sul tasto*.[19] Our conversation had ranged across the map of Europe, where I discovered that my companion's knowledge of the great cities rivalled mine but in different and complimentary ways. We dissected the theatre, quoted *Antony and Cleopatra* at each other, and compared experiences of eccentric producers and yet more eccentric venues.

"Could our minds have met like this," I wondered aloud, "if you were

---

15 The tragic opera *Lucia di Lammermoor* was written by Gaetano Donizetti in 1835, based upon Sir Walter Scott's historical novel *The Bride of Lammermoor*. The story's dramatic apex comes when Lucia, forced into marriage against her will, stabs her husband on their wedding night and, driven mad by her deeds, descends to the wedding company believing that she is instead married to her true love Edgardo. Her "madness scene" and the demanding aria "Il Dolce Suerno" springboarded the careers of many coloratura sopranos.

16 "As written", rather than embellished with the flourishes and variations that were often added by performers to show off their own skills.

17 The fifth and final part of Bach's *Partita in D Minor for Solo Violin*, or *Partita for Violin No 2*, once described by Yehudi Menhuin as "the greatest structure of solo violin that exists".

18 Jenny Lind (1820-1887), "the Swedish Nightingale", and Adelina Patti (1843-1919) were amongst the foremost sopranos of their eras.

19 Advanced violin bow techniques where the bow intersects the string closer to the bridge for an intense sound or over the end of the fingerboard for an ethereal quality.

still the detective in Baker Street? Or does the Norwegian Sigerson have liberty that the great mind of Baker Street has not?"

"An interesting query," Sherlock replied. He furrowed his brow, as he does when he turns his intellect inward, and pondered for a while. "I confess that I am, at the present, disconnected from those bulwarks which have formerly tethered me. Circumstance has required me to separate from friends and family, from my familiar haunts and accustomed patterns. I am versed in setting aside routine for a time to pursue some disguise and settle a case, but what I now face is a magnitude greater than what I have experienced before."

"You still have work to do," I understood. "Like a soldier under fire, you take cover and seek a way to flank your enemies anew."

"There is still unfinished business between Moriarty and me, in the persons of Colonel Moran and other remnants of my enemy's organisation. I am, however, much comforted to find respite in the company of..."

"A friend?"

"A friend."

Our gazes met and neither of us shied away.

Then Cosi tapped on my door, breaking the moment. "Madame," she called without entering, "I am sorry to interrupt but there are men here to see M. Sigerson."

I saw the mantle of Sherlock Holmes wrap around my guest again, like a tragedian of old donning a stage mask. That massive mind which had been turned inward and on me moved outward, encompassing every detail of the room and the situation.

Sherlock gestured that I should shift to a corner of the room away from the door, then indicated when I should call Cosi to admit the visitors.

Three pungent local shepherds shuffled into my dressing room, uncomfortable in such unfamiliar surroundings. As Sherlock relaxed I moved my hand away from the Beretta Stampede Gemini[20] in my laundry hamper.

"Ah, Miss Adler," Sherlock called, "may I introduce the men who have been running certain errands and keeping watch for me? They have lately returned from the passes and clearly have news for me."

The English-speaker amongst them shuffled forward. He was the oldest and most whiskered of the group, and from his resemblance to the others may well have been their father. He fingered a feathered alpine hat in his hands as he spoke.

"Sir, there were travellers of the sort you said," he reported. "Five men

---

20 A single action .45 revolver, a very substantial and powerful weapon for a lady to use.

on strong horses, travelling quickly and in military order. They crossed the high cleft this morning an hour after sunrise."

"Then they may be in Cettigne by now," Holmes observed. "Their method of travel is considerably swifter than yours. What else did you discern? Detail, man! Give me detail!"

Under the detective's precise questioning the shepherds disgorged observations they had not even realised they had made. The five horsemen wore city-cut civilian clothes. They had rifles slung across their backs. One man advanced as outrider ahead of the others. Their horses had a harness unlike the local saddles. The mounts were fresh, meaning that the travellers had camped overnight amongst the passes.

Finally satisfied that he had wrung from them what information he might, Sherlock paid his sentinels and sent them back to their vigil.

"Colonel Moran has found your trail again," I surmised. "Or is this some other pursuer?"

"There are few men other than Sebastian Moran who could stay on my trail this far," Sherlock considered. "None whom I would expect to have an interest and opportunity to do so. Even so, I am uncertain that those hillmen watchers saw the Colonel's arrival in Montenegro."

I followed my companion's thinking; to do so with Sherlock is always exhilarating. "You questioned the shepherds closely on the weapons the riders carried, and on any other they might have stowed in their baggage."

"Colonel Moran is much attached to a peculiar air rifle of unique design. I mentioned its use at Milan. It is possible he had discarded it or lost it, but its absence amongst the weapons of the newcomers from the Jankovici pass suggests that the old *shikari* was not amongst them."

I thought there was the faintest quiver of a smile fighting for existence at the sides of Sherlock's lips. "What am I missing?" I demanded. "Wait... let me fathom it for myself."

He spread his fingers in a gesture which meant 'help yourself.'

"You expected Moran to find your trail again. You cannot return home in safety until he is dealt with. So you came here, to Montenegro, an enclosed and isolated place where he might be able to corner you and where you might learn of any strangers who came in hunt."

"I apologise for bringing trouble to Cettigne while you are here."

"Nonsense. The scenario also allows you to test my loyalties, does it not? At one stroke you learn whether I ever had affiliations to Professor Moriarty, you attract Moran to a closed environment where you can get to grips with him, and... what else? Those riders..."

"I do not believe they are with the Colonel. I do not think they tracked me here."

"They are following *him!*" I realised. "He is hunting you. They are chasing Moran!"

Sherlock nodded a respectful bow. "Moriarty's fall leaves a void amongst the criminal classes. There are those who will seek to fill it."

"The Professor's most faithful lieutenant cannot be ignored. He is too dangerous to live. He might set himself against the new management, even seek to supplant them. He might still be operating on instructions left for him by his late employer."

"He remains the single and most knowledgeable source of information about Moriarty's schemes and minions. An interrogation would yield up data beyond measure of value to those who sought to take Moriarty's place."

"Moran is valuable dead or alive. And you believe those riders mean to take him." Something in Sherlock's expression alerted me that there was more. "No, wait… They are not here by accident. They did not pick up Moran's trail by chance or cleverness. They were warned!"

"Intelligence was passed on to them," my companion admitted.

"By you! Moran believes he has cornered you here, fled in desperation for solace from a woman you once admired. You have brought him to a trap where his enemies can eliminate him."

Sherlock snorted. "I trust my schemes are not as transparent to them as they are to you, my dear Irene."

I poked a finger at his chest. "You want them too! You said you needed to wrap up all the consequences of Moriarty's fall. That includes finding and stopping those who would rebuild what you have so recently demolished."

"That is so. But now I apologise for weaving you into the plot. An error, I perceive."

"I take it as a compliment, Mr Sherlock Holmes. What is your intent now?"

"A flight to Antivari as if I sought ship, then an ambush on the road."

I shook my head. "No."

"No?"

"The odds do not favour you, Sherlock. Your plan sets one lone detective scrambling over unfamiliar territory against a proven deadly hunter in a contest where he is expert, and against five gunmen who can split up and task you from different directions. There are too many incalculables that render your strongest skills void."

The schemer winced. "I *have* to finish this, Irene."

There it was; that confession of desperation. Holmes' war with Moriarty had cost him something, almost everything. He was hurt and tired and stripped of the comforts of his usual existence. He would gamble all for a chance to win back what he had lost; his friend Watson, his career and calling, his case-files and Persian tobacco-slipper and Baker Street hearth.

Such yearning could kill him.

"Your plan is the best that a hero all alone could possibly devise to seek a swift conclusion, Sherlock," I told him. "But you are not alone."

The account of Dr John Watson, 28th June 1891:

Inspector Lestrade arrived so early that the maid was still clearing away breakfast things. He swiped his hat off his head in a belated gesture of respect and apology to Mary. "I wouldn't disturb you on a Saturday, Doctor Watson, except that after last night..."

My wife recognised the signs of a man who had worked without sleep. She retrieved the teapot from the tray that Lucy was removing and poured our guest a reviving cup. "I'm sure you would not come like this if it were not urgent," she assured Lestrade. "A general practitioner and his wife become accustomed to sudden crises."

Mary generously did not add that she had seen that red-eyed ill-shaven countenance before, at times when Holmes had roused me from my domestic comfort for one of his sudden investigations.

"It's been a bit hectic since..." Lestrade edited his comments, "since last night."

"My husband has informed me of his excursion," Mary assured the Inspector. "I take it you would prefer some privacy to consult alone?"

"If you don't mind, ma'am. It's not... I just... certain things are confidential."

"Help yourself to sugar, Mr Lestrade." Mary paused only to give me a smile that comforted me despite our guest's agitation. Then the Scotland Yard detective and I were alone in the dining room.

Lestrade let out a great breath that was almost a sob. "You have no idea what our trip last night has set running! Half the force don't even believe me that I was at the meeting. Most of the rest doubt that Moriarty could be back. The Chief Constable said… well, no matter. And there was a very sharp interview with a snotty fellow from the Home Secretary's office."

"You did not reveal Billy's part in this?" I checked.

"I kept his name out of it. I know how to protect sources. But you could not grasp the furore that claim has caused. If I hadn't received a big share of the credit for taking down Moriarty's gang I don't think anyone would have believed me at all."

"You are assuming that it was Moriarty whom we saw in the warehouse."

"I don't know, doctor. I really don't. I know my superiors hope that I am mistaken, that this is some fabrication. A few even suspect me of raising the canard in the hopes of grabbing more glory and staying in the public spotlight." Lestrade forced himself to calm. He slurped a mouthful of tea and bottom-lipped his moustache to strain the liquid from it after. "The destruction of what we now call Moriarty's crime ring was a feather in a great many caps. Many careers were enhanced by it. I'll not deny that mine was one of them. But that glory depends upon the prosecutions we have begun being successful, and upon the damage wrought on the illegal society of criminal activities that Holmes exposed."

"You worry that if the fellows you have arrested fear Moriarty's return they will fall silent once more, revoke their testimonies, wait for orders. That politicians who have ridden high on Moriarty's fall will deny his resurrection and so hamper any chance of the police effectively pursuing him. That…"

The words stuck in my throat so Lestrade voiced them: "That with Mr Holmes gone there is no defence against that madman. That genius."

I understood. The possibility of a world with Moriarty but without Holmes chilled me to the core.

"I do not think it was him," I declared to Lestrade. "A clever fake, perhaps, but not the Professor. I trust Holmes, though he is gone. He would not die without ensuring that black spider was removed from the world also."

"How do you know that?"

"I know Sherlock Holmes."

"That is a great leap of faith, Doctor Watson."

"It is the ineluctable conclusion from the information available to me. I know my friend. If he is dead then so is Moriarty. The man we saw was a pretender."

Lestrade had doubts. He always did. "But if…"

I raised a hand. "Let us suppose for a moment that the 'Napoleon of Crime' really has survived to reclaim his place. Do you believe that there would be any chance of stopping him? That you or I could match wits with that evil intellect and prevail?"

The Inspector shook his head, flushing angrily at his admission.

"Then let us concentrate on other possibilities where we might make a difference," I advised. "Assume now that the 'Moriarty' we saw is a fake. Who is he? Whom does he represent? Some surviving fragment of the Professor's shattered organisation? Or some new menace?"

"Not part of the old school," Lestrade considered. "Holmes dismantled them pretty thoroughly. We got almost all their leadership. Those that escaped our net are being hunted across the Continent. Besides, if it was somebody already in Moriarty's hierarchy then he would not need to resort to terror tactics and torture executions to stake his claim."

I remembered the dismembered man in the box and shuddered. "What of these Germans, then? The ones who have been warring with the leaderless remnants of London's illicit enterprises."

"That's more likely. Say they find a bloke who can play a good Moriarty. The Professor was pretty anonymous in his glory days, behind the scenes. Anyone who could tell the difference between him and an impostor is dead or in chokey[21] now. All who's left is small fry—medium at best—and the name of Moriarty is known to them now and carries a lot of weight."

Lestrade and I exchanged troubled, baffled looks.

"Scotland Yard is paralysed," the Inspector confessed at last. "There will be no action. Not until things are a lot worse."

I didn't want to find out how much worse things could be than Lonnie Dyson's corpse.

"Then we must act," I decided. "We need to formulate a plan."

"If we go in assuming it is not Professor Moriarty and we are wrong…"

"Do you imagine either of us will have long happy lives if he has truly returned, Inspector? No, we shall cast our nets for a pretender… and whoever is behind him."

"That tall Kraut, 'Herr Falkenrath'," Lestrade remembered. "What about him?"

I hurried the detective into my consulting room. There on a top shelf above copies of *The Lancet* and the *British Medical Journal* were a row of battered and scorched scrapbooks containing the notes of Mr Sherlock Holmes.

"You'll have to check again with the index and note-boxes that Holmes bequeathed to Scotland Yard," I warned the Inspector, "but these might help us with a starting place."

---

21 Prison

The leather covers of the journals were singed and cracked from a fire that Moriarty's agents had set at Baker Street in the final days of Holmes' investigation. I counted off the volume that covered 'F' and leafed through until I found the name Falkenrath.

"Bavarian," I reported as I flicked through a clip of cuttings and scrawled notations. The German material was beyond me but fortunately Holmes had provided glossary marginalia to assist me in comprehension. "A significant force in organised criminal activity in the kingdom of Bavaria and across the whole *Deutsches Reich*.[22] But hold on! There's not one Falkenrath here. There's two of them!"

Lestrade leaned over my shoulder to examine the documents. "Ulrich and Ehrlich Falkenrath. Brothers."

"And both bad sorts, by these accounts. Gun-smuggling, extortion, immoral houses, kidnapping… but no convictions. Witnesses vanished. Policemen fell silent."

I found a yellowed clipping from some German newspaper dated three years earlier. From what I could read of it there had been some kind of incident in which nine constables of the *Bayeriche Polizi* had been lured to an abandoned *bierhof* which had then been destroyed by arson. I presume 'Nicht genügend Beweise' meant that there was insufficient evidence to convict the Falkenraths of complicence.

"They kill policemen," I noted.

"That could never happen here," the Inspector swore.

"If the Falkenraths have come to Britain seeking new opportunities then you might be wrong," I worried. "With the kind of support they might call upon from their operations in Nuremberg, Munich, and Ingolstadt they might have access to the very resources they require to cow a disrupted and uncoordinated London underworld."

"They would be dangerous even without the Moriarty gambit."

I stared down at the fire-curled edges of Holmes' ledger. I clenched my fists and made a choice. "It seems we must find a way to stop them."

✼ ✼ ✼

---

22 The *Norddeutscher Bund* (North German Federation) was renamed the *Deutsches Reich* (German Empire) in 1871 and included the Kingdom of Bavaria as a semi-autonomous part that retained its own monarch and standing army.

A Private Memoir of Madame Irene Adler, 28th June 1891:

A seedy florist's clerk shuffled the large spray of flowers and its tripod stand into my dressing room.

I sniffed an orchid. "Why thank you, Mr Sherlock Holmes."

The clerk snorted, amused to have been caught out. "What gave me away this time?"

"The tip. It was small enough that any real delivery man would have scowled. Add in the stoop to disguise your height, the prominent teeth changing your jaw line profile, and your unquenchable taste for low theatrics and the matter was elementary."

Sherlock retreated to my dresser to pull out the false teeth and dab away the ruddy make-up of his failed disguise. "I have been sightseeing," he explained.

"There is much to see in Cettigne," I agreed. "The Vlaska church dates from the fifteenth century. Its fence is made from the barrels of captured enemy rifles. And of course the monastery guards the remains of St Peter of Cettigne,[23] the right hand of John the Baptist, and particles of the True Cross."

"I have been looking at different sights," the detective replied.

"You have been checking *pensions* and hotels for the men who came over the pass," I predicted. "Also for an Englishman, or some foreigner at least, travelling alone or with a few companions and with little luggage. You have not found them."

The ratty wig came off. "I have eliminated a number of places where they might go. I have established that the riders who came in yesterday have been asking some of the same questions of some of the same people regarding the whereabouts of Colonel Moran."

"If they are not in paid lodgings then where? Cettigne is not a large place."

"Possibilities remain. The Embassies. Private houses, as guests or usurpers. Moran is capable of living rough if it is required."

"The Embassies?" Cettigne is well blessed with diplomats from England, Germany, Turkey, France, Russia, Italy, and more. Indeed, some of their lodgings are the finest architecture in the city.

---

23 This is not the biblical disciple Peter but rather Petar I, Petrović Njegoš (1747–1830), ruler of the Prince-Bishopric of Montenegro, Metropolitan of Cetinje, and Exarch (legate) of the Serbian Orthodox Church throne, who defied both the Ottoman and French empires in defence of his nation and was canonised within the Serbian Orthodox Church by his successor Petar II.

"With the right-looking credentials it would be easy to claim a place," Sherlock estimated. "The slowness of outside communication beyond the black mountains would prevent receiving verification for two or three days."

"Many of the diplomats will be here at the Zetski Dom, the Royal Theatre, to hear my performance tonight. Prince Nicolas himself will be in attendance so all the important men of the city will attend."

My guest grimaced. "Your gala would be the ideal place for an assassin to lurk. If Moran sought to flush me out there, perhaps by offering a threat to you, or if the faction hunting him misjudged the security around the event, lives might be lost."

My pulse skipped. "You think Moriarty's man knows of me?"

"James Moriarty was nothing if not thorough. His study of me was intense. On at least one occasion he had an agent penetrate my rooms at Baker Street. He would be well aware that on my desk there is a portrait of the celebrated Mme. Adler."

My pulse skipped again for another reason entirely. "A portrait of me?"

"A fee I claimed off a client of mine, remembrance of a singular encounter."

Schoolgirls flush. Adventuresses of soiled reputation are supposed to be past that. "You acquired the picture I left behind. You retained it."

"The personage to whom you sent it did not understand its value or yours, Irene. It has remained on my desk since, to remind me of a most remarkable woman. Moriarty's study of me must surely have discovered it, and through it my admiration of you. He may well have been aware of my intervention in the matter of the despicable Norton. So long as I took no other action and showed no ongoing interest in you he had no reason to weave you into his plots."

Yet Sherlock has considered the possibility anyway. Was that measure of how much he feared and respected his archenemy or indication of unspoken regard for the defiant survivor in the lithograph? If it was the latter, what did that mean?

"In coming here you have confirmed to Colonel Moran that there is a connection between us," I recognised. "Am I then part of your trap?"

"I would not place you in such danger. Nor do I wish to place the patrons of your concert at risk. The idea that an attack might happen during tonight's *Rigoletto* is most disturbing."

"Then you will agree to my suggestion?"

Sherlock's brow furrowed. Behind those keen eyes the finest mind of

"A portrait of me?"

our age chased through a million options, sifting possibilities and laying plans. "So long as you and no others are placed in peril, it remains the most logical course of action."

"Then I shall perform," I promised.

Mr Sherlock Holmes is the finest sleuth in the world, of course. But I am the finest actress.

The account of Dr John Watson, 28th June 1891:

'The Lord St. Simon marriage, and its curious termination, have long ceased to be a subject of interest in those exalted circles in which the unfortunate bridegroom moves. Fresh scandals have eclipsed it, and their more piquant details have drawn the gossips away from this four-year-old drama. As I have reason to believe, however, that the full facts have never been revealed to the general public, and as my friend Sherlock Holmes had a considerable share in clearing the matter up, I feel that no memoir of him would be complete without some little sketch of this remarkable episode.'

It felt good to have a pen in my hand. I paused for a moment to consider the opening for the account I would call 'The Adventure of the Noble Bachelor'.[24] I pondered whether I had sufficiently disguised the identity of the young man whom I was referring to as Lord St Simon and decided that the subterfuge would suffice. The world would know of my dearest friend's brilliance without miring with scandal those he had helped.

I decided that I might rely upon my literary agent to make any necessary changes[25] and continued with my testimony:

---

24 This account was published in the April 1892 edition of the *Strand Magazine* and then collected in *The Adventures of Sherlock Holmes*, October 1892.

25 Watson's confidence may have been slightly misplaced, since in editing the story Arthur Conan Doyle mistakenly altered a reference to Watson's Afghan shoulder wound, "which shattered the bone and grazed the subclavian artery" according to *A Study in Scarlet*, to that of a limb injury.

A lively debate amongst Holmesian scholars about the apparent discrepancy of Watson's wound location has run on for well over a century. This has involved elaborate theories about the injury being psychosomatic or of an unpublished incident wherein Watson receives a second Jezail wound. One favoured theory is that the injury was sustained during 'The Little Affair of the Vatican Cameos' mentioned in *The Hound of the Baskervilles*. The least extraordinary reconciliation is that Doyle, editing some more

'It was a few weeks before my own marriage, during the days when I was still sharing rooms with Holmes in Baker Street, that he came home from an afternoon stroll to find a letter on the table waiting for him.'[26]

I was interrupted by the door being thrown open. A trio of unpleasant ruffians shouldered into my consulting room, their faces obscured by woolen scarves.

My hand began to move down to the middle drawer wherein I keep my Beaumont Adams but halted when I saw that one of the intruders had already levelled a snub-nosed foreign pistol at me.

The man in the rear closed the door they had slammed through and turned the key on the interior rim-lock. The others moved into the room, the one approaching my side of my writing desk, the other with the gun taking station beside the window where he had a clear field of fire at me.

These were desperate men. The penalty for using firearms in a criminal enterprise is always death.

"Do you have an appointment?" I asked them pointedly. Already my mind was racing. Mary was asleep upstairs; she was easily tired these days and had become accustomed to an afternoon nap. My wife slumbered just one flight of steps away from armed criminals! Had I been able to grasp my service revolver I would have shot them like dogs.

The fellow who approached me had a long bayonet-knife in his left hand. He brandished it gloatingly, making it clear that he was willing to use it. "Here is my appointment, Herr Doktor."

---

medically precise description from Watson and not approving the medical jargon or not believing that readers would, amended the text to a more generalised and comprehensible but less precise description. Of such apparent errors are the Great Game made.

26 Another controversial feature of "The Adventure of the Noble Bachelor" is where to place it in Holmes' timeline. "A few weeks before my own marriage" seems simple enough, except that evidence from other parts of the Canon suggests that Watson was married from November 1886 to December 1887 (a period during which Watson gives no accounts of Holmes or himself), was single again until his marriage to Mary Morstan in May 1889, was widowed during the period in which Holmes was thought dead, and married yet again in October 1902. Some commentators have posited as many as *seven* wives for the good doctor.

The prosaic possibility is that Watson's accounts obfuscate dates in order to protect the identities of those described and that therefore marital dating evidence is inherently unreliable. Holmes' most venerable biographer, W.S. Baring-Gould, is a proponent of the "three wives" hypothesis, and his timeline for the misfortunes of Lord St Simon places the incident on Saturday 9th October 1886, before Watson's first marriage. Others argue for an April 1889 date before the confirmed Morstan wedding.

Yet others maintain that Dr Watson's entire body of work is fictional, made up wholly by Sir Arthur Conan Doyle and subsequent writers, which is, of course, ridiculous.

His Teutonic accent would have betrayed him even without his linguistic flaws. So these were the 'Krauts' whom we had observed at the docks, the men who served the supposed Moriarty and his German lieutenant.

"What do you want, sirrah?"

The bruiser glanced down at the case notes spread across my table. "You were close to Herr Holmes. You have his papers. His *dateien*—his files."

They meant Holmes' commonplace books, his meticulous indexed compilations of information about the criminal elite of Britain, the Empire, and Europe. Such material would be invaluable to any ambitious outlaw seeking to command a new underworld network.

"Holmes bequeathed his case notes to Scotland Yard," I told the intruders. "I suggest that you go there to look for them."

I never saw the blow coming when the knife-wielder drubbed his hilt-filled fist into my head. I clattered from my chair and sprawled across the rug.

"We know you have some files, Herr Doktor." The bruiser pulled a copy of *Lippincott's Monthly Magazine* from his jacket, the edition which published my recounting of *The Sign of the Four*.[27] "You are the detective's *chronist, ja?*"

Holmes' invaluable handwritten files were ranged on the top shelf behind me. I cursed myself for not thinking of their usefulness to malefactors. In my grief and sentiment I had thought such papers mere keepsakes, source material for my tribute accounts of Holmes' genius. Were they now to be used to undo much of the good work he had paid with his life to complete?

As I fretted on that question I realised that even a perfunctory search of the house would discover Mary, and once she was in these brutes' hands all was lost.

"I have a few things," I answered sullenly. I dragged myself up, ignoring the dribble of blood from my lip. I've had rougher beatings at prep school rugby.

"You will show us."

"In my surgery." I led them through the interconnecting door to the

---

27 That is the February 1890 issue. Sir Conan Doyle's autobiography describes a Langham Hotel dinner on 30th August 1889 with Lippincott's managing editor Joseph M. Stoddart, who was seeking to develop a British version of his successful American magazine. It was at this meeting that *The Sign of the Four* was commissioned, along with a contribution from fellow guest Oscar Wilde whose *A Picture of Dorian Grey* appeared in the July 1890 issue.

inner room where I prepare my medicines and occasionally perform minor operations. The room was quite small, requiring only a workbench, a padded examination table, and the paraphernalia of a working medical room. The far wall was stacked high with boxes, most of them medical periodicals and unrequired text-books.

The three intruders followed into the surgery after me. As before, one closed the door and another took station where he had a line of fire on me.

I pointed to the stacked boxes. "I hope you brought a cart."

"Which ones?" the knifeman demanded.

"All of them, of course. But if you want the index, reach up to that one in the corner, the one with the packing tape hanging loose."

There was a moment when he had to cross between me and the gunman. At that instant I scooped up the bell jar on the counter beside me and hurled it with all my strength. The heavy glass container hit the pistol wielder square on the forehead, shattering.

The contents burst out into the room. Only I knew to hold my breath as the pressurised nitrous oxide burst free, filling the room with the medical anaesthetic commonly known as 'laughing gas.'

The villains turned on me, failing to recognise the threat from the heavy fumes. I have previous experience of the chemical[28] and was careful not to inhale while the gas did its work.

The fellow with the knife came at me first. I caught him in the face with a reflex mallet and scooped his legs out from under him to wind him further. The gunman had dropped his weapon to claw at his glass-torn face. He had taken the deepest breath of nitrous oxide and was at once giggling and groaning as the effect overtook him. The guard at the door had been furthest away and now he drew a heavy gat and leaped towards me.

Those desperate days avoiding Jezail fanatics came back to me. I caught and blunted the cosh's blow on my good shoulder and buried my fist in the fellow's solar plexus. He folded over like a house of cards, but to be certain I stamped down on the hand that gripped his weapon and kicked him in the head. Afghanistan rules.

The knife-wielder tried to rise again, but now he was slashing aimlessly at the air. My chest was getting tight for want of oxygen so I simply thumped him until he lay still.

I staggered to the door, forcing myself to ignore burning lungs and reflex inhalation until I was out. I dropped to my consulting room floor and

---

28 As described by I.A. Watson in "The Lucky Leprechaun" in *Sherlock Holmes: Consulting Detective* volume 3 and *Sherlock Holmes Mysteries* volume 1.

allowed myself a period of desperate gasping. I couldn't help but giggle at my survival; some of the nitrous oxide had followed me from the room and more seeped beneath the door, but I was able to crawl away and outside, where a constable might be summoned.

A Private Memoir of Madame Irene Adler, 28th June 1891:

I felt quite sorry for M. Duvoir. My manager often had to cope with my obsessive demands about the readiness of our troupe, about the conditions of a stage or the welfare of a crew member. He is not accustomed to women who so carefully read and parse their contracts, nor who so volubly object to being publicly matched with swains who might win column inches in provincial broadsheets. Over the two years he has suffered me I have presented him with even more than the usual grief a *prima donna* wreaks upon her management.

Now he clutched his hair as if he was about to tear his whiskers from his face. "What? What do you mean? How can you…? Why would you…?"

I had announced to Duvoir that I did not intend to take up the option to continue our tour into Albania and Servia and so down to Greece. Our company's manager was not taking it well.

"The theatre in Sentari is already booked!" he objected.

"That is well," I told him. "The troupe will have somewhere to go from here. Carlotta is ready for the lead. Put on *La Traviata* and let her loose to sing Violetta."[29]

"But she is not Irene Adler!"

"Nor will she be unless she has her moment in the limelight, M. Duvoir. Give her that moment. She will not disappoint."

The poor man shook his head in bafflement. "I do not understand. Why would you throw away…" He looked up, his expression suddenly calculating. "His highness attends our performance tonight. He wishes to meet you."

"My reasons for declining a further tour are my own, M. Duvoir. I regret the inconvenience my decision makes but am fixed in my mind that it is the right course. Tonight shall be my farewell performance."

---

29 Verdi's *La Traviata* ("The Fallen Women"), based on Alexandre Dumas' 1852 novel *La Dame Aux Camélias*, is famed as a vehicle for a soprano soloist in the title role of courtesane Violetta Valéry.

There was more dialogue of course; a tedious amount of it, but a woman is entitled to skip over the trivial parts and diary only the juicy things, is she not?

Eventually my bereft manager departed to change his arrangements for the second week following and to consider the shifted fortunes of the company. Cosi had been present in my dressing room for the exchange and regarded me now with wide, surprised eyes.

"Madame..." she breathed. "What have you done? What will you do?"

"As ever, I shall do whatever I wish," I told the girl. "Will you mind dressing Carlotta?"

"She has a temper, madame."

"Remember that there is nobody you cannot slap if it is required."

"But you, madame? What...?"

I help up a hand to silence her questions. What the girl needed now was instructions, tasks to busy her hands and quieten her mind. "I have some unusual jobs for you, Cosette. First off, I require a picnic hamper, the very finest you can purchase. I want quail *fois gras*, oysters in aspic, a splendid cheese tray, everything required for an intimate meal for two."

My maid's eyes widened more as she understood that there was to be an assignation. "Oh..."

"I want a second hamper too. That must have enough fine provisions for two people to dine comfortably *al fresco* for... shall we say three days?"

"Three days?" Little Cosi's imagination was running wild now.

"Perhaps. Who knows? Make sure there is a good selection of wines suitable for the fare. Something that travels well. Take this note to the address on the front. The gentleman there will supply you with the bottles I require."

My maid was almost exploding to ask who might share this protracted repast with me. "Madame..."

"There is more, Cosi. I also require you to purchase for me a good divan, a comfortable couch where a lady might recline if she wished. And a dozen down-stuffed cushions to scatter upon and around it. And a carpet rug, say three yards in diameter, to place beneath it."

The girl nodded, her mind reeling with fantasies.

"Then acquire a canopy, something tasteful in silk that will cover the furniture and create a little bower. Buy two stands with sprays of roses, I think. Acquire candelabras, enough to hold a hundred of the best beeswax candles you can find. Another two gross candles to spare, in case."

"Candelabras? And many candles?"

"I like candlelight," I confided.

"Is this for M Sigerson?" Cosi blurted. "Or for the Prince?"

I ignored the impertinent enquiry. "When you have assembled the items I have ordered, find some strong men who can porter them for you. You have heard of the Lipa Cave? The *Lipsca Pećhina*?"

"It is some famous cave a few miles outside the city. They say it goes on forever. The interior is supposed to be very beautiful. There are great columns holding up fantastic roofs, and even a river that runs underground." Cosi caught up with the question's meaning. "They say it is a very romantic place! A trysting spot, very private, with only one entrance."[30]

"I want you to have some reliable fellows take my purchases there. I want them find a good spot and set things out, carpet, divan, lights, and canopy. I expect my hamper to be ready when I arrive for an underground picnic."

Cosi bit her bottom lip in excitement. She could not have been happier if it had been her own midnight meeting in that secret cavern. "Oh, I shall see to it, madame! Everything will be perfect! I swear it!"

I lifted a cautionary finger. "Absolute discretion, Cosi. Nobody must hear of this. Not one word to anybody, understand?"

"*Oui!* Yes. My lips are sealed."

I was gambling that they were not, but I nodded my satisfaction and set the girl about her tasks.

Cosi is a dear child and diligent in most of her duties; but she cannot keep a secret to save her life. I was counting on it.

Moran hunted Sherlock and knew about me. A man of his talents would soon learn of Cosi's covert mission and of my assignation in Lipa Cave. It would not be a great leap for a hunter of his savvy to realise that provisions for three days of an *assignment d'amour* might equate to six days of rations for a fugitive escaping through unguarded subterranean passageways under Vrtijeljka's peaks. Once in those deep tunnels, Sherlock might

---

30 The *Lipsca Pećhina* is a karst cave chain that runs from Dobrosko Seto, seven miles outside Cetinje down the eastern side of the Lovcen plateau for 3,512 metres (2.2 miles). It was first documented in 1839 by an English traveller called Lejard and was more comprehensively described by the Russian geographer Pavel Rovinsky in 1887, four years before the time of our current narrative. Cosi is wrong in stating that there is only one entrance but that was the common belief of her time. The current main access, 480 meters above sea level, was excavated by the Austrian army in 1918.

From 1905 to 1950 the Lipa Cave was open to the public as a show cave attraction. The walkways are still accessible today through an unlocked gate but visitors need to bring torches and beware of bats. A new tour company offers a range of guided visits at http://lipa-cave.me/ Beyond the old tourist routes there are a number of difficult-to-access side-tunnels that have not been fully documented.

even lie in wait for those who hunted him and spring a trap of his own.

Moran must go to the cave first then, and be ready for his enemy to arrive.

Meanwhile, that bumbling delivery agent who had shambled into my chamber earlier or some other stock character from the great detective's repertoire would be shuffling around Cettigne, speaking a word here, dropping a hint there, about a strange foreigner with a military aspect and his interest in *Lipsca Pećhina*. Hence those who sought Moriarty's right hand would also migrate into those isolated caves to corner the old tiger-hunter at last.

None of them would trouble the Royal Theatre or its final performance of *Rigoletto*.

At least so Sherlock and I hoped, on our last day in Cettigne.

The account of Dr John Watson, 28th June 1891:

Half a dozen burly fellows in worker's clothes and caps arrived before the constabulary. In my half-gassed state I worried that more Germans had come to finish the job, but then I saw that amongst the larger toughs were yet more anxious-looking urchins of tenderer years. Here were the scrub-kneed 'Baker Street Irregulars' whom Holmes had employed to such effect.

I recognised Albert Sutter, to whom informal leadership of the troupe had fallen since Wiggins' graduation. He leaned over me and asked, "Are you awlright then, Doctor Watson?"

I coughed away the last of the laughing gas and wiped my face. "I shall be," I assured the anxious young Arabs. "Some unpleasant types inside my surgery will need a trip to Scotland Yard."

My wits caught up with me. I realised that the Irregulars had come in force, bringing some of their former number that had come in force, bulked by some of their former number that had grown up and moved on to other things. Most of the older ones carried a club or stick, ready for affray.

"Them Krauts turned up at Baker Street an' all!" Sutter reported. "But Wiggins said we 'ad ter keep a watch-like on the old place, so when they turned up Reg and Judy was ready to run and get th' rest of us. We chased them bad-uns off right sharpish. Din't want a fuss, did they? An' then Mrs H said that if they was after 221B then they might 'ave a go at you, doctor. 'Get over there sharpish,' she tells us, so 'ere we are!"

I chuckled and it had nothing to do with the laughing gas. "The tip for this one will be very generous," I promised.

The constable rounded the corner from Cromwell Road at last. Sutter's confederates began to drift away.

"Keep an eye on Mrs Hudson," I instructed them. "And Sutter, drop by later on, will you? I might have a job for your lads, looking for the fellows behind all this."

The urchin winked and sped away.

The next hour was filled with policemen and a prison dray to drag away the drowsing intruders who had entered my home. I spent the time arranging for Mary to go visit her dear friend Miss Hunter where she would be safe. My worried wife was reluctant to leave me but recognised that I might act more freely without need to fear for her wellbeing.

"James, do be as careful as you can," she pleaded. "I had thought these interruptions were behind us."

"They will be," I promised. "First, though, there is some unpleasantness to settle."

"You would not be John Watson if you did not feel the need to settle it," she acknowledged as she kissed me goodbye.

Scarcely had Mary's trap rattled away than a growler sped up bearing Lestrade and Hopkins. The Scotland Yard men had learned of the attempt on Holmes' records and had sped over to consult.

"Every dock and dive is buzzing with rumour of Moriarty's return," Hopkins reported when we had retreated to my now-aired consulting room. "I daresay that these German interlopers would have had a rougher reception to their takeover otherwise."

Lestrade grunted agreement. He unfolded a wad of papers from his inner pocket. "I found these."

I recognised Holmes' script. "'Notations on the *Bayerische Unterwelt Vereinigung*'" I read.

"The Bavarian Underworld Organisation," Hopkins supplied. "Holmes had evidently made a study of it—along with everything else. There is correspondence from senior officers in the Bavarian *polezai* and some scribbled accounts from sources whose identities seem to have been encoded. Most of all there is a diagram."

Lestrade pulled out the relevant page. It was a convoluted chart of places and criminal enterprises, bulked out by names and assignments within the criminal hierarchy.

"They were nothing like as organised as Moriarty's lot," Hopkins opined, "but they were getting there. The professor liked to consult, didn't he?"

My eye was drawn to the name Falkenrath. It appeared many times, with spidery lines drawn between entries to suggest associations and spheres of influence. "We encountered one of these chaps," I observed.

"Ulrich and Ehrlich," said Lestrade. "No idea which one we saw in the warehouse."

"Not much to choose between them," Hopkins warned. "Sons of a mercenary soldier who led a band of rogues during the Franco-Prussian war and got rich from the sack of Mars-la-Tour and the Siege of Metz.[31] Educated but brutal fellows who traded on their father's infamy to horn in on illegal enterprises in Nuremberg They've built up quite an empire in the past ten years but have been cautious about treading on the toes of their rivals in Franconia and Swabia."

"And now they have scented opportunity in England," growled Lestrade. "Von Bismarck's behind this, be certain of it!"[32]

"Holmes' files on Bismarck were not sent to us," Hopkins admitted. "They and some other folders on political figures were forwarded to Mr Holmes' brother."

Lestrade dismissed that as irrelevant. "The point is what's to be done? If Moriarty is back then it's as bad as it gets. Even if people just believe he's back it's going to get very nasty. Armed robbers breaking into a respectable doctor's practice in Kensington? *The Times* will have a field day! There'll be questions in the House and a sharp note from the Home Secretary."

---

31 The "War of 1870" was a conflict between the second French Empire and the North German Confederation, ostensibly about the succession of the Spanish throne. The Battle of Mars-la-Tour on 16th August 1870 is often cited as the last successful cavalry charge, "Von Bredow's Death Ride". In any event, a Prussian force managed to defeat and rout a French army four times its size and to capture the town. The consequence was the Siege of Metz, in which German forces trapped the French army inside the city and eventually achieved decisive victory on 27th October 1870 by forcing surrender by starvation. Amongst the Prussian attackers was medical attendant Friedrich Nietzsche who contracted dysentery and diphtheria during the siege.

32 Otto Eduard Leopold, Prince of Bismarck, Duke of Lauenburg (1815 - 1898), "the Iron Chancellor", was the Prussian statesman and master-schemer who dominated European affairs from the 1860s until his death. He provoked a series of wars that ensured German unity and won an overseas empire but he was also a peacekeeper who managed to prevent much European conflict. In Britain he was regarded with respect, suspicion, and fear.

"We have to nip this in the bud," agreed Hopkins. "Otherwise we'll have more and more criminals turning to firearms and brute force, and then we'll be like the Wild West. It's not fair to expect a bobby with a night-stick to chase after lawbreakers carrying guns."

"It's got to stop. We have to stamp on it hard. But how?"

I looked down at the papers I'd had on my desk when the intrusion began. How much I wished then for Sherlock Holmes to be amongst us, that vast intelligence and unstoppable character which could reduce the most intractable problem to a reasoned solution. A new pang of loss shivered through me.

And then an idea…

"Gentlemen," I declared to the Inspectors, filled with inspiration, "it is my belief that the Moriarty we spied in the Murcheson Warehouse is an impostor. He has been set to facilitate the Falkenraths' take-over of London's illegal endeavours. The mere fiction that Moriarty has escaped Reichenbach is sufficient to do the job."

"That might be true," Lestrade responded, shrugging. "Makes no matter. We still face…"

"It matters," I insisted. "Don't you see? If rumour of Moriarty surviving can cause all this, then what we need is rumour of our own. If Professor Moriarty could survive the Falls to make a secret return, then why not Sherlock Holmes?"

A Private Memoir of Madame Irene Adler, 28th June 1891:

I am sometimes too in love with my own schemes. I have to admit it. I am so good at convincing others that I also convince myself. So it was with my lover the Crown Prince and with the man whom I supposedly married; in each case I talked myself into believing it was what I wanted, what I should do.

So it was with my deception about Lipa Cave.

The plan was so clever. I had drawn it so well, manipulated everyone just so. Between M. Duvoir and Cosi, after conversation with my understudy Carlotta and with friends and colleagues in the orchestra and chorus, I was certain that my trap was well baited. I had done well in aiding Sherlock.

I never underestimated Mr Sherlock Holmes. I made that mistake with Colonel Moran though.

I returned to my dressing room after my matinee performance. The first thing I saw was Cosi, tied to the chair at my make-up table, gagged to silence. The second thing was the man awaiting me behind the door.

The distraction of spotting my bound maid was enough for Moran to catch me off guard. The barrel of his pistol pressed into my neck, right over the jugular where a shot would most certainly end my life.

"A nice performance, Mme. Adler," the soldier praised me. "I'm more a music hall man myself but I know class when I hear it."

"Did you wish me to sign your programme?" I asked, being careful not to move.

"The last autograph of La Adler?" the Colonel considered. "That would be valuable."

"Are you here to kill me then?"

"Are you not afraid of death?"

I considered the question. "I would prefer not to die. If I do, then I have lived a life remarkable enough to satisfy the dreams of a young girl from Trenton. And you, Colonel Moran? Which frightens you more now, death or life?"

"Don't be clever with me. Professor Moriarty would have played word games with you—played and won, I guarantee it. He kept me around for when the talking stopped."

"But Professor Moriarty is dead."

Even with peripheral vision I could see the ripple of anguish that momentarily flickered across the killer's face. Whatever else Sebastian Moran was, he had been Moriarty's true friend.

"The Professor is gone. Holmes did it. Moriarty's last order to me was to kill Holmes if the detective survived an encounter with him. I'm going to do that."

There was no bravado in Moran's statement. I heard only deadly, focussed intent.

"Sherlock Holmes is not an easy man to kill," I observed. "I'm given to understand that every scrap of your commander's organisation is now in ruins. Nothing remains. You who hunt Mr Holmes are yourself hunted by those who would replace you."

"Jackals chasing a tiger! They think their numbers can bring me down? Let the Falkenraths and any others come against me! All of them who try to take what was the Professor's will end the same way!"

"Are you here to kill me then?"

"Even those men already in Cettigne to seek your death?"

Moran snorted. "Ulrich Falkenrath and his assassins? All I'll need are five bullets." There was still no boast in his voice.

"Then you know the men who follow you?"

"Yes. They think they have trapped me here in the Black Mountains? They should be careful chasing a tiger into a drain."[33]

Moran had given me the clue to survive him when he confessed Moriarty the speaker and he the man of action. I had drawn the hunter into conversation regardless; now we fought on my terrain.

"What is your intention for me then, Colonel? If it was simple murder then you could have killed me as I entered the room."

"Gad, you have pluck," Moran admitted. "So then, here's the thing. I'm a gambling man. Cards, mostly, and hunting."

"Hunting?"

"My kind, yes. Some fellows bag harmless game; grouse, deer, that kind of thing. Others like to chase dangerous prey in safe ways; on elephant-back with native beaters in the way, using a long-barrel rifle from a comfortable distance. My bag is filled with proper hunts, with treks through trackless jungle taking my turn as chaser and chased against creatures that can kill me as easily as I can them. In the Yellagiri Hills or the African veldt I'm gambling that my skill is greater then my quarry's."

"Wagering your life."

"The best kind of bet. And I'm going to stake it again now—and yours."

"What do you mean?"

"I mean that I'm turning Holmes' trap against him. When I leave here your little maid is coming with me. I'll be heading for that cave system just like Holmes wanted, just where he wants me to tangle with Falkenrath and his gunmen. But the girl will be there too."

Cosi heard Moran's intention. She shook her head wildly, desperately, too afraid to scream through her gag.

The Colonel went on. "When you have finished your performance tonight, when everybody has clapped and cheered and gone home, you'll keep your supposed assignation at *Lipsca Pećhina*. You will go there in earnest. You'll find to your canopied divan and set out your picnic and await your guest. Otherwise you will need a new maid and I shall find you tomorrow and kill you too."

"I am to be the lamb you stake out to lure Sherlock Holmes to your killing ground?"

33 In "The Adventure of the Empty House", Holmes comments upon Moran's own brave exploit in following a wounded man-eating Indian tiger into a drain

"You are a very perceptive woman. Holmes has set the game but I am changing the rules. Tell him so."

"And if he does not come into your trap?"

"Then he will still have a picture to remember you by."

The account of Dr John Watson, 28th June 1891:

'*Thayer, George Henry*, born Ealing June 11th 1843, third son of rag and bone collector; juvenile convictions for theft and petty larceny, served three years in HM Armley Jail; two arrests for receiving stolen goods, no convictions. Small independent operator, runs 'fencing' business from junkyard at Shoreditch. Principal employees Hector 'the Grab' Drewer and 'Flash' Tom Mottle, low-end enforcers. Goods stashes at 16, Burton Street and 1, Flagstone Yard. Long time illicit liaison with Meg Copperditch (formerly of Mme. Crope's on Knockpenny Lane, rtd.), two children. Not affiliated with any single theft ring, handles small-to-middle size hauls, gold and watches preferred. Retain watching brief.'

Thayer looked up from the paper whereon Holmes had written his analysis of the man.

"He knew you," I assured the handler of stolen articles. "He might have had you arrested at any time."

"Then why did he not?" Thayer was as I had seen him at the warehouse meeting, a seedy balding man running to fat. Dressed as he was in waistcoat and shirt sleeves it was easy to see the damp sweat-stains beneath his armpits. His prominent pink forehead was shiny with perspiration.

"Why bother, Georgie?" Billy challenged the fence. "When Mr 'Olmes could come down here whenever 'e pleased and watch 'oo it was came to you to pass on their loot? A gold mine, you were, Mr Thayer. You helped 'im catch no end of bad-uns."

Two unpleasant bodyguards whom I deduced to be Hector 'the Grab' and 'Flash' Tom shifted uneasily, unsure what to do.

"It is true that Sherlock Holmes found you more useful outside prison than in—barely," I agreed. "Of course, he had enough evidence that he might have had you arrested at any time had he deemed it necessary."

Thayer blinked up at me and swallowed hard. "Dr Watson, isn't it? I read about you."

"If you know who I am then you know that I am—was Holmes' friend. You might guess that some of his notebooks passed on to me."

The fence sneered. "So what is this? Blackmail? You want a payoff, is it?"

"Don't insult me, sir! I have no interest in squeezing you for money, you repellent oik!"

Flash and the Grab took steps forward. Billy moved defensively to cover my back, reaching into his coat pocket as if to draw a weapon.

"What, then?" Thayer demanded. "Why come to me with this?"

"Because I know you were at a South Bank meeting last night in the Murchison Sheds. I know with whom you met. I know what became of Lonnie Dyson. I know who did it."

Thayer's already troubled face now filled with terror. "How? I never said… I don't know nuffink!"

"Perhaps the Germans will believe you," I reflected. "Herr Falkenrath is probably a kind and forgiving chap when you get to know him."

Thayer exchanged panicked, helpless looks with his henchmen.

"Not as much fun moving up in the world as you expected, eh?" Billy noted. "Them Krauts play for keeps."

Thayer leaned over his desk towards me, speaking low and urgently. "If you know that much then you know who is behind them. What's a man to do, Dr Watson? Tell me that!"

I answered coldly. "I have no interest in helping out a man who deals in burgled goods, Thayer. I *am* concerned when German hoodlums come to my practice, to my family home, to try and steal these notes from me. Armed men, in broad daylight, in England."

If Thayer could have opened his eyes any wider he would have. Instead he swore a vile oath. "Those fools! That's the kind of thing what has the peelers slam down like a hob-nailed boot! We'll have coppers everywhere, swarming like wasps from a broken nest. And never mind Judge's Rules, they won't be playing games!"

"Inspector Lestrade did seem somewhat perturbed. I gather there will be directives from the Home Office."

"Gad! It's going to be…" Thayer's troubled thoughts latched on to the next bit of information I had fed him. "You said they came after you. But you're here."

"They were dealt with," Billy announced ominously. "Do you think Sherlock Holmes would 'ave left Dr Watson unprotected? And all 'is files, covering all the criminals in London?"

The fence was catching up now. "The Krauts, they wanted those files, so they'd 'ave us all by the throat. That's what they intended."

"They have over-reached," I declared.

Thayer forced himself to calm as best he could. He reached into a drawer of his cluttered desk and poured himself a generous three fingers of rum. When he had downed them in one he asked, "Why did you come, then, Dr Watson?"

"You and your colleagues should be aware of what Falkenrath's agents are attempting. Whoever they purport to work for, you should be cautious about joining their organisation. The Bavarians are seeking to establish an absolute hold over you—and over Henson, Gaxton, Bromsgrove, the Bruces, and all the rest."

"How could you know...?"

"We have our methods. Discovering information of that kind is... elementary."

"Pass on the message, Georgie," Billy advised. "The Krauts ain't getting London. The days of organisations like Moriarty's are over. We just got rid of one. There won't be another."

"Who's going to stop them?" the fence challenged the former page boy. "You?"

"My next stop is at the Army and Navy Club," I mentioned. "I'm meeting my old regimental commander and a few of his comrades-in-arms. German thugs might be very intimidating against Lonnie Dyson's brawlers. How do you think they would fare against the Berkshire Regiment of Foot? Would you bet against the 66ᵗʰ? Or the 5ᵗʰ Northumberland Fusiliers? Or the Connaught Rangers?"[34]

Thayer stared at me, aghast. "That would be... it would be war."

"I do not take kindly to intruders threatening my wife."

"Pass the word, squire," Billy suggested, with a wicked grin.

We departed the junkyard while our shock tactics still had the fence

---

34 Resolving yet another potential Canonical continuity conundrum, Holmesians now generally acknowledge that Dr John H. Watson of the Army Medical Department was first sent to India as part of the 5th Northumberland Fusiliers before being transferred to the 66th Foot, also known as the Berkshires. It was with his second unit that Watson participated in the Second Anglo-Afghan War and was wounded at the Battle of Maiwand.

Watson and Holmes' association with and goodwill from the 99th Regiment of Foot (the Scots Brigade), which merged in 1881 with the 88th Foot as the Connaught Rangers ("the Devil's Own"), was revealed in I.A. Watson's "Spring-Heeled Jack" in *Sherlock Holmes: Consulting Detective* volume 7.

and his employees reeling. We passed beyond the wooden gates, chuckling to each other.

"Do you think they'll spread the word, doctor?" Billy asked.

"I imagine they will, lad. Now we'd best get off to our other meetings. Holmes will require a detailed account of all we have done when we meet with him tonight."

We hailed a cab and rattled away; leaving the secret spies that Falkenrath had left watching Thayer's yard to report what they heard.

✹✹✹

A Private Memoir of Madame Irene Adler, 28th June 1891:

ettigne's great Royal Theatre, the Zetski Dom, was not quite finished.[35] The stately white façade and clock tower were complete and the elaborate interior of the main auditorium was stuccoed and gilded. The first production had been Prince Nikola I Petrović's play *Balkanska Carica*[36] some three years earlier. But the backstage areas were still swathed in scaffolding, some walls were not yet plastered, and corridors and dressing rooms tended to be littered with construction materials. The planned museum, library, and hall of public records were not yet installed.

There are many tasks to do on a closing night gala when the crowned head of the nation is attending with his court and ambassadors of the powers of Europe. Before our final performance M. Duvoir was rushing around so red-faced and panicked that many of the company were concerned for his heart. The last I saw of the poor man before the curtain rose he was berating the men erecting the trestles of floral displays, arguing with some captain of police about security arrangements, and trying to resolve some dispute between the dancing master and the orchestra conductor about precedence in Act Two.

I only had time for passing sympathy, however. I sought out our new second violin, a lanky fellow in his formal tuxedo who sat quietly at his place amidst the chaos, tuning his borrowed fiddle.

---

35 Josip Slade's distinctive design is now regarded as a classic of its era. Although the façade was modified in the early 1900s, the Zetski Dom (Zeta House) is considered a treasure of Montevidean architecture and is included in the European Route of Historic Theatres.

36 "The Balkan Princess"

I stopped to speak to the newcomer, as any gracious First Lady should to welcome another member of the company but as so few do.

"I had an unexpected visit from your Colonel," I warned him in a muted whisper. "In my very dressing room. He has taken Cosette."

Sherlock very carefully laid down his instrument before clenching his fists until they went white. "I have erred," he confessed, as if it were as unlikely as the moon moving backwards in the heavens.

"You said he was dangerous. He anticipated your trap and has set one of his own. If I do not go to the caves tonight then Cosi's life is forfeit. He knows that if I am there you will follow."

Holmes touched his long fingers to his brow as if to stimulate his calculations. "He has foreseen me and he knows I will have directed the Bavarians to him also. It was a mistake to come here."

My heart churned with dismay. "Really?" The Lipa cave trap had been my idea, alternative to a dismal showdown at some barren pass; or had Sherlock foreseen how my mind worked and manipulated me into suggesting the ploy? "Is it not natural to seek out whatever resources are available in a crisis? Or do you still believe me one of Moriarty's pawns and another problem to solve? *La donna è mobile.*"[37]

"You are a problem," Sherlock Holmes confessed, "but not one set by Professor Moriarty."

"What shall we do? I cannot abandon Cosi."

Holmes gestured to the bustle around us as the first of the audience were admitted. "We must follow our plan as much as we might. It is possible that Moran may have taken your maid as a false lure, intending to focus my attentions on the *Lipsca Pećhina* when he still intends to strike at me here. There are also five German gunmen loose in Cettigne. Herr Falkenrath may decide that the Colonel will attend this event in spite of the cave trap and may have deployed some of his forces in this very theatre. Tonight we must deal with them all."

"Even though Colonel Moran has Cosi hostage?"

"Even then." Holmes penetrating eyes locked onto mine. "If he has indeed taken your dresser to the caves then you will need to go there too if she is to be saved. It will be dangerous. You will accompany me?"

"Yes. I shall."

He clapped his hands together in a gesture of approval, as if all his opinions were validated. "There is no other woman whose qualities I

---

37 "The woman is fickle", the first line and title of the Duke of Mantua's canzone at the start of *Rigoletto* Act 3. It is probably Verdi's best known song and one of relatively few opera tunes to still be recognised by the wider public.

would trust in this, whom I would ask to face such adversity. I believe I can rely upon you as I would my closest companion."

"You regard me and so you would risk me?" That was as akin to a declaration of affection as Mr Sherlock Holmes might ever utter.

"There are many variables in play tonight. The odds of resolving matters properly are considerably enhanced if I can count upon your aid, Irene. It is, of course, unquestionably safer for you to remain here."

"I have never shied from adventure. I have been led astray by men before. It is too late for me to change my nature now."

We parted as the auditorium began to fill. I wondered at Sherlock's raw courage, sitting in full view in the orchestra pit preparing his instrument as the public thronged to their seats. Any one of them might be Falkenrath's assassin. Even now Moran might be concealed somewhere setting up that lethal airgun that Sherlock had described.

Had I betrayed the detective's disguise by speaking with him for too long?

I hastened back to my dressing room, calling for other assistance to dress since Cosi was taken from me. I halted only to stop Carlotta vapouring as she tends to do before a big performance. She decided that she might overcome her hysterics to avoid a slap from the *prima donna*. Wise child.

As I was laced into my first costume I spared a worry for little Cosi, held fast somewhere by a ruthless hunter. I determined to do what I must to see her safe. One must take care of one's people. I wondered whether I would betray Sherlock to rescue her if I must, then realised that I would not. I would burn the world rather than harm him.

A hasty thump on my door warned me of curtain in three minutes. I proceeded backstage and used a star's privilege to peer through the gap in the drapes to examine the house.

The Zetski Dom is laid out in a traditional manner, with three tiers of galleries on sides and rear looking down over the stalls. The boxes are arrayed in the Continental fashion, some of them actually angled slightly away from the stage; those who occupy such seats have come to see and be seen, not to watch the production. The first circle is atypically low, so that only a four foot balcony separates the royal box from the edge of the stage and the orchestra pit. A charming actress might lean across and flirt with a visiting prince face to face if she so chose.

Box number one was still unoccupied except for two guardsmen in elaborate livery, dressed up like those tin soldiers one sees in a child's playroom. Their rifles were new and bright. Box three, the next one, was no longer reserved for my guest Herr Sigerson. Instead it was occupied with the next rank of dignitaries deemed worthy of proximity to the sovereign prince of Montenegro.[38] Box two, opposite the royal enclosure, was filled with the French and Italian ambassadors.

Then it was too late for any further observation, too late for evaluation or any other conscious thought save that required to perform. I had to be poor Gilda, to go on stage and fall in love with a scheming, cursed man for whom I would sacrifice my life.[39]

"Col pensier il mio desir
a te sempre volerà,
e fin l'ultimo mio sospir,
caro nome, tuo sarà."[40]

The account of Dr John Watson, 28th June 1891:

We avoided meeting at Baker Street. I told myself it was because it was watched by the enemy. In truth I think I did not want to pass through that well-remembered door into the rooms where Holmes and I had enjoyed long fellowship.

Nor did we gather behind the ancient brick walls of the Detective Branch's headquarters that back onto Great Scotland Yard. Wiggins and his fellows were uncomfortable appearing there, and in any case the Metropolitan Police investigators were in the midst of relocating themselves to larger premises that would be known as New Scotland Yard.[41]

---

38 Nicholas I Mirkov Petrovich-Nyegosh (1841-1921) reigned as sovereign prince of Montenegro from 1860 but did not claim the title king until 1910.

39 Gilda, beautiful daughter of the hunchbacked jester Rigoletto, falls disastrously in love with his master the licentious Duke of Mantua, as a result of a curse laid by the father of one of the Duke's sexual conquests. She eventually sacrifices her life to save the Duke from assassins sent by Rigoletto.

40 "In my thoughts, my desire will ever fly to you, and my last breath of life shall be, beloved name, of thee." Gilda, *Rigoletto*, Act 1, Giuseppe Verdi.

41 "Scotland Yard", the informal name for both the investigative branch of the London Metropolitan Police and its headquarters, has moved several times since its inception at 4, Whitehall Place after the Metropolitan Police Act 1829 established the force. Great Scotland Yard, allegedly named because centuries earlier it had housed roy-

Instead we assembled in my Kensington practice, where signs of recent intrusion has been so recently erased. Clustered into my consulting room were Lestrade and Hopkins, very different models of a police investigator, Billy, our former buttons, and Wiggins, resplendent now in the superior livery of the Diogenes Club.

These four between them represented a wealth of data and resource. Lestrade was now amongst the most experienced of the Scotland Yard men, sharing with his rival Gregson the mantle of head of the old guard. There were few "old lags" or traditional dodges and wheezes that he did not know and could not thwart. Holmes thought him plodding and dull, yet oftentimes that steady diligence is what police work requires and yields eventual success.[42]

Stanley Hopkins was the coming man. New then to the Detective Branch he was a great admirer of Holmes' methods and tried to apply them in his work to the irritation of his compeers. Time would season his skills.[43] Of all the Scotland Yard men he was the most organised and had spent the most time sifting Holmes' indexes for vital information.

Billy had been our runner when first Holmes and I took lodging with Mrs Hudson. We had watched him grow from a cheeky irrepressible boy to an adventurous young man. The unusual errands he had been set over

---

al Scottish prisoners, was Whitehall Place's "backyard" and the entrance by which the Detective Branch accessed the site.

In 1888 the Detective Branch had grown considerably from its original roster of eight and a new site was acquired overlooking the Thames on Victoria Embankment. This site, dubbed New Scotland Yard, was occupied from 1890. During demolition and reconstruction for the police headquarters a partial corpse was discovered. The so-called "Whitehall Mystery" remains one of the Yard's most famous unsolved cases. *Sherlock Holmes, Consulting Detective* readers may wish to await "The Scotland Yard Corpse" by I.A. Watson in a future volume.

In the 1960s New Scotland Yard moved again to a modern concrete and glass office block on Broadway. This building houses the "national crime computer", the Home Office Large Major Enquiry System, or HOLMES; it's training program is called Elementary.

Current plans are for the police headquarters to move again to the Curtis Green Building, back on the Embankment, and that site will also be renamed Scotland Yard.

42 "Rat-faced" Lestrade appears in no less than thirteen of the Canon stories including the first, usually playing the role of Holmes' critical rival and reluctant ally. The character has become pre-eminent in the public's perception amongst the many policemen whom Holmes encounters in his investigations. In film and modern Holmes literature he is often selected as the representative police inspector who serves as the great detective's foil and stooge.

43 Hopkins is the investigating officer in "The Adventure of the Abbey Grange", "The Adventure of the Pince-Nez", and the "Adventure of Black Peter", all set during the mid 1890s. He is sometimes portrayed as Holmes' protégé, pioneering modern forensic detection in a changing police force.

the years had won him a broad circle of eccentric acquaintances and he had become an invaluable means of harvesting intelligence from the oddest corners of the city.

I first knew Wiggins as a scrub-kneed lad running wild with one of the many gangs of street children whose neglect and circumstance disgrace our capital. Holmes occasionally employed these youngsters as spies and informants. Over the years he had moulded them into a disciplined, motivated troop of agents, quietly steering many of them away from grim lives of petty crime towards more positive pursuits. Wiggins' singular childhood experiences were no doubt of use to the Diogenes Club's most enigmatic member, Holmes' elder brother. The lad's former contacts and new associations gave him a unique sense of London's hidden tides.

We met now, these five us of, each holder of some part of Sherlock Holmes' legacy, to discuss what we should do next.

"Word is out," Billy announced, grinning from ear to ear. "There's whispers everywhere that if Moriarty is back then so is Mr 'Olmes. Not long after we went from old Thayer's yard 'e got a visit from some Krauts wanting answers. But by then it was too late to shut 'em up."

"So Moriarty or Falkenrath or whoever is against us has heard the doctor's threats about bringing in his army pals," Hopkins reflected.

"Surely he would know that the British Army cannot deploy in peacetime to address a police matter without a judge's order under the Riot Act?" I objected.

"I expect the Bavarians do it differently," Lestrade sniffed. "They might believe you could pull in a squad of Berkshires to sort them out."

"Word is out, anyhow," Wiggins agreed. "There's been more scuffles, a few quite nasty, between the fellows following the Krauts and the ones as won't go down quiet-like. The Moriarty name isn't cowing them as well as the Germans hoped."

"'Course not!" Billy exclaimed. "Even if it was the old Professor, you think every cracksman, dip, and rumbler in London was 'appy 'e was there lurking behind them? That they 'ad to peel off a wedge from the top of their cash-pile to keep 'im sweet? Looking over their shoulder all the time in case they got a bullet in the back from one of Moriarty's enforcers?"

Hopkins nodded. "Some of the bosses who benefited from Moriarty's organisation might miss him. A lot of folks might fear him. But there's plenty more, including a lot of low types who had to knuckle under to him, who wouldn't welcome him back."

"And we have started the debate," I ventured. "So what now?"

"We need to find this so-called Moriarty and arrest him. That Falkenrath cove too!" Lestrade determined. "We witnessed him displaying Dyson's tortured remains. The testimony of a Scotland Yard Inspector and Dr Watson, that's enough for a conviction. I should have pinched him then and there."

"We'd 'ave ended up pegged out in crates next to Lonnie the Slash," Billy objected.

Lestrade had to acknowledge that our situation had not been ideal for a successful arrest.

Hopkins returned to the problem "What now, then? We've turned the Germans' trick against them a little—if trick it is! We have provoked some trouble. If Falkenrath's men chased down Thayer to find out what Dr Watson said, won't they also want to speak to the good doctor in person?"

"That's why we're taking precautions," Lestrade rumbled. My practice was watched now, not only by the constable standing sentry beneath my surgery lamp but also by hidden guards carrying firearms. I doubted that our opponents would be so stupid as to send more thugs to my home but we had made provision all the same.

"Those three you gassed are refusing to speak," Hopkins reported to me. "We're letting them have a night in the cells. There are some hard cases in there with no love for the Krauts. We'll see if your attackers are still so close-mouthed come the morning."

"They won't know anything," scoffed Lestrade. "Their kind never do."

"There was much to learn from them," young Hopkins argued. "There was all kinds of dust on their trousers, for example, and iron filings and a smell of tea-leaves."

"The Murcheson Warehouse was packed with cases from Shanghai, all carrying char,"[44] the senior Inspector pointed out. "Leave it, lad. You're not Sherlock Holmes."

I suppressed a pang of mourning and determined to take charge. "We need to find this Falkenrath character and the chap claiming to be Moriarty. An arrest warrant sounds to be simple enough, but it's no use unless we can serve it. We must discover their hideout and go in there with sufficient manpower to overwhelm whatever guards they have."

"They're keeping that pretty dark," Billy pointed out. "It's not like I 'aven't asked about."

"Same here," Wiggins agreed. "But there's got to be a trail. At the back

---

44 Tea

of all this is an attempt to revive and control Professor Moriarty's net-work. And that was all about money an' power. Moriarty took a slice of the operations he oversaw. New Moriarty will want to do the same. The Falkenraths need that cash to fund their takeover. So follow the money."

As the lad spoke I heard a colder, more sophisticated analysis behind his suggestion. I wondered whether he had been primed by consultation with that aloof civil servant Mr Mycroft Holmes. In any case his idea was a good one.

"I'll get Albie Sutter to send a few of the lads out," Wiggins offered. "They'll follow on after some of the racketeers and chase where the pay-offs go. Eventually the Krauts will get their cut and we'll see where it ends up."

"Carefully," I cautioned. "We've seen how brutal these Germans can be. Don't put children in danger."

"Credit us for knowing 'ow to slip away, Dr Watson."

"I'll have another go at the prisoners, then," Hopkins offered. "See if they ever collected or delivered any cash for their employer."

"And I'll try and find out if there's to be another meeting called," announced Billy. "They thought they'd got it all sewn up with that last 'un, but now they might need to gather the faces again to put the message one more time. Maybe even tonight, before rumour wrecks everything for them."

"If they do," Inspector Lestrade said with relish, "*that* is when we strike!"

✱✱✱

A Private Memoir of Madame Irene Adler, 28th June 1891:

n every performance there comes a moment of clarity where one watches oneself perform. For me, in *Rigoletto*, it is usually that moment where the chorus sings *"Zitti, zitti, moviamo a vendetta"*—Softly, softly, the trap is closing—and my abductors drag me off, leaving only my scarf behind as clue to my capture.

It's just before the curtain for Act One, and by then I know how well I have served my art. I see myself, my fellow actors, my audience, and there is a still instant of revelation wherein I assess all.

On that stage, in the Royal Theatre of Cettinge before that glittering

"We've seen how brutal these Germans can be."

crowd, I saw three things. There was the prince, leaned forward in his chair, utterly captured by the opera. Queen Milena and their nine children were not with him.

Behind him were his guards, carelessly enthralled as they had not expected to be by the production. They should have been looking outwards at the auditorium, at the packed lower and upper circles and the crowded stalls. Most especially they should have watched the curtained boxes where an assassin could assemble a weapon and aim it before he was spotted by casual observers.

Finally, there was Second Violin, scraping away in the orchestra, his face rapt as he produced music, a part of that well-matched machine of men and instruments that were every second heartbeat of our opera. And yet his eyes never stopped flicking across the hall, never deviated from vigilance for a hidden enemy.

It was at that instant of artistic awareness that loud reports echoed around the theatre and the wall behind the prince was marred by two exploding chunks of plaster. Someone screamed. A soldier seized Prince Nicholas and pressed him to the floor.

The orchestra faltered. The singers halted in mid phrase. Some of the audience stood up and looked around, shocked and surprised at the sound of gunfire, not thinking that by their prominence they exposed themselves to other shots.

Second Violin rose from his chair and pointed his bow. "There! On the upper balcony! Two men in box twelve!"

I saw them now, a pair of burly fellows in ill-fitting eveningwear. They were hastily vacating their seats and pressing out into the corridor behind their box.

"Get them!" a guard captain shouted in Montenegrin, parroting Sherlock's gesture and pointing at the fleeing spectators. The heavy tramp of booted soldiers added to the confused squaws of the crowd.

More soldiers arrived to hasten the Prince from his royal box, presumably to some prepared retreat route in case of danger. By the box door were two deep imprints in the wall where plaster had been sprayed out by explosive force. They looked for all the world like bullet impacts. Only an expert would have determined that the divots were caused by explosives already concealed beneath the fresh-painted dado, that twists of paper had held gunpowder which had simulated gunshots.

I marvelled at Sherlock's forensic calculations to conceal exactly the right amount of sulphur, charcoal, and saltpetre at exactly the right spots where accumulated heat from the box's wall gas mantle would ignite them at the right time.

The effect he had sought was achieved. Two men he had identified as watching for Moriarty were now themselves exposed and on the run, suspected of attempted regicide. No other spectators would have reached for their own weapons at the report of gunfire. Two of the Germans were exposed and fleeing.

The theatre was one moment from panic. It was time to take control.

"Ladies and gentlemen!" I called, then repeated myself in French and Serbo-Croatian.[45] "Please remain calm and keep to your seats. There has been an unfortunate incident but it is now over. The Prince is safe and is being escorted from the building. Stewards will shortly come to guide you to the exits. Please follow their instructions. We are civilised people here and we will comport ourselves as such, shall we not? I regret that we cannot complete our performance for you but hope that you will remember our endeavours so far with favour."

I took a bow. A house of shocked patrons applauded my words. I am that good.

The curtains closed behind me and the gas lights were turned up to facilitate evacuation. I heard Germanic swearing from the upper gallery and saw that the soldiers had grappled their quarries. Both men were disarmed and close held, trying to explain that they had not fired the shots at the sovereign of Montevideo. Nobody was listening to them.

I glanced to the orchestra. The borrowed violin was back in its case. Its borrower had gone.

I gathered my skirts and hastened backstage to change and join him for the most dangerous part of our adventure.

The account of Dr John Watson, 28th and 29th June 1891:

ews came in that night, independently verified by three of Sutter's runners, that another summit had been called. The same criminal operators were expected to assemble at the same warehouse as before.

That was why Lestrade and I found ourselves again scrambling after

---

45 Montevidean, the national language of Montevideo, is a dialect of Shtovakian, itself derived from Serbo-Croatian.

Billy over the weed-slick mouldy timbers under the Murcheson sheds, while the foetid ripples of the tide-swollen Thames washed only inches below us—and sometimes over our boots!

The journey was more treacherous than before. This morning's rain had swollen the river and the Thames basin was at its highest as the tide turned. The brown water washing beneath us was something between mud and ordure. The rank stench below the timber pier's gloomy under-drawings made it difficult to breathe. I held my lantern tentatively, afraid that some pocket of gas might be detonated by its flickering flame.

Our voyage before had seemed long and difficult. This one seemed harder still. I heard Lestrade wheezing behind me. At one point he may have retched; it was impossible to tell from the liquid below us.

We slithered and struggled until we found the chalk marks and rag from before. Billy signalled for me to point the lens of my storm-lamp downwards so it would not betray us as he tested the hatch. The trap-door hinged open and he slipped through it to investigate the warehouse.

A long time seemed to pass, although I suspect it was only a few seconds. Long enough for me to reflect upon my hubris in attempting such adventure without Holmes to back me up. Schemes which had seemed so clever in the warm comfort of my surgery now revealed themselves to be flimsy, desperate things, ploys too weak for Holmes to ever have considered. What pride in association with the great detective had goaded us to take up his mantle? What terrible fall would follow when we encountered events that only he might correct?

The slightest whisper from above bade us pass through the hatch. I heaved myself upwards, trying not to wheeze at the exertion. Lestrade climbed after, puce-faced with his efforts at silence.

Billy gestured for me to completely cover the lantern. I hooded it and blinked to accustom myself to the gloom.

There was light. A single brazier in the circle already burned. A sole sentry warmed his hands by it. He had a rifle strapped over one shoulder.

Lestrade hissed at the firearm. He fingered his police whistle but knew it was not yet time to shrill it. Fifty good men awaited in cover outside the dock tonight. When all the felons were assembled, a sharp series of blasts on that instrument would bring them in ready to scoop up 'Moriarty', Falkenrath, and their whole set of criminals.

At least so we had planned.

Billy had got us into place just in time. We had scarcely settled when the sentinel was joined by another. The two men exchanged words in

German and began to light the other braziers. In the improved light we could see that the warehouse was fuller than before. New boxes were stacked up behind the meeting area; all stamped with Shanghai marks and tea company stencils.

Within the quarter hour more people arrived. Even as the church clocks jangled midnight and the sonorous tolling of Big Ben confirmed their opinion, a mixed huddle of hooligans were chivvied into the circle of firelight. Amongst them was the fence Thayer, but not his bodyguards. In fact none of the illegal operators had attendants protecting them tonight. All looked nervous.

The men who shepherded them were all armed. They were young and fit, short-cropped or shaven-headed in the Teutonic style. Most carried long guns though a few preferred hand weapons. Any deference they had shown to the indigenous criminals last time was gone now. I saw one man shove the older Bruce's back to speed him on. The younger Bruce glared as if ready to kill but could do nothing.

When the nine 'guests' were in position there was other movement. The grim thin figure who claimed himself Professor Moriarty moved to one edge of the firelit ring as he had before. Falkenrath flanked him like a predator waiting to pounce upon the lesser villains.

"So you came," 'Moriarty' said at last. "That was wise. Very wise."

"Where are they?" demanded Gaxton the Enforcer. I heard genuine fear in the strong-man's voice. "Bring them out."

"But certainly. Bring them."

Falkenrath turned to his fellows. *"Führe sie heraus."*

More brutes dragged a very mixed selection of newcomers into the shed. Here were five women of various ages, a pair or boys of twelve or thirteen, and three infants. One of the younger females clutched close a swaddled babe.

"Hostages!" gasped Lestrade. "I don't know all of them, but that woman there is Gaxton's wife. *That's* how Falkenrath got everyone to attend again tonight! How devilish!"

"Your families are returned to you," 'Moriarty' declared. "Perhaps you will not be so foolish as to spread alarming rumours and plot disobedience in future?"

"What *about* Sherlock Holmes, then?" Thayer demanded. "I told you what I over'eard, and your people 'eard it too!" The fence's face was swollen with contusions. He clung now to one of the boys and to a golden-haired girl-child who sobbed into his shoulder.

"This is getting harder," Billy whispered to us. "Do we call in help now?

If so what's to stop them Krauts from grabbing the little-un's as hostages again?"

Falkenrath addressed the fence's argument. "Sherlock Holmes' survival was only a rumour. A false rumour. He's dead. Dr Watson was trying to be clever, casting doubts to interfere with the Professor's plans. I'll prove it."

Too swiftly to anticipate, the German seized the blonde girl from Thayer's grasp and pressed a Lancaster pistol to her temple. "Come out, Dr Watson. Appear now or this *kinder* will suffer an injury you will not be able to treat."

"Ah, yes," 'Moriarty' announced to his captive audience. "Did I neglect to mention that we have other visitors, tonight? They set a trap for us, but I am afraid that the trap has rather been sprung upon them."

A Private Memoir of Madame Irene Adler, 29th June 1891:

Sherlock Holmes had selected a covered wagon, a two-horse dray with a high canopy that could conceal the driver on the running board and a passenger behind. I appreciated the precaution, which would make it harder for a rifleman perched on a high building or overhanging cliff to target us on our departure from Cettigne.

Harder to target, but not impossible.

We took the Eastern road from the city, beginning along the same route by which the Bavarians had arrived. We diverted south after only a few miles, under the looming peak of Mount Caba into a steep valley descent towards the village of Lipa. The way was completely unlit, illuminated only by the swaying yellow arcs of our carriage lamps and the constellations above us.

The road was little more than a farmer's track. Sherlock indicated marks of earlier passage, including several well-shod horses whose strides suggested they were not of agricultural stock. Three of the tracks were spread in proportion as if men rode together. A fourth set of prints was singular but heavy as if the mount had carried a double burden.

We passed one farmhouse, closed up and silent for the night. It was beyond midnight as we dog-legged between brooding black rocks towards the entrance to the rendezvous cave.

My fears were more palpable in the lonely darkness. "Do you think Cosi is alive?" I ventured.

"Yes," Sherlock answered at once. "Alive she is an advantage to the man holding her; a hostage or bargaining chip. There is no gain in Moran killing her unless she becomes a burden. We must prevent that."

"When you calculated a confrontation in *Lipsca Pećhina* you did not expect Cosi or me to be present."

"Adjustments must be made based upon circumstances. If the parameters have been varied then the options available vary too."

Sherlock seemed as cold and remote as the stars.

I checked my skirts, where I concealed a pair of pistols from my dressing room and a good sharp thin-bladed dagger. A lady accustomed to travelling alone requires certain insurances.

We rattled past another unlit hovel and dropped sharply into the lee of an outcrop. Sherlock reigned in the horses and paused to inspect the road ahead. "If I were to set a trap for travellers then this is where I would place it," he noted. "Around this tight bend, before any light can warn a rider of danger."

He slipped from his seat, took one of the lamps, and edged around the bend. "Ah," he sighed.

"What is it?"

"Blood on the road. A substantial amount. A lethal amount. Let us see..."

I peered after the detective as he studied the marks upon the muddy bend. There was a glistening coil of thin wire discarded at the side of the track.

"Cheesewire," Sherlock informed me. "It was stretched taut across the road here at such a height as to catch a rider in the throat. Judging by the traces here it succeeded in its task."

"A man died here tonight?"

"Yes. One of three riders, as I read these tracks. He fell from his horse here, to the left. His companion scarcely avoided the same fate—a minor injury to an upflung arm, perhaps? The severely-hurt rider toppled from his steed and landed upon his back, so, bleeding profusely. Judging from the spray effect, he had sustained..."

Holmes remembered that he was not now reeling off deductions to his Dr Watson but to a member of the fairer sex.

"Please proceed," I prompted him.

"He died here," Sherlock abbreviated his account. "His comrades loaded him back on his horse, cut down the wire, and proceeded more cautiously thereafter. Judging by levels of coagulation and allowing for local climate variables I would say the incident took place around two hours ago."

"So Moran was not in the theatre. He came here to prepare and he set that trap for those who might follow."

"He has already reduced their numbers by one. Now there are but three deadly adversaries remaining in the Lipa Cave."

Before we proceeded on Holmes rigged a pair of wooden staves at the forward corners of our carriage to protrude above our head height. He did not expect another cheesewire trap but it was a prudent precaution. We left the gory ground behind and followed the winding track.

Lipa was no more than half a dozen buildings and barns. A loosed dog barked at our passing but nothing else stirred. A scant two hundred yards beyond the last house the forest pressed in close and another trail switched back from the road we had been following. A hand-carved sign and arrow proclaimed the way to *Lipsca Pećhina.*

The new path rose steeply. It was almost too narrow for our wheelbase. Low branches scraped our canopy. We followed a ridge north, cliff towering above us to our right and a tree-choked drop on our left. Forest insects swarmed us, attracted by our lamps.

The trail hairpinned again, leading us back along the top of the cliff-ridge. We found a clearing where three horses were tied. A dead man was strapped onto one of the saddles.

Of course Sherlock examined him. "Clothing bought in Bavaria. Boots from Bamberg. A cartridge belt... .22 long rifle cartridges, I see. His weapon has been removed by his comrades. Passport papers in the name of Shultz."

"He is certainly one of the Germans that hunt Moran, then?"

"Indubitably, Irene. His knuckles betray the grazes of an habitual fist fighter. He has served as a boxer at some time but has also utilised less disciplined combat forms. Recent calluses indicate a protracted mounted journey, which supports what we know of his arrival. And yet he is not well equipped for mountainous or subterranean environments. He was more experienced and better suited for urban lawbreaking than for this wild terrain."

"I know how he felt," I confessed. What use my manipulation skills and careful planning on this lonely hillside surrounded by murderers?

"The game is afoot, Miss Irene Adler," Sherlock Holmes told me. Or was that a challenge?

Ahead of us were steps cut into the rock and the looming mouth of the *Lipsca Pećhina.*

"Let us play," I told Sherlock, and began to climb.

* * *

The account of Dr John Watson, 29th June 1891:

We came out and surrendered. What other choice did we have, with a gun pointed at an innocent child's temple?

"Gentlemen, may I present Dr J. H. Watson, Inspector G. Lestrade, and... some nonentity who once answered the door at 221B Baker Street," the pretender Moriarty announced.

We were marched under guard from our place of concealment and divested of our firearms. Falkenrath's thugs discovered the handcuffs in our pockets and used them to shackle our hands behind our backs.

I faced off against the man who claimed to have killed Sherlock Holmes. "Professor James Moriarty?" I began.

"The same. It was foolish for you to try the same trick twice, doctor. When it became evident that our previous meeting had been spied upon it was not difficult to locate the point of entry by which you gained your intelligence. The whole reason for calling another *rendezvous* here in the same place was to tempt you to such boldness a second time."

"What are the names of your brothers?" I asked.

The impostor frowned. "What?"

"Your brothers. If you are Professor Moriarty you should know your siblings. Or tell me, in what year and from what university did you graduate? What was the title of your first thesis? By which words did you first address Sherlock Holmes? If I am thirteen stone seven pounds here then how much would I weigh upon the moon? What is Newton's Second Law? Who was the abominable Merridew?"

'Moriarty' glanced for guidance to Herr Falkenrath.

"He can't help you," I declared. "Your imposture is discovered! The real Professor could answer any and all of those questions in an instant."

"He's a fake!" One-Ear Henson spat. His face was killing-set. Only the firearms trained upon the brute saved the false Moriarty from immediate death.

"A ruse," Falkenrath admitted. "It has served us well enough." He turned to his agents and snapped, *"Box sie!"*

While the would-be ruler of London's underworld kept his pistol at a child's forehead, the remainder of the Kraut gang prised open packing crates and bundled local criminals and hostages alike inside them. The lids were hammered down, trapping everyone inside.

Only Lestrade, Billy, and I were not so confined. When the last of the captives was boxed—Thayer's hostage daughter was tossed in with him at the last minute—Falkenrath had the three of us bound to one of the warehouse's timber support columns with a length of chain looped through our handcuffs.

"You were almost clever enough, Herr Doktor," the Bavarian told us. "You exposed our Moriarty double quite nicely. It would have caused a problem had we intended any of the men we brought here tonight to live. Fortunately we had already determined their loyalties too compromised, their credence too stretched by your confidence trick. They were already scheduled to die."

"You brought their families here too!" Billy objected, rattling his shackles in vain.

No, not in vain. While our captors' attention was on the former page they were not watching Lestrade fumbling his police whistle from inside his shirt.

"Tonight is about sending a message," Falkenrath explained. "A declaration of intent."

I sneered at him. "You think mass murder will get you what you want? You do not understand our nation at all. We do not truckle to bullies."

"Then you have not yet been bullied hard enough."

Lestrade brought his silver whistle to his lips and let off three sharp blasts, then three more. "There!" he shouted triumphantly. "Whatever you do now, you'll never do it again. This place will be surrounded by inspectors and unformed men in no time at all! The trap is sprung!"

"Indeed it is," Falkenrath agreed. "Dekker, set the fuses."

The man who had claimed to be Moriarty scuttled off to uncover a rats' nest of fusewire. The military fuses ran regulation lengths to those new tea crates that occupied half the floor.

"Gunpowder comes from China as well as Lapsang souchon," Falkenrath observed. "There is enough explosive here to destroy this warehouse, the wharf beyond, and many of the dwellings that ring it. It will decimate this part of the harbour. It will most certainly kill the officers who are trying to batter down the reinforced doors of this shed long before they get in-

*"Thank you so much, **Doktor** Watson, for your assistance."* Falkenrath gloated.

side." He yanked the warning whistle from Lestrade's neck. "Thank you for bringing them here to be part of the lesson."

"Oh G---!" the Inspector breathed. "They're all outside! Hopkins, Gregson, Forrester, Forbes, Barton…"

"Many problems removed with one stroke," Dekker crowed.

"Thank you so much, Doktor Watson, for your assistance," Falkenrath gloated. "We could not have managed without you."

They checked that the fuses were burning steadily and retreated for the very trapdoor by which we had arrived. Once down under the building there were too many lines of retreat for the constabulary to cover. The Krauts would get away, mass murdering their opposition as they had in Nuremberg, criminal and policeman alike.

Falkenrath gave me a last insolent wave as he lowered the hatch and vanished. We were left in darkness save for damped dying braziers and the deadly sparking of a dozen shortening fuses.

A Private Memoir of Madame Irene Adler, 29th June 1891:

Hardy voyagers tramping through Montenegro may purchase a locally-printed pamphlet about Lipa Cave, badly typeset in Serbo-Croatian, English, and what its translator fondly imagined was French. No more than sixteen pages long it distils what is known about the extensive and fascinating *Lipsca Pećhina*: that it is over three thousand yards long, switchbacking through lower and higher levels down to an underground river; that there are spectacular cascades of stalagmites and stalactites, many of them now joined into "organ-pipe" columns of remarkable beauty; that many side-tunnels branch away from the main cave and vanish into uncharted darkness.

That leaflet and the travel books it has informed refer to "the Englishman Lejard's" 1839 exploration, and to more recent investigations by "the Frenchman Rovinski" and his discovery of "extraordinary speleothems". They do not reference the fact that in season the upper passageway of *Lipsca Pećhina* is a favourite illicit trysting place, as evidenced by the carved initials etched on the walls and the discarded bottles and jugs abandoned after midnight revels. Cosi had been unsurprised by my instruction to arrange such a liaison for me with a gentleman friend.

Crude brackets were affixed to certain alcoves where torches might be placed to light trysts and to warm caves that usually remained a constant fifty degrees Fahrenheit all year round. The wind that came from the deeper tunnels like a chill breath must have caused those brands to gutter and dance but I suppose passion can ignore such inconveniences.

There were no lovers hiding in the deep shadows tonight. A murderous big game hunter and the killers who chased him had deterred all amour.

Sherlock paused and shone our covered storm lantern at the dusty trail we followed. "The Germans discovered Moran's tracks here. They moved after him cautiously; see the way they separated to opposite walls, moving on their toes, treading carefully for silence? They believed they had the Colonel cornered."

"Would a hunter like Moran leave such obvious marks to follow?"

"Only if it suited him. I wonder if Falkenrath has your acuity, Irene?"

I pushed the compliment aside and chided myself for feminine preening. Instead I tried to anticipate what the contending killers might have planned. It seemed that the Bavarians had not yet realised that Holmes was alive and in Montenegro. Their whole concern was to capture or destroy the last significant lieutenant of the criminal mastermind whom they intended to replace. What did they imagine Moran was doing in this vast cave? Did they know he had abducted a frightened dresser from the Zetski Dom? Did they understand why?

They must be aware that Moran hunted someone or something, I concluded. As they followed the Colonel across Europe they could not have failed to realise that he travelled with purpose. Perhaps they thought he hunted out another of Moriarty's key men, or perhaps sought some cache of weapons, money, or secret information set aside for a day of disaster. Possibly they had decided that the trove was concealed in Lipa Cave, and poor Cosette the key to its recovery?

Moran knew all, though. He was aware that Holmes was close, drawn by the bait he had set for me and therefore for Sherlock. He had lured his Bavarian pursuers in and had eliminated half their strength already. The 'second-most dangerous man in London' after James Moriarty himself was loose in the darkness carrying out whatever strategy he had prepared.

A voice echoed up from the chamber ahead, reflecting my confusion back to me. "You think you have me trapped, Ulrich? You have gambled too much on your weak hand."

Moran's voice had the cultured sneer of an upper-class Englishman, arrogant in his entitlement to rule the world, confident in his ability to seize it. The tone stirred up every republican sentiment in my blood, ready to dash tea into any harbour and wipe the smirk that voice implied from the speaker's face. In just a few words Moran became my enemy as few others had. Here was a bully who sought to murder the man I regarded most in all the world, an assassin who killed like a coward from a hidden distance, whose long rifle overcame the cleverness and courage of any whom he opposed. I hated him.

Sherlock was always tracking my mind. He laid a hand across mine and gestured that we should move forward quietly with the lamp covered except for a tiny slit.

"Moran!" boomed the reply from a speaker whose voice had a Teutonic tinge. "You have run out of places to hide at last. We have you now!"

"You think so? There's a lot you don't know. It'll be my pleasure to show you."

"You bargain for your life?"

"No. I'm bargaining for this girl's. Scream, Cosi. Announce yourself."

A full-throated shriek set bats flapping in the pitch black heights. Sherlock's hand tightened on mine.

"He intends to turn the trap about," my detective murmured urgently, either to me or to himself. "I sought to pit Falkenrath against Moran. He intends to pit Falkenrath against me. Next, he will..."

"You think we care about some *Shlampe Hure* that you snatched from the theatre?" Falkenrath sneered. "You're done, Herr Colonel. My brother is already in England, patching together the remnants of your dead master's organisation. We will rebuild it stronger and better than before and all your nation will be ours. Nothing you can offer will preserve you from destruction."

"I was not bargaining with you," Moran replied. "Shall we deal, Mme. Adler?"

"He intends to draw you out," Sherlock finished. "Irene, you are in grave danger. There are several ways that this confrontation can go..."

"All of which end in Cosi's death if I do not present myself," I pointed out. "We have no time to revisit this conversation. No time for anything now."

If I kissed Sherlock then it is not your concern, nor anybody's save ours. Decide for yourself what you wish to believe.

"Do what you must," I breathed to him. "He is ruthless and cunning. *You* are Sherlock Holmes."

I parted hastily, scrambling by touch down the steep slope to the Njegoš Hall, the furthest chamber that can be safely reached without climbing equipment. As I entered I saw a campfire at the far end and Cosi huddled beside it. She knelt near the hampers I had ordered delivered, uplit by the flames from a firepit that had been prepared at my instruction. The light cast her shadow high and huge over the rock formation that the guide leaflet called the *Gusle* after the single-stringed bow-played Balkan musical instrument it resembled.

Cosi was gagged and bound, her arms pinioned behind her, but seemed otherwise unharmed. Outlined by the flames she made a perfect target for any concealed marksman in one of a score of concealed crevices around the cavern.

"You are not aware of Mme. Adler?" Moran mocked the Germans. "There is a lot you don't know. Come out where you can be admired, *bella donna.*"

Bella Donna is Italian for 'beautiful lady', but as I moved forward I reflected that the name has also become attached to the poison which those ladies once dripped into their eyes to make their pupils wide and attractive. Belladonna is Deadly Nightshade, the most lethal herb in the Western world. Play with it at your peril.

I smiled to myself. Sebastian Moran should beware me!

"Move over to your maid, madame," the Colonel instructed. "Do you know her, Falkenrath? Do you know who she is? What she is?"

"Why should I care?" the German replied. With all the echoes bouncing around it was impossible to know where either speaker was hidden.

"She is regarded by my deadliest foe as the epitome of her sex. Irene Adler is the only woman in the world to have defeated Sherlock Holmes."

I reached the platform and scrambled up. While Moran was taunting the Bavarians I hitched the ribbon from Cosi's mouth and cut her bonds.

"Madame, there is a man...!" the poor girl gasped out. "He said..."

"I know about the man," I assured her. "He will be dealt with."

"He is looking for M. Sigerson!"

"He will find him. Now be a good girl and unpack the *fois gras*. We may be here for some time but there is no need to go hungry while we wait, is there? Your abductor did not tamper with our meal?"

"He searched the boxes but took nothing."

"Splendid. Then please allow the Bignon Cognac to breathe. No, leave the Larios Benefique for later. Pass it here. When you have unpacked the plates, be sure to light the candelabras."

Cosi regarded me as if I had gone mad to order our picnic as we were menaced by gunmen.

"We cannot prevent lunatics with firearms shooting us," I advised her. "We can be sure there are pleasant tastes in our mouths as they do so."

Ulrich Falkenrath continued his dialogue with Moran. "I fail to see how you think bringing this madwoman into these affairs will save your life, Herr Colonel."

"I have told you: Sherlock Holmes admires her."

"Sherlock Holmes is dead."

Moran's laugh was a disturbing thing. "You think so? You think I would have trailed across the whole damned Continent hunting any smaller game? The detective lives, you idiot! He is here in Cettigne, here in this cave with us now!"

There was a long pause from the German before he replied, "Your lies cannot save you."

"Tell them, Mme. Adler. Explain your lover's plan."

I sipped my drink and set my plate down. "Herr Falkenrath, Colonel Moran believes he has lured Sherlock Holmes to *Lipsca Pećhina*. He has forced my presence where he can threaten my life to command Mr. Holmes' actions. He intends to compel the detective to eliminate you Bavarians before Holmes too is shot down by the hunter's own gun. Colonel Moran thinks he has been very clever."

"Be careful, madame," Moran warned. "I am not a man to be mocked."

"You have overlooked certain possibilities," I advised my unseen adversary. "If, as you believe, the cunning Sherlock Holmes escaped his final confrontation with Professor Moriarty, what might he do? Fly to the ends of Europe dragging you after him? Or secretly return to London to deal with Herr Falkenrath's brother and others who seek to benefit from the chaos of Moriarty's fall? And if the latter, would he not send some trusted double who might distract you with a desperate chase across Europe while he deals with more significant problems?"

I am a consummate actress. I can sell a lie. For five long heartbeats Moran was stunned into considering the option.

"You think us fools!" Falkenrath shouted. His cry scattered bats from the roof and send them plunging away down stygian tunnels to trackless depths. "All this tale of opera singers and Sherlock Holmes? You are desperate, Moran. Face your end like a man!"

A single shot shattered the cognac bottle beside me. My heart leaped to my throat.

"You spin a convincing tale, madame," Moran called out. "I hope for your sake it was false. Holmes, if you are indeed present in this cave then eliminate these Kraut fools and show yourself. If they are not dead and you are not visible in my sights in one minute from now, the exquisite Irene Adler dies!"

✱✱✱

The account of Dr John Watson, 29th June 1891:

"hat do we do?" moaned Lestrade, struggling uselessly at the cuffs that held him fast to the warehouse pillar. "I've killed them all! I've led the whole Yard to their deaths!"

"Can you pick the lock, Dr Watson?" Billy asked optimistically. Alas, Holmes had never shown me how.

The dim shed echoed with the regular crashes of the police ram, drowning out the muffled whimpers and ineffective hammerings of captives nailed and strapped inside packing cases.

"Sit down," I instructed Billy and the Inspector. "Work the chain that holds us all down to ground level."

Neither man wasted time asking why. We shuffled the links down until our cuffs were touching the floor. Then I could get my hands to my laces and pull off a boot.

That was where I had the spare handcuff key. As Holmes once observed, I am somewhat careless in certain habits. Tracking lost keys was one of my friend's many regular services to me. I had deemed it prudent in his absence to supply myself with a second copy of the Tower handcuff key to avoid embarrassment.

I had not expected it to save my life. When I produced the duplicate, Lestrade and Billy exclaimed in wonderment as if I was Sherlock Holmes himself managing a miracle.

I quickly loosed myself from my gyves and scrambled over to the hissing fuses. There were no less than twelve tapers to stamp out, all lit from the same junction but now branched out to detonate different cases of black powder. I danced upon the threads, hastening from one to the next as the last of them closed upon the boxes they were to detonate.

I caught the last one scant inches from the powder chest.

"Now free us!" yelled Lestrade, but I had no time. I kicked his discarded revolver back to him so he might shoot through his restraining chain, and hastened to the trapdoor through which Falkenrath had departed.

A red rage was upon me. With his false Moriarty, his attack upon a home where my wife slept, and his stirring up of all my bruised bereavement over Holmes, the German interloper had pressed me too far. That he might now escape to plot anew and further his schemes again was an insult I would not endure.

I dropped down onto the slippery beam below the hatch, balancing my lantern in one hand, grabbing for rotting timber supports with the other. My service revolver was once again heavy in my pocket.

"Come, Watson," I murmured to myself. "The game's afoot. Hurry up, old chap!"

Bobbing lights of other torches in the distant darkness betrayed the direction of Falkenrath's retreat. I hurled myself from joist to joist heedless of the risk, splashing though inch-deep spillwater where pylons had sunk too far.

Falkenrath had twenty men with him. That should have given him an absolute advantage; except that the Krauts had never faced Jezail assaults on a retreating refugee train by night.

There is one simple rule about fighting in the dark: kill the men with the lamps.

I had shuttered my own lantern when I first spied theirs. It made passage over the crusted groynes more dangerous still but it also meant I had clear targets who did not yet suspect I was there. I braced myself beside one of the heavy tree-timbers that supported the main weight of the pier, raised my Beaumont Adams, and squeezed off three 54-bore cartridges at the lead men with hand-lights.

I don't know if all three shots hit. Certainly the first man went down, screaming as the .442 calibre bullet entered his side. The next man may have taken a glancing wound but it was enough to surprise him into dropping his lamp. My third round probably went wide but my target swivelled too quickly, overbalanced, and toppled into the pungent ooze; his light was doused.

I ducked low behind my support beam. There was confused German shouting from Falkenrath's attendants. They had not seen from whence the shots had come. I took the opportunity to reload then snapped off another three, aiming again at those men still shining lantern lenses in my general direction.

"*Decken diese Lampen!*" Falkenrath shouted at his men; but by then I had got two more of them, dousing their lanterns the hard way. A third thug panicked and tossed his light aside, drowning it in the mud.

Dekker was the last of them to carry a light. I saw him flip the shutter to cover it. Then all of us were plunged into darkness in the deep shadows beneath the pier.

I tried to judge distance. We were no longer beneath the Murcheson Warehouse. We had moved upriver, probably far enough to be at the edge of the range of the detonation that the Krauts were expecting.

It was time to talk. "Falkenrath, you're done!" I called out. "Defeated. Your fuses are out. Lestrade and Billy will be free by now. They'll have let the police into the shed. The criminals you tried to murder will be rescued. Word of what you tried will spread through their whole fraternity. Do you think there is any safe place for you now in the whole of England?"

It was the false Moriarty who replied. "This is only a setback. London is weak. Britannia is weak. Vulnerable. We have the resources, the backing, to do whatever we must to make it ours."

"Doesn't seem to be going that well just now," I mocked.

I heard a cry and a splash. Some unfortunate fellow had tried to move in the abject gloom and had slipped into the stinking sucking mud.

"You can't get away in pitch darkness," I pointed out. "Uncover a light and I'll shoot you like dogs. Stay where you are and Scotland Yard will come. The Thames or the noose. What are you going to do?"

I could not follow Dekker's language but I gather it was profane. Moriarty would never resort to such crudity.

"You are being distracted, Watson."

The voice came into my head so strongly that Holmes might have spoken in my ear. It seems that our years of association had told upon me. Some small part of the detective's cunning had rubbed off.

Dekker was speaking loudly and long. He was keeping me occupied. Falkenrath had fallen silent. I did not know where he was.

What if that deadly opponent had instructed his minion to keep talking while he took the same risks that I had in fumbling round to discover an enemy?

What if he was close now?

I listened but could hear nothing over the creaking of the wharf, the sloshing of the tide, the distant sounds of the port of London. Dekker still mouthed off, perhaps even foaming in his vitriolic tirade. Why was he so intent on gaining my attention?

I reached for my own lantern, made sure I was under cover from the bulk of the German gunmen, and snatched the hood away.

Ehrlich Falkenrath was not six feet away from me, groping his way across a flood-washed plank to close to killing range.

He blinked at the sudden illumination in his face.

I emptied the full contents of my Beaumont Adams into his chest.

Holmes might have overpowered and arrested him. Holmes was a better man than I.

✳ ✳ ✳

A Private Memoir of Madame Irene Adler, 29th June 1891:

I closed my eyes and instructed Cosi to do the same.

Sherlock replied at last to Colonel Moran. "You cannot expect me to do your work for you, Moran. However, I shall give you a chance to finish matters for yourself."

"The clock is ticking, Holmes!"

"Indeed it is. You have cleverly anticipated that I would set this place as a trap for you, to bring you and the murderous hooligans who hunt you to some enclosed space where you might eliminate each other or where I might overcome you all. You have turned that trap around upon me. But when Miss Adler sent provisions here in simulation of an escape from Cettigne, I had opportunity to visit as one of the labourers who delivered them, and thus to lay down supplies of my own."

"I've searched this place, detective. I found your cache of hidden weapons."

"You did not find my stepladder, though, since I took it with me and erased all trace of its former presence."

"Stepladder?"

"*Was is das?*" interrupted Falkenrath, his nerves and his patience exhausted. "Who speaks?"

I heard the catch of fear in his voice. *What if it was Sherlock Holmes?*

"A stepladder," Holmes explained. "To fasten things in the upper shadows where you would not look. It might not have occurred to you. Tigers do not use ladders. Or chemists."

I kept my face hidden in my hands as the magnesium strips flared up. The long strands that Sherlock had previously tacked to the roof and higher walls of the cavern had fast fuse-cord coiled about them. They ignited virtually the whole web of metallic ribbon in a simultaneous burst of actinic light.

In that instant the Njegoš Hall was illuminated as bright as day, exposing the hidden positions of Moran, Falkenrath, and his final minion.

Never forget that Sherlock is a talented scientist who has published a number of unreadable monographs on chemical matters. Magnesium thread is well within his metier. A prepared Sherlock Holmes is an un-stoppable force.

Moran was entrenched on a high ledge with a fine view of the length of the cavern. There were half a dozen places like that in the cave and Sherlock had wired them all with his magnesium threads.

The Colonel recovered from shock before the Bavarians. He blinked away the seared light-images and fired almost by reflex before the flares dimmed out. The first shot took Falkenrath's agent in the throat. That air-propelled pellet exploded through the back of the man's neck, jerking him like an Italian marionette before spilling him to the ground.

A second bullet caught Falkenrath in the shoulder as the German raised his gun to fire. The third shot followed while Falkenrath recoiled from the impact. It took the would-be criminal mastermind straight in the forehead, as clean a kill as any hunter might desire.

Sherlock was still in an area of the cave that was shadowed. He knew the pattern of light he had laid out and where best to remain in cover. His own revolver shot reverberated through *Lipsca Pećhina* as he targeted Moran.

The deadly Colonel rolled aside. He must have been moving even as he took the fatal shot on Falkenrath. His predator instincts had trumped Sherlock's calculations. Subsequent bullets came within inches of Moran but none hit him.

That lethal air rifle changed direction and found the place from which Holmes had fired. I saw Moran lever back the action and position his shot.

I will say this for the Colonel: had he chosen the craven course and aimed his weapon at me he might yet have won the day. Instead he chose a soldier's shot, a gentleman's shot, and bracketed Sherlock in his sights.

The Larios Benefique was still at my right hand. Well, the bottle was. Sad to say its Andalusian contents were long since consumed, replaced at my command by a rather less potable liquid developed by the Italian chemist Ascanio Sobrero in 1847. He called his creation pyroglycerine. It is better known today by Alfred Noble's preferred term, nitroglycerine.[46]

A significant amount fits very handily into a wine bottle, and as many a *prima donna* knows wine bottles have an excellent heft when thrown.

---

46 Although Sobrero had strongly warned that his creation should not be used as an explosive, Alfred and Emil Nobel worked to find a means of creating a more stable solid form that could be used for demolitions work. A laboratory accident cost the lives of Emil and several colleagues in 1864 but within two years of that Alfred had shipped out the first sticks of his new invention, 'dynamite'.

Sherlock is a very clever man but sometimes the cleverest of men needs a woman there when his cleverness fails.

Preferably a woman with a wine bottle filled with liquid explosive.

I hurled the bottle at the ledge where Moran lay in cover.

I did not hear the glass shatter in the vast detonation that it caused.

✲ ✲ ✲

The account of Dr John Watson, 29th June 1891:

The remaining events of that troubled night were what Holmes would no doubt have termed routine.

My definition was somewhat different. First there was the tricky problem of keeping a score of armed men immobilised while reinforcements arrived. The loss of their leader proved a sufficient shock to cow most of them. Falkenrath had been their talisman, guarantee of success in a strange country. To see him suddenly illuminated in a flash of light and then shot down a second later had a morbid effect upon even the bravest of them.

Only Dekker attempted escape. Indeed he eluded the approaching members of the Metropolitan Police Force and got clean away; or so we thought until his mutilated body was washed ashore at Greenwich two days later. London's indigenous lowlife had not been kind to the pretender. Perhaps they finally had their opportunity to pay their last respects to the late Professor Moriarty, to penalise an impostor or to punish a surrogate.

Lestrade, Gregson, and Hopkins scrambled for arrest credits; there were enough to go around. The massive plot to bomb a significant part of the bowl of London was never made public, to prevent panic and avoid emulation. Various seedy career criminals were chastened and sent about their dodgy business, aware of Scotland Yard's watchful eye.

Billy and Wiggins joined Mary and me for a splendid high tea that celebrated the final end of Professor James Moriarty.

"From now on I shall stick to my wife, my practice, and my memoirs," I promised them.

"Them stories should set a few ears burning," Billy warned me.

"I shall be discreet," I promised. "Names will be altered as required. Some accounts must be stored away for decades, for a century or more, before they can be released."

"Will the public still be interested in Sherlock Holmes at that time?" Mary doubted.

"They shall have the accounts in any case. My dear friend shall not be forgotten."

And that is my memorial to Mr Sherlock Holmes.

❋ ❋ ❋

A Private Memoir of Madame Irene Adler, 5th July 1891:

From Montenegro we crossed the Adriatic Sea to Barletta. We progressed in easy stages up the Eastern Italian coast, pausing at Pescara and Rimini before making for Milan and Geneva.

We travelled for anonymity as Herr and Frau Sigerson. Holmes was not convinced that Colonel Moran had died in the cave explosion that had certainly finished the Bavarian contingent. Of the old *shikari* we found little trace save a smear of blood towards the underground river that torrents through unfathomed deeps.

"There is still much work to do," Sherlock lectured me as we crossed into France before dog-legging north to Switzerland once more. "Even if Moran is gone there are other agents, other cells of Moriarty's European web that remain active and dangerous. Mr Holmes of Baker Street is a liability now to his friends and allies. I must remain in the shadows until every last link in the Professor's chain is shattered beyond repair. It will be a lengthy journey."

"If I cannot travel with Mr Sherlock Holmes," I answered, "I may accompany Herr Sigerson for a time. It appears I am wedded to him."

"That was merely an efficient cover to…"

"Have you ever bested me, Sherlock?"

"That is a matter of…"

"Do not strive to now. Sometimes it is wiser to lose."

We were in Strasbourg by the time the post that Cosi had forwarded caught up with us. The mail brought me another of dear Dr Watson's accounts of our great detective. This one was of special interest to me.

I read it while I awaited Herr Sigerson's return from the investigative business in which he was engaged:

'To Sherlock Holmes she is always *the* woman. I have seldom heard him mention her under any other name. In his eyes she eclipses and predominates the whole of her sex. It was not that he felt any emotion akin to love for Irene Adler. All emotions, and that one particularly, were abhorrent to his cold, precise but admirably balanced mind. He was, I take it, the most perfect reasoning and observing machine that the world has seen, but as a lover he would have placed himself in a false position. He never spoke of the softer passions, save with a gibe and a sneer. They were admirable things for the observer—excellent for drawing the veil from men's motives and actions. But for the trained reasoner to admit such intrusions into his own delicate and finely adjusted temperament was to introduce a distracting factor which might throw a doubt upon all his mental results. Grit in a sensitive instrument, or a crack in one of his own high-power lenses, would not be more disturbing than a strong emotion in a nature such as his. And yet there was but one woman to him, and that woman was the late Irene Adler, of dubious and questionable memory.'[47]

Which goes to show that even the good Doctor Watson does not know everything about Mr Sherlock Holmes.

The End

---

[47] These are the closing words of "A Scandal in Bohemia".

The Apocryphal Holmes

"You may marry him, murder him, or do anything you like to him."

Sir Arthur Conan Doyle's response to an enquiry about a stage adaptation of Sherlock Holmes.

In the closing days of the 19th century, Sir Arthur Conan Doyle went to the railway station to meet a literary collaborator from America. He was confronted by a tall eccentric gentleman in an Ulster cape and deerstalker hat who drew out a magnifying glass and inspected Doyle's face carefully. Finally, the man stood back and proclaimed, "Unquestionably, an author!"

Doyle exploded with laughter and the two men became lifelong friends.

The be-deerstalkered detective was Connecticut-born actor and playwright William Gillette, and he had come to ask permission to be Sherlock Holmes.

Gillette was a colourful figure who could count Mark Twain amongst his mentors. He held patents for a modern method of simulating the sound of hoofbeats off stage and for the first office time-and-date stamp. His 1887 production *Held By the Enemy*, which he wrote, directed, and starred in, was the first American play to achieve success in British theatres.

Gillette came to Doyle at the behest of impresario Charles Frohman, who had approached Doyle about a Sherlock Holmes play some time earlier. Doyle at last penned a script but Frohman deemed it unworkable. Frohman suggested that the successful playwright Gillette might rework the manuscript. Now Gillette had travelled from America to present his proposed work to Holmes' creator.[48]

Doyle's original script was a five-act play featuring Holmes against Professor Moriarty. Gillette rewrote from scratch, drawing heavily from *A Study in Scarlet*, "The Final Problem", and "A Scandal in Bohemia". In

---

48 Holmes had featured in stage productions even before this. He debuted in *Under the Clock*, an 1893 skit by Charles Brookfield, and then in James Webb's 1894 production *Sherlock Holmes*.

Doyle had already sought to interest Henry Beerbohm Tree in the stage role of Sherlock Holmes for the draft he had written, but had been turned down. Discussions with Henry Irving had failed when Irving had demanded that the part be rewritten to suit his acting preferences and that he also be given the role of Moriarty.

fact he wrote the play twice, since his original manuscript was destroyed in a theatre fire. Some of the production's dialogue is drawn directly from the stories.

Picking up on an illustration by Sidney Paget, Gillette and his play popularised the archetypal image of Holmes in a deerstalker cap. In the same way, Gillette's use of Inverness cape, curved pipe, violin, magnifying glass, and syringe cemented those tropes in popular culture. It was in this play, rather than in the Canon, that Holmes utters the phrase, "Oh, this is elementary, my dear Watson!"[49]

Since Doyle had not yet mentioned a forename for Moriarty in his Canon, the play supplies one: Robert. The character of Irene Adler was renamed Alice Faulkner, whose sister has been murdered, and Holmes marries her at the play's end. Indeed, the play's original title was *Sherlock Holmes, or The Strange Case of Miss Faulkner* before it became *Sherlock Holmes—A Drama in Four Acts*.

It is perhaps the inclusion of Moriarty and a substitute Adler in the highly popular stage production which first promoted them from their original one-story appearances to be essential parts of Holmes' mythos.

The unnamed Baker Street page-boy from "A Case of Identity" was included in the play and given the name Billy the Buttons. Billy's inclusion in the play and in three subsequent Sherlock Holmes stage productions raised public perception of the character's significance. Doyle transported Billy back into three of his written works; the page plays a significant part in catching the malefactor in "The Mazarin Stone". On the London stage, the part of Billy was the debut performance of a juvenile actor called Charlie Chaplin.

Sherlock Holmes - A Drama in Four Acts was a very successful show, running for 260 performances in New York from 1899 before touring the States and crossing to London's Lyceum Theatre in September 1901 for another 200 performances. It was revived four times between then and 1915 and spawned other Holmes stage productions, *The Stonor Case*, *The Crown Diamond*, and the comedy *The Painful Predicament of Sherlock Holmes*. Gillette portrayed Holmes on stage over 1,300 times, as well as playing the role in a silent movie and twice on radio.

I recount this to illustrate that even during the period when Doyle was still producing the Sherlock Holmes magazine stories that fans now account "the Canon" there were other sources that influenced public per-

---

49 The shortened epigram "Elementary, my dear Watson!" was originally uttered by Clive Brook portraying Holmes in the first "talkie" cinema version, *The Return of Sherlock Holmes*, 1929.

ception of the character and even shaped some later content of Doyle's own narratives.

"A Scandal in Bohemia" is the third Holmes tale in print, his first short story, written before the massive popularity of the character came to shape Doyle's presentation. It offers Holmes at his most fallible; Irene Adler actually sees through Holmes' plots and disguises, and prevents the detective from recovering the documents that he has been retained to confiscate. Only her word to him that she will never use the material resolves the problem. In short, The Woman wins.

This oddity of a tale is exactly the sort of material that provokes the imagination of Holmesians. There are a number of apparent errors in the narrative, including some legal detail about marriages. Fans playing "the Great Game" admit no such flaws and must explain them some other way. Hence much suspicion has fallen upon Irene's supposed husband, the scarcely-described Geoffrey Norton.

But more than that, in the entire Canon Irene Adler is one of only two women in whom Holmes takes much interest. The other is Miss Violet Hunter of "The Copper Beeches", about whom Dr and Mrs Watson entertained hope of romance with their friend, but in whom Holmes lost interest once her case was solved. Only one female's photograph adorned Holmes' desk, and she seemed ever denied to him.

There seems, then, something unresolved in the Holmes/Adler relationship. That their whole story was encompassed by two meetings while Holmes was disguised and by a brief pass-by farewell encounter on the steps of 221B seems impossible to many aficionados.

The first rebellion comes with Gillette's play, in which the Adleresque heroine stays to become Mrs Sherlock Holmes. Soon after, speculative theories and non-Canon accounts of subsequent meetings of the two characters began to circulate. In a 1930 Christmas greeting to The Baker Street Irregulars, Inc., the Holmes 'fan club', Sherlockian James Montgomery revealed that he had discovered papers in the estate of his late aunt Miss Clara Stevens of Trenton, New Jersey, revealing her to have performed under the stage name Irene Adler, along with correspondence demonstrating a prolonged liaison with Sherlock Holmes. The papers included "the only known photograph" of the detective, which Montgomery circulated with the revelation.[50]

In 1956, John D. Clark hypothesised in *The Baker Street Journal* that

---

50 Baring-Gould attributes information about Holmes' secretly solving the Ripper murders to this same source.

Rex Stout's Mycroft Holmes-like detective Nero Wolfe might be a son born of a 1892 liaison between Sherlock Holmes and Adler. The idea was expanded by Ellery Queen in 'The Great O-E Theory', *In the Queen's Parlor*, 1957. This very apocryphal idea even makes it into Sabine Baring-Gould's seminal *Sherlock Holmes* biography.[51]

Opportunity comes from the periods in Holmes' career which are not chronicled by Dr Watson. There are no firm accounts of investigations between April 1883 ("The Adventure of the Speckled Band") and October 1886 ("The Resident Patient"), although some later-mentioned cases probably occurred during that time.[52] Proponents of "The First Mrs Watson" assume that the doctor's marriage took place during this period. Baring-Gould proposes this wife to be San Franciscan Constance Adams, and that Watson removed to the United States until her premature death in August 1886.

That gap is no help with Holmes and Adler, however, since conventional Holmesian chronology places their first encounter in May 1887. Of much greater use is the period from 4th May 1891 to 5th April 1894 when Holmes was assumed lost in the Falls at Reichenbach. It is in this time that "the Norwegian Sigerson" undertook his "remarkable explorations". Holmes spent time in Tibet during which he visited the Dali Lama, then "passed through Persia", "looked in at Mecca", visited the Khalifa at Omdurman in Sudan, and still found time to research coal-tar derivatives in Montpelier.[53]

During a period when Holmes was unable to return to England without endangering his friends it seems entirely feasible to romantic readers

---

51 The idea predated Clark's article. When asked to comment upon Wolfe's lineage, Rex Stout wrote to the *Baker Street Journal* on 14th June 1955: "As the literary agent of [name deleted], I am of course privy to many details of [name deleted]'s past which to the general public... must remain moot for some time. If and when it becomes permissible for me to disclose any of those details, your distinguished journal would be a most appropriate medium for the disclosure. The constraint of my loyalty to my client makes it impossible for me to say more now."

52 "The Delicate Case of the King of Scandinavia", "The Service for Lord Backwater", and "The Little Problem of the Grosvenor Square Furniture Van" are referenced in "The Adventure of the Noble Bachelor". "The Case of the Woman at Margate" is touched upon in "The Adventure of the Second Stain". "The Darlington Substitution Scandal" and "The Arnsworth Castle Business" happen prior to "A Scandal in Bohemia".

53 Beyond the Canon references to Holmes' journeys, other chroniclers have sought to unearth details of those fascinating missing years. Foremost amongst them is surely A. Carson Simpson, who between 1953 and 1956 published six volumes of *Sherlock Holmes' Wander-jahre* (Philadelphia, International Printing Co.); these researches are summarised and added to Holmes' timeline in the Baring-Gould biography.

that he might seek out the fascinating Miss Adler, were she now properly separated again from the dubious Norton.

There are later, shorter gaps in Holmes' recorded career but none so helpful to the Adler romance supporter.

So to *Sherlock Holmes, Consulting Detective* volume 10. The present volume is something of a landmark. With its publication, Airship 27 exceeds the nine books in the official Canon and matches the Canon's 658,000 words. Doyle's accounts tend to be briefer that those of modern chroniclers. His short stories average at 7,200 words, whereas *Consulting Detective*'s usual narratives weigh in at 15,000 words. *A Study in Scarlet* is only 48,000 words long while even a slim modern novel averages 60,000; my recent *Holmes and Houdini* book is still modest at 68,500.[54]

While in no way seeking to rival Doyle's initial achievements and worldwide prestige, the *Consulting Detective* series has garnered some critical success. Volumes have been shortlisted for Pulp Factory industry awards for Best Short Story almost every year since the first volume debuted in 2010 and have won twice. The series has won Best Cover and Best Interior Art once each, and has been shortlisted for Best Short Story and for Best Cover twice more, for Best Anthology once, and for Best Interior Art three times.[55] It has also featured several times in nominations for the popular-vote Pulp Ark Awards.

These are notable successes to those of us in the small press pulp industry. These—and strong sales—tell us that there is still an appetite for traditional Holmes stories told in line with the original Canon. Our own apocrypha still operates on the rules that our content must not contradict the original material, must not introduce elements that do not match the "world" that Doyle established for the great detective (so no aliens, magic, revelations that Holmes was a woman etc.), and mostly follow the same

---

54 Not counting the inevitable footnotes, of course.

55 Sherlock Holmes, Consulting Detective volume 1 received awards for Best Cover (Mark Maddox) and Best Interior Art (Rob Davis), and was shortlisted for Best Short Story (Andrew Salmon, "The Adventure of the Locked Room") in the 2010 awards. Volume 2 won Best Short Story (I.A. Watson, "The Last Deposit") and was nominated for Best Cover (Ingrid Hardy) in the 2011 awards. Volume 3 won Best Short Story (Andrew Salmon, "The Adventure of the Limehouse Werewolf") and was shortlisted for Best Interior Art (Rob Davis), and volume 4 was nominated for Best Short Story (I.A. Watson, "The Adventure of the Clockwork Courtesan") and Best Cover (Chad Hardin) in the 2012 awards. Both volumes 4 and 5 were nominated for Best Interior Art (Rob Davis) in the 2013 awards. Volume 6 was nominated for Best Pulp Anthology (ed. Ron Fortier) and Best Interior Illustrations (Rob Davis) in the 2015 awards. Volume 7 won Best Interior Illustrations (Rob Davis) and was nominated for Best Pulp Anthology (ed. Ron Fortier), Best Short Story ("Spring-Heeled Jack, I.A. Watson), and Best Cover (Michael Youngblood) in the 2016 awards.

narrative pattern established in Dr Watson's original accounts; I had to get special permission to feature Mme Adler as co-narrator in my story for this volume.

Landmarks must be celebrated. So on the occasion of our own output matching that of the master it seemed appropriate to stretch the boundary and explore some of the "traditional" apocrypha which have been held in respect by prominent Holmesians for so long as to be close to Canon. Foremost amongst those interests is that "lost" period when Holmes was "dead", and what might have happened had he ever encountered The Woman again.

It also occurred to me that I have never read a story that covered what happened with Watson and the London cast in the days following the supposed demise of Holmes and the fall of Moriarty. It interested me to imagine the consequences of an underworld power vacuum and what waves might crash over the criminal fraternity of England with its Napoleon gone. And I wanted to describe Holmes' funeral.

What started as one story rapidly separated into two and then twisted together again as I realised that the two narratives occurred simultaneously in Britain and the Continent. Holmes' encounters with Irene and Moran paralleled Watson's struggles beside Lestrade and Billy. Both situations allow for different kinds of plotlines without ever doing violence to Airship 27's editorial policies.

I hope, then, that readers will permit a milestone indulgence and accept another apocryphal attempt to imagine a link in the story-chain that the Canon left untold.

IW
Travelling under an alias,
December 2015

I.A Watson has contributed to each of the *Sherlock Holmes: Consulting Detective* volumes and apparently nothing can be done about it. Voting him Best Pulp Author 2016 in the popular-vote Pulp Ark Awards has not deterred him. His novel *Holmes and Houdini* debuted earlier this year. His other recent books include *Labours of Hercules* and *Blackthorn: Spires of Mars*. Full lists of his fifty or so published works appear at http://www.chillwater.org.uk/writing/iawatsonhome.htm and at https://www.amazon.com/I.A.-Watson/e/B00E47RJFE

Sherlock Holmes

in

"The Problem of the Unearned Beard"

By
Aaron Smith

When I accepted an invitation to dine at the home of my old army friend Captain David Foster, I did not anticipate that the evening would begin a new case in which I would assist Sherlock Holmes.

The Foster residence was a handsome house, the aroma coming from the kitchen was immensely appetizing, and David's wife greeted me warmly. I was the first to arrive and so sat savoring a glass of wine and watching the other guests enter one by one.

The assembly included the Fosters' nearest neighbors, a tall thin man and his short, portly wife; a Catholic priest; two junior solicitors of the law firm David had run since leaving the military; a local pharmacist and his rather lovely daughter; and, finally, a man whose unusual appearance caught my attention immediately upon his being welcomed in by my friend and his wife.

This man was, I guessed, several years older than I, quite tall, walked with a slight limp for which he compensated by using a cane, and wore one of the most unusual beards I had ever seen. His facial hair was arranged in a full moustache and a flowing beard which must have taken many years to grow to such an extent. But, despite its length, the beard was kept neatly in place by the furthermost segments of whisker being tied together by pieces of twine at several intervals, leading to a narrowing, conical shape that reached halfway down the man's chest.

David introduced him as Mr. Winston Oldham.

As we all sat down for a friendly meal of delicious food accented by polite and varied conversation, I considered inquiring as to the reason for such an unusual beard, and I noticed the others glancing at the sculpture of whiskers too, though they tried to conceal their interest. At some point between the main course and the meal's end, as my courage was bolstered by drink, I made up my mind to question Mr. Oldham should I happen to find opportunity to do so without making it a scene which all the others would have to witness, for I did not want to embarrass the fellow.

As the evening grew late, the chance I hoped for arose. Oldham drew a thick cigar from his jacket pocket, held it up for our host to see, and announced, "I shall return soon, David." With that, he rose and exited through the front door.

"I could do with a bit of air myself," I said, and followed my fellow guest.

As I left the dining area, I heard Mrs. Foster laugh and say, "The poor doctor will be quite surprised how little air remains outside once Winston gets his fire going!"

Outdoors, I found Oldham sitting on a wooden bench beside the tall hedgerow of the Fosters' yard. Above his head floated a thick cloud of smoke of a strong but not altogether unpleasant aroma.

"May I join you?" I asked.

"Of course, Dr. Watson," Oldham said. "Would you like to try one? Mrs. Foster dislikes the scent of my cigars, but I love this brand, a Turkish blend that comes at a rather steep price."

"No, thank you," I replied, lighting one of my own cigarettes. "Although I must admit I too disagree with our hostess's judgment. It smells quite delicious."

"David has told me of your rather interesting work," Oldham said as I sat beside him.

"My medical practice is nothing so unusual," I said.

"No, Doctor, I refer to your chronicles of the experiences you have shared with the famous detective."

"Then you know of Sherlock Holmes?"

"What man or boy in London capable of reading does not? You have made your associate into a man of great renown through your words. My compliments."

"Thank you."

"Tell me, Doctor, does Holmes' interest in the unusual aspects of life overlap into your mind as well? Are you of a curious disposition?"

"I suppose so, perhaps more so since being involved in Holmes' career."

"Then you have no doubt wondered about my beard."

I laughed. "Mr. Oldham, every guest at this gathering, I am sure, is curious about it!"

"Please call me Winston."

"I shall. And you must call me John."

"Well, then, John, if you will permit me to explain the origin of my whiskers, perhaps you will agree that you and your noteworthy friend Holmes might consider taking me on as a new client."

"Continue, please, Winston. If you require Holmes' aid, I will listen most eagerly. I hope the situation is not one that poses danger toward you or your family."

"I have no family, I am afraid, and it is not, at least as yet, a perilous situation, but more a strange sequence of events for which I truly wish to discover an explanation."

"Then tell your tale."

"Like you and David," Oldham said, "I served in the army, although not in Afghanistan as the two of you did, but in India. Tell me, have you ever heard of Morgan's Marauders?"

"Indeed I have!" I told him. "Though I admit to being ignorant of the details of that unit's activities, I understand they were soldiers of great reputation some years ago."

"We were good soldiers, yes," Oldham continued. "I am proud to have served under Colonel Morgan. We operated in India, often assisting local villages in defense of their homes. We were a small unit, able to move from area to area swiftly and with little fuss. I was a sergeant.

"At one point in time, a group of Thuggee—I assume you know of them …"

"The cult of Kali!" I had certainly heard of the bloodthirsty society of thieves and assassins.

"Yes," Oldham confirmed, "the Thuggee menaced many villages in India at the time. And my fellow Marauders and I were assigned to put an end to one particular reign of terror and death. We journeyed to the general vicinity of the latest killings, but found that our foes had eluded us, vanished into the surrounding lands, leaving us no clue as to where they might strike next. To make matters worse, the local people wanted no part in helping us, as they resented the British presence in their lands. Having no clues and receiving no assistance, we were afraid our mission might fail. Then, our chaplain, Rutherford, looked up from his Bible one night as we sat around our campfire and said, 'Seek, ye shall find.'"

"A well known biblical quote," I said.

"Or so we thought at first," Oldham said with a chuckle. "In fact, the colonel scolded Rutherford for his habit of quoting scripture before we realized what he actually meant. He was trying to say, '*Sikh*, ye shall find.' And by that he meant that if we disguised ourselves as members of one of India's native religions, we might find the indigenous people more cooperative! We could not assume the guises of the more common Hindu people of India, for we certainly did not share their dark complexions and black hair. But if we donned turbans and grew our beards, perhaps those accoutrements would distract others from examining our facial features too carefully."

I nodded. "I have observed such an effect at work when Sherlock

Holmes has seen fit to alter his appearance."

"We ceased shaving immediately," Oldham went on, "and used false whiskers made from camel hair to augment our beards while they grew. We took to wearing the traditional Sikh headgear and speaking local languages in which some of us had grown quite fluent during several years on the continent."

"Was the plan successful?" I asked, as I had found myself fully interested in Oldham's tale.

"It was," he answered. "The natives trusted us once they believed us to be merely of a different religion rather than an altogether alien origin. We soon gained several trustworthy informants and picked up the trail of the Thuggee band. The chase was on!

"We tracked our foes to a series of caves and the battle was joined. We did not know the numbers of the enemy and were surprised to find ourselves vastly outmanned, some hundred of them to our mere twenty men. They were fierce merciless warriors and the fight raged in the tight corridors of the caverns. We of Morgan's Marauders won, but at great cost. We slew all the Thugs, but lost more than half our men. Colonel Morgan died, along with eleven others. Of the eight survivors, most suffered wounds, including a knife stroke to my leg, which is why I still limp to this day.

"We buried our dead and traveled slowly back to the nearest city, and then finally joined a caravan to Delhi. There, when the highest ranking British general in India at the time made his evaluation of what we had done, he offered us the choice of returning to civilian life or assignment to other companies. Captain Elswood, who had been Morgan's second-in-command, elected to remain in the army. The rest of us took our retirement and sailed back to England together, each to pursue a peaceful profession after having had our fill of war and bloodshed. I studied law, which is how I began my friendship with our host; the chaplain Rutherford became a country vicar, and others took up their own trades. On the way back, the seven of us made a mutual oath to forever remember and pay tribute to our fallen friends by wearing these beards for all the years we would continue to live and breathe upon the earth.

"Now, years later, four of us remain. Captain Elswood, we were informed not long after our return to England, died in battle in another part of India. One man perished in a train accident, and two died of illness between then and now. Our quartet of survivors includes me, Father Rutherford, a tailor named John Maxwell, and the somewhat famous novelist Bruce Brant. We all reside in England, all keep in contact through letters or the occasional social visit, and, most important, we all gather together thrice yearly to remember Colonel Morgan and all our other lost friends."

"That," I said, "is truly commendable, that you should feel such a strong bond so many years later that you join each other so often in memorial of your fellow soldiers."

"Yes," Oldham said, "Morgan's Marauders was a close group, loyal to each other to the end and beyond. And it is those meetings, once every four months, and the strange occurrences that have stained them over the past year, that have made me think perhaps it is time to make one other aware of them; namely, Mr. Sherlock Holmes."

"I have," I assured him, "become an able judge of the cases which may or may not interest Holmes. Tell me of these strange occurrences, if you will."

"Certainly," said Oldham. He took a long drag on his cigar and let the smoke flow back out of his mouth to drift up toward the night sky. When it seemed he had braced himself for the revelation of whatever events had him so eager to relate, he resumed his narrative.

"Father Rutherford's church is located just outside the village of Castle Combe, in Wiltshire, among the Cotswold Hills. It is a beautiful country region, and it is there we have chosen to hold our thrice yearly vigils of remembrance. The setting is lovely, and Rutherford does not have to leave his congregation to undertake a journey, while the rest of us have the luxury of being able to travel.

"It is in an open field behind the small stone church that we gather. The church is on one side and several wooded hills make up the rest of the perimeter. The four of us meet at the church and walk into the field together. We have a wooden cross that Rutherford made, engraved with the letter M, which, of course, stands for either Morgan or Marauders, and we plant the cross in the ground and stand around it. We pray and then spend some time reminiscing about our days in India and those we lost in battle or over the following years. After our ceremony, we return to the church and share a bottle of wine before going our separate ways until the next meeting four months later.

"On the first handful of such gatherings, all was peaceful and we enjoyed our time together, even if it did have its mournful moments. But then, for the past three meetings, things have been quite different and we cannot discover the reason for what has happened.

"You see, John, it has not been only the four of us these last three times.

We have had a visitor and we do not know his identity or his reasons for appearing. It was in the middle of our night in the field when one of us—I no longer remember who—glanced up at one of the hills and spotted the figure of a man silhouetted against the moonlit sky that shone between the trees. We thought nothing of it at first and assumed it was merely a local citizen out for a walk who had happened upon our ritual and stopped to look out of curiosity. But, as we gazed up at him, he turned and we could see him in profile. To our surprise, he sported a beard as long as any of ours!

"We were all shocked and simply stared for a moment, watching him shuffle off into the woods atop the hill and vanish. By the end of the night's gathering, we had mostly written it off as chance, as there are many men with beards in the world, though it is rare to see one with whiskers of our length. And Rutherford, who has lived near Castle Combe for years now, claims to know of no local residents sporting such facial decoration. Still, coincidence seemed the most likely explanation that first time."

"A reasonable assumption," I commented. "But the next time?"

"Exactly four months later," Oldham continued, "we assembled again. As we stood out in the field and prayed, I looked over at the hills and saw the bearded stranger again. I called the others' attention to his presence and we stood and watched as he looked back at us. Finally, after several moments, Bruce Brant took several steps forward and waved to our visitor. The effect of this gesture was to send the man running off into the woods, his long beard waving in the wind as he fled. We briefly considered following him, but decided to not allow his appearance to interrupt what had become the traditional order of events. We stoically continued our prayers and reminiscences."

"And on the third occasion?" I asked.

"Before venturing forth from the church," Oldham said, "we talked and came to the decision to get to the truth of this strange matter if our mysterious guest returned. And he did appear again. This time, Brant and Maxwell ran toward the hills at first sight of the stranger. Rutherford is quite fat now, and I, as you have surely noticed, do not walk well. But the others are still in good health and eagerly gave chase. Unfortunately, it was to no avail and our visitor eluded them.

"John, we truly resent this odd interruption of our gatherings. We are quite angry that this man, whoever he is, feels compelled to appear and stare down at us as we pay tribute to our fallen friends and their bravery and sacrifice. And that damned beard makes it worse! He has not earned it! Four of Morgan's Marauders remain and we wear our beards proudly as badges of a unique brotherhood. I want this man's purpose discovered before ..."

I waited for Oldham to finish his statement, but his voice trailed off as he hesitated.

"Before what?" I asked.

"Before Brant loses his temper. He is a good man with a creative mind and a strong heart, but he is given to fits of anger and drinks too often. He has hinted that he is prepared to bring a rifle to our next meeting and fire at the man upon the hill if he should interrupt us again. I do not wish to see any more bloodshed and I certainly do not want Bruce to face legal difficulties for anything he does in response to this stranger's inexplicable actions. Maxwell, Rutherford, and I want only answers."

"Do you have any theories?"

"Two. Perhaps it is all just coincidence, but that is doubtful, as we have already learned that no man with such a long beard, except Rutherford, of course, lives in that area. The other is that this man somehow learned of our coming together there every three months and has decided, for a reason I cannot fathom, to taunt us; perhaps his beard is false and he dons it only on those occasions. But why, John, would he want to do such a thing? Few men alive today know anything of Morgan's Marauders outside what may be learned from books regarding the British army's activities in India. I do not often speak to others of my time with Colonel Morgan or of the reason for my beard, and I know that the others do not either. I had not considered asking assistance from any man outside our circle of four old soldiers, but your presence this evening and your partnership with Sherlock Holmes has caused me to ponder the idea. Do you think Mr. Holmes would be willing to investigate the matter?"

"Indeed I do, Winston," I said, and I asked my new acquaintance to call at Baker Street the next afternoon.

✳✳✳

"At the very least, Watson, this matter of the unearned beard will be a welcome diversion from the string of dull cases I have been immersed in of late," said Sherlock Holmes when I had finished relating Winston Oldham's strange story.

Shortly past two o'clock, Oldham arrived. I introduced him to Holmes and he settled into a chair with a cup of Mrs. Hudson's tea.

"Although Watson has already told me of your situation, Mr. Oldham," Holmes said, "I would appreciate a repetition of the tale, in your words, so I may become aware of any detail the good doctor has left out."

Winston Oldham related, once again, what he had told me at Foster's home the night before. I listened for any inconsistencies, but the details were just as they had been upon the first telling of the story.

"When is the next scheduled gathering of the four bearded former soldiers?" Holmes asked.

"One week from today," Oldham said.

"Very well, then," Holmes declared. "I trust you have no objection to outsiders being present at your traditional assembly."

"Better outsiders I have invited than those who appear for reasons unknown," Oldham said.

"Excellent," Holmes said, his words accompanied by a single clap of his hands. "To Castle Combe we shall go."

✻ ✻ ✻

The hills of Wiltshire are truly beautiful, and I found Castle Combe to be a charming little village. Holmes and I arrived by train in the early afternoon one week after our visit from Winston Oldham. Our client had promised to rendezvous with us later in the day. Following our disembarking—and we were the only two passengers to get off at Castle Combe's tiny station—Holmes found a small wooden bench upon which to sit and smoke his pipe, while I set out to explore the village, with my first destination being St. Andrew's Church, home of the Castle Combe Clock, one of the few timekeeping devices from the medieval era to still function in modern times.

When Oldham arrived, he escorted us, driven by a local with a carriage for hire, to the small church looked after by his friend Rutherford, which was located two miles outside the borders of Castle Combe proper. The country grew even more breathtaking as we left the little village.

Father Rutherford, a round, red-faced man, greeted us warmly and welcomed us into his small hut of a vicarage, where he brewed tea and fed us sandwiches. As Oldham and Rutherford related a few anecdotes, of the amusing sort rather than the tragic, of their military days, Holmes loudly cleared his throat to interrupt.

"Watson," he said, "I wish to survey the surrounding area while a hint of light remains. I shall return by dark. By then, I assume the other two celebrants of their Indian adventures will have arrived."

✱✱✱

By nightfall, five of us had gathered within the church. John Maxwell, the tailor, was a shy, quiet man of medium build. Bruce Brant, the writer, was the opposite, a serious sort with strong opinions and a tall, thin body.

"I have my mind made up," he said, showing us the rifle he had brought with him, "to put a stop to this nuisance. He has no right to intrude upon our solemn remembrance. A threat should be enough to send him running, but if it is not …"

At that moment, Sherlock Holmes reached out, firmly gripped the end of the barrel, and pulled the weapon from Brant's hand.

"No," the detective said. "Mr. Oldham has enlisted me to find a peaceful solution to this situation and determine the reason for the appearance of the stranger with the beard like yours. That is what I will do. No bullets will fly tonight. No blood will stain this land."

"Mr. Holmes is right," added Rutherford. "This is God's land, and the field beyond these walls is as sacred as the church itself. I will not allow violence."

"Think of it this way, Bruce," said Winston Oldham. "Perhaps the truth we uncover with Holmes' and Watson's help will be something suitable for one of your books."

"Rubbish!" Brant shouted. "Whoever he is, he displays utter disrespect for all of us by standing up there in the shadows with that beard blowing in the breeze! He mocks us and I will tolerate it no more!"

"Then, Mr. Brant," Sherlock Holmes said with fire in his voice, for he had heard enough of the author's protestations, "you may leave this place! I had already intended to ask one of you to remain within the church tonight so that I might take your place. You have now given me two reasons to choose you. First, you most closely resemble me in physical figure. Second, your insistence on wielding this firearm and your refusal to listen to reason make you a danger to us all!"

"Very well, Holmes!" Brant shouted. "Good evening to you all!"

With that, the number of bearded men present was reduced to three.

"But you look nothing like Bruce, Holmes, except for similarity in size," said Oldham.

"A situation most easily remedied," Holmes replied as he put a hand into the deep pocket of his coat and pulled it out again, now holding a false beard. He held it up in front of his face to reveal that it was as long as the natural beards of the four friends. It did not surprise me in the least to see that Holmes, always a master of disguises, had manufactured such a thing during the week since we had arranged our visit to the hills. "Now, for the details of our plan. Watson, I trust your revolver is at the ready."

"It is, Holmes," I said, patting the place where my trusted service weapon rested within my coat.

"Bruce Brant," Holmes explained, "is a man I neither know nor trust, but Watson will, I assure you, make use of his firearm only out of the utmost necessity."

Oldham, Rutherford, and Maxwell nodded their understanding.

Holmes continued, "Using the skills you, like our friends here, learned during your army days, Watson, you will climb to the top of the hill upon which the mysterious visitor usually appears and conceal yourself among the brush. When he makes himself seen, you will approach him, but do so carefully, as I do not wish injury to befall you. Although the night will be dark, observe what you can of his appearance: his face, clothing, shoes, and anything else that might catch your attention. Capture his image in your mind as you have seen me do many times. While you examine this man with your eyes, I shall call to him from below and make my way up there to join the two of you. If he runs, we shall try to stop him, but gently, nonviolently, for there has, as yet, been no indication that he means any harm to these gentlemen who have sought our help. We shall speak with him if he is so inclined. If not, we shall either catch him or chase him and learn what we can in the process."

With that, Holmes turned his attention away from me and toward the • three former members of Morgan's marauders. "You three will remain in the clearing. As you are the targets of the visitor's attentions, and we have not yet determined his reasons for coming here, it would be unwise for any of you to join in the pursuit. Is that understood?"

Oldham, Rutherford, and Maxwell nodded once again.

"Very well," Holmes said, glancing out the window, "dusk has arrived. Watson, go and make your nest atop the hill."

✴✴✴

As I climbed the hill, I wondered why Holmes had assigned the task of approaching the bearded stranger to me rather than undertake the job himself, for surely his skill at observation was a thousand times more powerful than my own. He had his reasons, I was certain; perhaps he hoped to learn something by seeing the man from afar, a different sort of observation from a different angle. Or, perhaps, he felt he should be the one to gather in the field with the others, for his ability in disguise would better convince the visitor, should he appear, that it was Bruce Brant who stood with Oldham, Rutherford, and Maxwell.

I was fortunate, upon reaching the crest of the hill, to find a row of bushes behind which to crouch, so that I was able to hide mere feet from the place Oldham had described as being the spot where the mystery man would stand and look down upon the others.

When night had fallen fully over the Wiltshire hills, I looked down from my hiding place to see Holmes, who now wore the long false beard he had created, and the three others exit the church and walk slowly into the clearing. Maxwell and Oldham carried lanterns to light the way, while Father Rutherford held his large wooden cross.

Rutherford drove the cross into the ground and the white wood reflected the light of the lanterns. In the sky above, the moon was large, lending illumination to my surroundings. I watched as the men below prayed. Rutherford and Maxwell kneeled, while Oldham leaned on his cane. Holmes stood straight up, bowing only his head.

As the ceremony in the field went on, I became aware of the sound of movement not far from my position. My senses now on alert, I watched the silhouette of a man come into view from within the nearby line of trees. He was quite tall and had the thick upper body of a strong athlete. Even in the semi-darkness, I could see the long beard hanging from his face to halfway down his chest. He walked with purpose, shoulders straight, head held high, like a proud soldier. I could not quite make out his face, though I squinted and peered through the shadows the best I could.

He emerged fully from the trees and stared down at the ritual of remembrance, just as Oldham had said he had done on three previous occasions.

At that instant, Sherlock Holmes looked up from below. "You there, stop!" he shouted. "Watson, catch him!"

I moved from my hiding spot as I saw Holmes begin his run up the front of the hill. The bearded man, surprised, turned to flee.

"Halt," I cried, racing toward him, "we only wish to talk!"

"Halt, we only wish to talk!"

I was almost upon him when he turned back in my direction and slammed a powerful fist into my jaw. I toppled backwards, falling. As I lost balance, I reached out with both hands, felt my fingers take hold of two separate soft items, one with the left hand and one with the right. The right hand pulled as I fell but released what it held, while the left's object came away from its possessor and I retained my hold on it.

I felt the grassy ground collide with my back and lay there stunned and breathless as the running footsteps of the mysterious visitor grew fainter in the distance.

"Watson, are you badly hurt?" Holmes asked as he knelt beside me, tearing the false whiskers from his face and flinging the beard aside.

"Only my pride is truly injured," I said. "I shall bear a bruise upon my face for several days, I expect, but no blood has been drawn and my teeth are firmly attached to their roots."

"What is that in your hand?" Holmes asked.

Remembering I had captured something from the target of our investigation, I held it up for Holmes to see.

"A scarf!"

I handed the long piece of cloth to Holmes. I stood and we walked carefully down the hill, toward the two lanterns and the wooden cross.

Inside the church, I sipped brandy to dull the ache in my jaw. Oldham, Rutherford, and Maxwell stood there looking disappointed that we had failed to apprehend the stranger, but Holmes appeared unconcerned.

"Do not worry, gentlemen," the detective assured our clients, "for Watson's and my observations, added to the facts we may learn from this scarf, shall lead us to this man's identity and the reasons for his interest in your gathering here!"

"The man was certainly a soldier once," I said. "His posture and movements, as well as the punch he threw, told me that he has had discipline drilled into him and is no stranger to violence."

"I concur, Watson," Holmes said. "From my vantage point in the field, I looked up and immediately judged him to be a man of military experience."

"And his beard is authentic," I added. "I took advantage of our close tangle to give it a good tug!"

Holmes was now intently examining the scarf. It was a long, grey piece of cloth. He held it close to his face, scrutinizing every inch with his eyes, then placed it under his nose and inhaled deeply. He had caught an interesting scent, I knew, when he closed his eyes as if searching the vast halls of his memory for a name or place to match what he had detected on the scarf. Finally, after we had all waited for what seemed half the night, Holmes opened his eyes.

"Elephants!" he shouted.

"What?" some combination of Oldham, Maxwell, and Rutherford asked all at once.

"The man who wore this scarf," Holmes elaborated, "has very recently been in close proximity to elephants, for those large beasts have a particular odor, which has permeated the fabric of this garment. And, as there are not many of those animals in England, the field in which we must search for this man has now narrowed considerably."

"But," Rutherford protested, "Perhaps he simply visited a zoo or traveling circus. Many men go to such places."

"True," said Holmes, "but they watch the animals from afar and do not go home stinking of them. This man has been close enough to touch an elephant, and that is a clue we must not ignore."

"Salisbury!" a voice from the church doorway suddenly shouted.

We all turned to look. It was Bruce Brant, his expression calmer than it had been earlier. He walked over and looked at each of us in turn.

"I apologize for my behavior earlier," the novelist said. "You were right, Holmes, to insist on a peaceful solution to this mystery. I entered just as you commented on the scent of the scarf, and I think I may be of some help."

"You mentioned Salisbury," Holmes said.

Salisbury is far to the south of Castle Combe, though still within the county of Wiltshire. It is the only proper city within Wiltshire and is home to a famous cathedral.

"A bit over a year ago, I think it was," Brant explained, "I had gone down to Salisbury to get a look around that bloody old church for a chapter I was writing that concerned the habits of the clergy in centuries gone by. While in the region, I was surprised to see a long caravan of wagons heading into the surrounding valley. I thought I heard, from one of the carriages, the cry of an elephant, and the noise brought back memories of my days in India. I interrogated one of the locals and learned that some rich bloke had bought a piece of land and was importing animals from the East. The whole matter sounded quite eccentric and caught my attention, though I soon put it out of my mind and got back to my book."

Sherlock Holmes nodded. "Yes," he said. "Salisbury is where we shall begin the next step of our investigation. Watson, we will travel there tomorrow."

"What of the rest of us?" Winston Oldham asked.

"Go back to your individual concerns in life," Holmes advised. "We do not know if we will find anything of use in Salisbury. Perhaps it will be a dead end and another thread will have to be explored. In either event, you will all be kept informed of our progress."

On the subject of Sherlock Holmes, policemen across England held widely varying opinions. Some thought of him as an interfering amateur who often stuck his nose into matters better left to the official agencies, while others, such as our frequent allies at Scotland Yard, considered him a friend and colleague, though he wore no uniform. In either case, his name was known far and wide, and he had a reputation which was interpreted in different ways according to the whims of each officer of the law.

We were fortunate, upon arriving in Salisbury, to discover that the constabulary of that city were quite interested in Holmes' methods and considered him a celebrity of the most fascinating sort.

"I've long hoped to meet you!" said a round-bellied sergeant when I introduced him to Holmes. "I've spent many an hour reading accounts of your cases and have often wished I had such a man serving here under my command. What can I do for you today, Mr. Holmes?"

"I am in search of elephants," Holmes said.

The sergeant laughed. "It ought to be difficult to hide one of those monsters! Is it a murderous elephant? Did he trample some poor fellow to pudding?"

"Nothing of the sort," said Holmes, without as much as a chuckle. He leaned closer to the sergeant, said in a whisper, "I am afraid, my dear man, that I am at work on a most sensitive case and am not yet at liberty to reveal its particulars, but you have my word that you will be the first to know the details when such a time arrives. Now ... if an elephant, or perhaps more than one, were to be found near Salisbury, where would that be?"

The sergeant, his voice now a serious whisper to match Holmes', glanced around as if to make certain nobody but Holmes and I might hear, and said, "There's a large estate a few miles west of the city, bought by a retired soldier about two years ago. He's a strange one, I hear, though I have not met him. He's taken to keeping wild animals from faraway lands on his grounds, elephants included! I don't know if such livestock is legal in these parts or not, but I say if he's not hurting anybody he ought to be left alone to do as he pleases, elephants or not!"

"A sensible attitude, sergeant," Holmes replied. "I commend you for your open-mindedness. If you would kindly tell us how to get to this estate, I would be in your debt."

"I had better draw you a map, Mr. Holmes," the sergeant said as he reached for a pencil.

✳✳✳

The next morning, after a night's stay in a charming local inn, Holmes and I followed the crude diagram the sergeant had drawn. We rented two horses, rather than hire a driver, as we were not sure what we might find at the designated estate.

The policeman's directions were adequate and we soon found ourselves outside a large set of gates which barred us from a private road that cut through a thickly forested area of the valley.

"Shall we find a way around the fences, Holmes?" I asked.

"No, Watson, I would prefer to be invited in rather than invade."

"But no one is here to admit us."

"Lend me your revolver."

I took out the weapon, handed it to Holmes. The detective aimed at the sky, pulled the trigger, and one loud shot rang out like brief thunder.

"That will bring attention to our presence," Holmes said as he handed the gun back to me.

Holmes was correct. His gambit soon produced results. Three men appeared, rushing into sight inside the gates. They were Indian, but wore English clothing, and each bore a hunting rifle, which were aimed straight at us.

"Gentlemen!" Holmes said rather loudly. "Please forgive the noise I have made. I merely wished for some attention and did not know how to go about getting it in a more subtle fashion."

"Who are you?" one of them snapped back. "What do you want?"

"If you cease pointing your rifles at us," Holmes responded, "I will happily explain."

"Quickly!" the Indian who seemed to be the leader barked.

"It is quite simple, really," Holmes said, keeping his voice calm and even as he spoke. "My friend and I are on holiday here in the Salisbury region and we heard, much to our delight that some animals that are rarely seen in this part of the world reside on the grounds behind these gates. We were especially excited to learn of the presence of elephants, which are, as I am sure you know, fascinating creatures. I have seen them only a few times in zoos, and John here has been fortunate enough to witness them in the wild during his days as a soldier. We were hoping to see elephants again, if, that is, the man who owns this land would be kind enough to allow us the privilege. You have my promise that we mean no harm to anyone who lives here, man or beast."

The Indians talked amongst themselves for a few moments before the leader turned back toward Holmes and me.

"Wait here," he said sternly. "I will ask Colonel Woodsall if he will grant your request. Who shall I say you are?"

"I am Sherlock Holmes. Perhaps your colonel has heard of me. My friend is Dr. John Watson."

"Very well. Do not wander far from the gates."

With that, our new acquaintances left us.

"Holmes," I said, "what if this colonel, should he prove to be the man we seek, recognizes me from our struggle on the hilltop. True, it was dark, but ..."

"You will not meet him, Watson, at least not yet. For even if he did not know your face, he surely remembers—and his bruised knuckles will remind him of it—the blow he landed to your face. The redness has not yet faded from your jaw. Take your horse, Watson, and ride back to Salisbury. I will tell this Colonel Woodsall, should I actually meet him, that you were not feeling well and regret missing the chance to view his estate from inside its fences."

"But, Holmes," I protested, "what if danger lurks within the grounds?"

"For a wealthy former officer to risk scandal by attempting to harm a celebrity," Holmes argued, "would be very foolish. There have been many occasions on which I have regretted that people recognize my name, but today is a day I welcome my reputation, for it may not only help to keep me safe, but could also increase my chances of being allowed to pass through the gates and witness the might of elephants and the correctness or lack thereof of a theory that is beginning to take quite solid form in my mind."

"Would you care to share this theory before I take my leave of you?" I asked, hopeful.

"I would not, Watson," Holmes replied. "I prefer to relate facts, not conjectures."

"At least let me lend you my revolver."

"Ha! No, Watson, the single shot I have fired today has been enough. Ride away now, and I suspect I will have a tale to tell when I rejoin you at our lodgings several hours from now."

Holmes returned in late afternoon, his face aglow with satisfaction, for he did possess a sizable appreciation of his own talents, which was certainly well-earned.

I let him into my room at the inn and he proceeded to sit at the window and go through the process of filling and lighting his pipe. Only after he had pulled in, held for a long while, and finally released the first mouthful of smoke did he start to speak.

"Shortly after you left the area," Holmes said, "the servants of Colonel Woodsall returned and graciously admitted me to the grounds of the estate. I saw elephants and various other animals rarely seen in this part of the world. I was then taken to the colonel's house, for he had indeed heard of me and wished to greet me in person. Yes, Watson, Woodsall—his first name, or so he told me, is Graham—is the man you met upon the hill outside Castle Combe. Tall, muscular, and wearing a very long beard!

"He was a generous host and had me served tea and sandwiches as he told how he had come to own such a large plot of land and provide a home for such wonderful beasts as his pet elephants.

"In the shortest possible summary, Watson, Woodsall served in India and Africa, came to admire the native population of both the human and animal varieties, retired to enjoy his family's fortune, to which he is the sole heir, moved here to the Salisbury region and took on this old estate after a fire ravaged his ancestral home—though he did manage to save from the blaze a collection of portraits of his father, grandfathers, and a long line of men with strings of the word 'great' prefixing their titles. Once settled here, he sent off to India for the Hindus who assisted him there so they could live as his loyal servants here. And, of course, he had the wildlife imported. The beard, when I questioned him, he explained as being a tribute to a Sikh who saved his life from a hungry tiger.

"Watson, a great deal of what the colonel told me and I have just repeated to you was a grand collection of lies! Colonel Graham Woodsall is certainly not his real name, although I believe his rank may be authentic."

With his summation at its end, Holmes puffed on his pipe as I digested all I had just been told.

"The flaws in his story, Holmes? Would you elaborate?"

"Most notably," Holmes explained, "the many portraits of previous Woodsall generations are fakes. They imitate the styles of past eras of art and the canvases and frames have been made to appear aged, but a sharp eye guided by a mind that contains at least a rudimentary knowledge of painter's methods—for I have at times been called upon to detect fraudulent masterpieces—will easily see that the brush strokes were made by modern tools of the portraiture trade.

"Second, there is the matter of the name this bearded former soldier is now known by."

"Woodsall?" I asked, not quite following Holmes' logic. "There is nothing so unusual about it. It is an English enough surname, I should think."

"Roll the name around in your mind, Watson. Hear its syllables and rearrange them."

"Ha! Yes, Holmes, I hear it now! I feel like a buffoon for not realizing sooner."

"Now that you understand, we shall proceed to the next step."

"Which is?"

"Colonel Woodsall has invited me to return to his estate this evening for a full meal prepared by his servants. You, of course, will also be present."

"But, as we discussed earlier, he may recognize me."

"It matters not. The time for our charade has passed."

We arrived at the Woodsall estate shortly after seven that evening. This time, the Indian servants came to our inn and drove us to the manor in the colonel's carriage. We were led into the large residence and up the stairway where the walls were adorned with the portraits that Holmes had found so revealing of the falsehood of Woodsall's claims.

We were led next to the large double doors of the dining hall, and when the doors opened and Holmes and I took our first few steps toward the feast that had been prepared for us, our host stood from his chair at the far end of the table and slammed his fist down with such force that it shook the plates and glasses.

"I should have known you had a motive beyond pleasant conversation and the sight of elephants!" Colonel Woodsall barked at us. "The renowned detective comes to call and now my life will be turned inside out! You," he pointed at me, "are the man who tried to assault me on the hilltop in the darkness. I see you still bear the imprint of my fist upon your face!"

Holmes immediately cut the colonel's shouting short with his own burst of words.

"Colonel Woodsall, sit down! I have made a career of my discretion and ability to keep secrets far greater that those you hold here in this mansion of yours, where you surround yourself with luxuries and exotic pets and portraits of men who never lived. I am certain you have good reasons for living in a nest of lies, and I should very much like to hear them. I believe I have already deduced much of it and my task here tonight is to confirm my theories and then decide what to tell the men who have hired me to learn the identity and motive of the man who stalks them from atop that hill by the church. You have nothing to fear from me or from Watson. Now let us eat before our meal goes cold, and let us talk like civilized men."

The food was delicious, with its flavor enhanced by a blend of exotic spices. As we ate, our host confirmed what Holmes had surmised, as well as adding the missing pieces to the story.

"Yes, Mr. Holmes, I am indeed the man who was once known as Captain Elswood, second-in-command of Morgan's Marauders. But the man I was then is officially dead according to all records kept by the British government. Also in those files can be found the full account of the career of Colonel Graham Woodsall.

"When the battle we of Morgan's company waged against the Thugs had ended and only eight of us remained, I was the sole member of the group to continue on in the service of my country. I was promoted to the rank of major and sent to lead a new troop against other threats in another part of India. However, while there, I learned of corruption and treason among the generals and colonels who oversaw the army's operations in that region. I managed to communicate what I had discovered to honorable men even higher in the chain of command and the problem was dealt with. But it was feared that allies of the corrupt factions would seek revenge against me and my family back here in England. I wanted, more than anything, to keep my loved ones safe, but I also wished to continue my military career.

"So a plan was devised to allow success on both those fronts. I would not see my parents or sisters again, for they, along with the men I served with, were informed that I had been killed on a mission of the utmost secrecy. A funeral was held for Major Elswood, and his story ended there, with his officers and men standing over a grave in which rested the body of a beggar—for weight had to be added to the coffin to provide a sense of reality to the ruse.

"Following my 'death,' with my continued existence known only to the highest of military authorities, the career record of Graham Woodsall came into being, every detail forged, of course, though with the accomplishments nearly matching those of Elswood, so my deeds and decorations would not be exaggerated or bestowed upon me without validity. I was then sent to Africa, where I continued to serve for several years, legitimately reaching the rank of colonel.

"The small lie I told you earlier today, Holmes, about the reason for my beard being that a Sikh saved me from a tiger was a reversal of the truth. You know the reason for my beard. It was I who saved the Sikh from the beast, and after that I learned that he was the possessor of a vast fortune, a small portion of which he gave to me in gratitude. It was then, after gaining a small fortune that I chose to retire from military life and return here to England. The guise of Woodsall had to be maintained, so a family history was concocted, complete with portraits of my forefathers. I chose to settle near Salisbury because it is the furthest point in the nation from the remaining family of Elswood; they must never know of my being alive. I purchased this land and filled this old house with new belongings. I then found that I missed my life abroad and sought to bring some of the magic of those exotic lands here where I could enjoy it again. I sent to India for my servants and to various lands for my animals. Life here is good. I do as I please, eat what I like, and bask in the beauty of the land. Yet memories of my time in India still rise to the surface of my thoughts quite often. I will never forget those times and the men I fought beside, so, as you see, I still wear the Sikh-like beard we all adopted as members of Morgan's Marauders.

"I had just come to feel as if this estate was home when I happened to drive into Salisbury sometime more than a year ago. While in the city, I was shocked to see a man wearing a beard very much like mine. Upon closer examination, though still intentionally keeping out of his line of sight, I realized it was Bruce Brant, my former fellow soldier. I could not risk him recognizing me, but curiosity burned in my heart and I had one of my servants keep watch on him as he went about his business. When he left Salisbury the next day, I followed him, taking the same train but remaining one car behind. We traveled to Castle Combe. I pursued him to the small church outside that little town.

"I was amazed when I stood upon that hill and watched four men, all old mates of mine, gathered in that field in tribute to those of us who had fallen in battle in India. I wanted, more than anything else in this world, to run down and join them in prayer and reminiscence ... but I did not dare, for I had cast aside my old life and name and could not risk revealing who I had once been or who I am now. I did not mean for them to see me, but I was so lost in emotion that I walked too far from the trees and into the moonlight and the brightness cast by their lanterns. Once they had gone back into the church and were drinking and talking, I snuck down and sat under an open window, listening. I learned the date of their next gathering and I attended again. This time, Bruce Brant gestured to me, but I was too afraid and I fled. On the third occasion, Brant and Maxwell chased me, but I managed to escape into the woods. Then, this last time, you were there and I was nearly trapped.

"Doctor Watson, you have my sincere apology for the violence with which I met you."

"It is all right, Colonel," I assured him. "I understand perfectly your reasons for being uncertain of what to do."

"As do I," Sherlock Holmes added. "You see, Colonel Woodsall, there was a period of time when I found it necessary to cause the world to believe that I had perished. During the years when I could not contact my closest friend, Watson, I often wished to send him a letter or some other sign of my continued survival, but I could not. But when the time for secrecy ended and I was able to emerge once again into the world of the living, it was a most joyous reunion. Was it not, Watson?"

"Yes," I replied, "after I too had returned to life from the fainting spell your resurrection caused!"

"I am conflicted as to what to do," Colonel Woodsall admitted. "What is your advice, Mr. Holmes?"

"You must weight what you know of the character of these men," Holmes said. "How fully do you trust Oldham, Rutherford, Maxwell, and Brant? You fought beside them, shed blood with them, and killed for the same cause. Does the brotherhood that develops in war carry over into the years of peace a soldier can expect if he lives long enough to escape the military routine? I know those four men as my clients, and I know you as a gracious host. But you know them far better than I ever will, and only you can decide what to do, or what not to do. You have my word that I will act no further in this matter. What occurs next is in your hands."

"Thank you, sir," Woodsall said. He then clapped his hands together three times to summon one of his servants and called out, "Drinks for our guests!"

Four months after our visit to the Woodsall estate, Holmes and I received a letter from Winston Oldham, thanking us for the fact that there were five bearded men present at the most recent gathering of the surviving soldiers of Morgan's Marauders. All present had been delighted by the reunion with their old superior officer, and all had sworn to remain forever silent to all outside the circle concerning his true history and identity.

Shortly after, another envelope arrived by post, this one containing a generous sum of money, as Colonel Woodsall had insisted to his old brothers-in-arms that he be the one to pay Holmes' fee.

I was happy to see the mystery of the seemingly (but certainly not) unearned beard reach its peaceful and satisfactory conclusion, and I laughed about the fact that the truth came to light because the vast storehouse of information that is the mind of Sherlock Holmes was able to recall the scent specific to elephants.

The End

Hair's How it Began

The Sherlock Holmes story you've just read, "The Problem of the Unearned Beard," was inspired by something I usually pay very little attention to. That something is fashion.

I've never been the sort of person who worries about what is or isn't in style. When it comes to my appearance, I'm more concerned with trying to look neat while still being comfortable. I wear what I want and, as long as I look presentable, don't concern myself with the details. The same goes for my hair. I keep it between very short and needing a haircut but not having time to get one.

When I do pay attention to fashion, style, or fads, it usually means either I'm doing research for a story or I've seen a trend that annoys me.

For example, the silly style of men wearing their pants drooping down around their backsides started when I was in high school. I'm happy to report that I never fell into that habit, not even for a minute. If my pants seem loose now and then, it's because I'm skinny, not because I have any intention of walking around looking like I have no idea what a belt is. The droopy pants phenomenon looked stupid then, when teenage boys were doing it. And now, I can't believe that of all the ridiculous fads I've seen come and go, that one has lasted this long! It was bad enough on kids, but on grown men, now in their late thirties, it's downright embarrassing! How can any man expect to be taken seriously as an adult if his pants are (intentionally) falling down all the time?

Now, along those lines, I must confess my own style screw-up of years past. When I was in my early twenties, I grew a big, bushy beard and kept it for a year or so. Nobody else my age (who I knew at the time) had one then, and my reason for growing it wasn't so much to make a statement as it was to be taken seriously. With my clean-shaven face, I looked younger than I was and I'd walk into a store and be looked at as if I was a teenager up to no good, but, with the beard, the salesperson would ask, "Can I help you, sir?" However, bushy beards are a pain to keep neat and when I look back on photos from the time, now almost two decades ago, I cringe. It just looked silly to see that thick a beard on such a young man.

So, here we are years later and big beards on very young men are in fashion now. I see them all over the place, whiskers fit for a lumberjack on faces that look a year or two removed from high school while the hair atop the head is neatly combed in a completely clashing style that makes a strange contrast to the facial hair. And, in my opinion, it just doesn't look right. (Yes, I'm being opinionated. Too bad!)

Some months ago, I saw such a beard on such a young man, and it set me off on one of the rants my wife finds so amusing. My little speech had to do with the idea that a big beard looks appropriate on a man who has lived life, been through some adventures, and developed some sort of toughness and experience. It looks right on the aforementioned lumber-jack, or a veteran, a truck driver, a leather jacket-wearing biker with his wallet attached to his pants by a chain, or a weather-beaten farmer. But on some young kid fresh out of high school or maybe in college or working his first job, it looks odd, as if it hasn't been earned! At that moment, with that judgmental tirade, I began referring to such beards on such boys as "unearned beards."

When one writes fiction, particularly mysteries, it's the little things that catch one's attention and plant the seeds of future mysteries in the mind. That was one such seed. It was then inevitable that a new Holmes mystery would form in my mind, concerning a beard that did not seem to belong in the circumstances in which it appeared. The phrase I began using in my rant about a fad that annoyed me for a moment turned out to be a fine title for my latest tale of Sherlock Holmes, "The Problem of the Unearned Beard."

***

Sherlock Holmes

in

"The Adventure of the Irregular's Innocence"

By
Greg Hatcher

In the years I spent sharing rooms with the consulting detective Sherlock Holmes, I had seen a great many desperate people appeal to him for aid. However, the young woman that appeared in our doorway that particular morning in April may have been the single most distraught visitor to our Baker Street quarters I had ever seen. She opened her mouth to speak but no words came out, and she tottered and would have collapsed in a heap were it not for the young man at her elbow. He caught her under her arms and looked rather wildly at Holmes and myself. "Mr. Sherlock..."

Holmes at once rose to his feet. "Here, put her in my chair, Davy. It is Davy, isn't it?"

The young man's eyebrows shot up. "Why—yes it is, sir. It's been so long—I thought sure you'd have forgotten. We was just kids then."

Holmes waved it away. "The contours of the human ear and the shape of the cheekbones do not change with age. I should have known you even as a man of eighty. Now let us get this young woman a pillow from the couch and while she recovers perhaps you would join us in a cup of coffee and tell us exactly what criminal enterprise has ensnared this poor woman's husband." He glanced over at me and added, "Watson, if you would be so good as to ring Mrs. Hudson."

I rose to do so, still looking at the young man.... Davy, Holmes had addressed him. "Is she ill, young man?" I asked him. "I'm a doctor. I can fetch my bag if..."

"No, I think she's just exhausted. But maybe we might arrange a slug of brandy in her coffee. It's been a rough couple of days." Abruptly Davy grinned at me. "Thought this sort of thing was well behind us, Doctor. It's been some years."

The smile did it. I had a sudden memory of a group of noisy and enthusiastic boys charging up the stairs past Mrs. Hudson, clamoring *Mister Sherlock! Mister Sherlock!* The realization dawned on me at last. "Good heavens! Davy Styles! You were one of Wiggins' street Arab crew!"

"The Irregulars, Mr. Sherlock called us. Almost a decade ago, aye. It was actually me what was standing watch over the *Aurora* that one time, to signal you and the police. You remember?"

"I shall never forget. That was the case where I met my dear wife." For a moment my thoughts went back to that wonderful and terrible night—the fearful motor-launch chase down the Thames after Jonathan Small and the Agra treasure, followed mere hours later with wild elation when Mary Morstan agreed to marry me. Her passing two years previously was still something of a fresh wound and I abandoned the subject, saying firmly, "But that is long ago. What has befallen you and the lady, Styles?"

"Not us, exactly—it's Fanny's husband, as Mr. Sherlock said." The young man shook his head. "Though I have no idea how he..."

Holmes snorted. "I told you lads a thousand times to observe. For example, I observe that the young lady is wearing a wedding ring. You are not. Thus she is married, but not to you. Her difficulty obviously concerns crime, for that is my field of expertise. Her emotional collapse demonstrates such pronounced dread that it must be a close family member that is in danger, and it is you that brings her to me, not her absent husband. Clearly she is prostrate with grief and fear but not a widow, else there would not be such urgency about the matter; a deceased spouse is no longer an emergency. Moreover, the recently-widowed ladies who consult a detective are usually seeking something in the way of vengeance for the loss, and the dominant emotion on such faces is anger, not fear. This woman is so terrified she cannot form words. Thus I must posit that it is the husband in danger, since for most young married women an endangered spouse would be the most likely one to cause this level of concern—and at her tender age any child of hers would be, one hopes, too young to fall afoul of some sinister criminal scheme. Therefore it follows that it is the husband that is somehow under threat, and a dire one indeed, if Davy persuaded her to seek my aid and not that of the police. But her eyes are open at last," he added. "Please, madam, you are among friends. Pray tell us what the problem is and we shall devote all our energies to assisting you. You can trust Doctor Watson and myself implicitly."

"I know that." The woman took a deep breath and her jaw set with determination. "My husband spoke of you often. My full name is Fanny *Wiggins.*"

"Great heavens!" I blurted, unable to help myself. "But....Wiggins was just a lad. Surely it cannot have been that long."

Holmes chuckled. "It is discomfiting to realize the passing of years, is it not, Watson? But the Sholto matter was over seven years ago. Wiggins was already fifteen, hardly a boy any longer even then."

"Yes," Fanny agreed. "We'd been together since we was fourteen, but our parents forbade us to marry until I turned eighteen and Mark had steady employment." She blushed. "I fear that our parents did not consider the jobs he did for you in the detective business entirely respectable. But he loved working for you, Mr. Holmes. Though he did indeed find a steady job at the docks three years ago, he never forgot those times. He was a devoted reader of Dr. Watson's magazine accounts of your cases. It greatly elated him to see his own name appear in some of them."

It was my turn to flush with embarrassment. I felt somewhat guilty to hear of such devotion when I had never even known Wiggins' first name was Mark.

Fanny Wiggins continued, "He was devastated to read the doctor's report of your passing at Reichenbach in '91, and there was a great celebration in our home when the news came of your return a few months ago."

"Yes," Holmes said. His mouth quirked in one of his half-smiles. "I confess I was rather relieved myself not to have perished at the hands of Professor Moriarty. It was a near thing. But that is a tale for another time."

"Of course. In fact we were talking about when we might to come round to see you, just to visit, you understand, when—when the..." Her shoulders shook and for a moment it seemed she might collapse again.

"Easy there, Fan," Davy Styles said softly. He laid a hand on her shoulder.

Fanny Wiggins smiled somewhat wanly and covered Davy's hand with her own. "Dear Davy. You have been my rock. Forgive me. I shan't faint again." Her attention returned to Holmes. "But you must understand you and Doctor Watson— that is to say, your encouragement and help with his leading the Irregulars, as you called his boys — it changed Mark's life. Without you, Mr. Holmes, I am certain that he would have fallen upon evil ways. It was his admiration for you and his pride at being your aide that kept him from the many criminal temptations offered on the streets of London. Were it not for his other boyhood experiences on the streets that caused such mistrust of the police I think he might well have sought to become a policeman himself." She fell silent for a moment.

"And yet despite this he has somehow fallen afoul of the law?" Holmes prompted her gently. She looked up, startled, and Holmes smiled. "Surely it is no great feat of deduction when you introduce the topic thus."

"It is so unjust!" Fanny burst out. "Anyone who knows Mark—he's the most honest and forthright man I ever knew! It's all just bad luck that he was even there! And now—now he's going to hang..." She began to weep.

"There, there, Fan," Davy Styles said. "Maybe you better let me tell it." He turned to Holmes. "It happened like this, Mr. Sherlock. Mark had been taking on extra work because he and Fan were looking for a better place, a house of their own..."

Fanny Wiggins took a deep breath and straightened. "We'd been wanting to start a family, see," she said, visibly struggling to keep her grief in check. "But we wanted to get out of the city first. Find a place in the country somewhere. I've been taking in washing, and Mark was working Sundays as a warehouse guard. Night watch, like."

Holmes leaned back and closed his eyes. "And there was some mishap at the warehouse? Some crime for which young Wiggins was blamed?"

"A murder, Mr. Sherlock." Young Styles was grim. "The police found Wiggins standing over Jimmy's body with blood on his hands. I myself cannot believe Mark Wiggins capable of such a brutal deed, but he refuses to offer a defense. He won't speak to anyone. He has refused even to see us. It looks very black."

At that last, Fanny Wiggins burst into tears again. Styles looked down at her helplessly, patting her shoulder again, in a futile attempt at reassurance. "Sorry, Fan, but it won't help to whitewash it. Mr. Holmes can't help unless we tell him everything."

"Indeed." Holmes opened his eyes. "Styles, can you describe the sequence of events as you know them? Facts, remember. As like a report in the old days as you can manage, if you have not forgotten all I taught you."

"Yes sir." I had to conceal a smile at Davy's furrowed brow. Though he was a man now, he clearly held 'Mr. Sherlock' in great esteem and was obviously still as fiercely determined to live up to the detective's standard as when he and Wiggins had been boys. "It was Sunday last. Mark was supposed to be standing guard at a wharfside concern, an importer of furs.... but the murder happened at the building a few doors down from that one, London Glass-works."

I could see Holmes straighten slightly at the name. "Indeed," he murmured. "Also on the wharf itself?"

"Yes sir. The back of the building has a loading dock that faces out on to the river where they load the glass bottles and lamps and such."

"This is a storage warehouse, or is the glass manufactory attached to the same building?"

"Both in the same building, Mr. Sherlock. Wiggins was on the night shift along with another old friend of ours, Jim Hornby. You remember him. That's who's dead, sir. I can't fathom it. Neither one of them had any business at the glass-works. And I can't see any reason why Wiggins would take a fish billy to our old mate and stave his head in. If only he would talk to us!"

Holmes nodded, his eyes slitted. I recalled young Hornby as being slightly more of a handful than Wiggins or the other lads; I remembered more than one incident when he tried to chivvy advance payment from Holmes or myself for services that were beyond the scope of what Holmes had assigned to his youthful crew. A scamp, certainly, but not malicious enough to warrant the kind of hatred that results in murder.

Holmes' voice roused me from my memories. "That was the weapon? A fisherman's billy club?"

"Something of the sort, anyway," Styles said. "A club is what we were told. No weapon was found. Just Mark with his hands all bloody. He clammed up when the cops arrived and hasn't said a word since. This morning we tried again to see him and when I couldn't get in, Fanny persuaded me that we must come round and see you and lay it all at your feet."

Fanny Wiggins added, "We've little money, Mr. Holmes, but I would give all I have to save my man from the gallows. We could manage payments, so much a month, if you..."

"Nonsense." Holmes' brow had been knitted in concentration but suddenly he smiled with great warmth upon the distraught woman. "Your husband is one of our Baker Street family, Mrs. Wiggins. There will be no fee. Nevertheless, you may rest assured that I shall do all I can. I venture to say that I have known Wiggins longer than you have, even, and I agree with your assessment. He cannot have done this terrible thing. Therefore someone else must have and the proof of this exists somewhere. We will find it."

He was already escorting her to the door as he spoke, and calmed by these reassurances, she and Styles were soon on their way. When the door closed behind them Holmes rubbed his hands with what seemed to me somewhat inappropriate anticipation. "It is a pretty problem, Watson. It promises complexities far beyond a simple dockside killing. These are—you must forgive the expression—deep waters."

"You must have seen much I did not."

"Ah, well, do not look so dejected over it, old fellow. In this case, it was not merely observation, though I did note one or two minor items that were suggestive about Davy's narrative." I started to ask him what he could possibly mean by this but he waved it off. "Later for that, Watson. It was a hint, no more. But more importantly, I have the advantage of special knowledge. You recall the affair of Cadogan West?"

"Certainly. The theft of the submarine plans. Are you suggesting there is a connection?"

"Indeed. It may help you to know that London Glass-works is a false front for one of Her Majesty's covert operations. One of my brother Mycroft's projects. It is where they are constructing the delicate breathing apparatus and filters for the very same Bruce-Partington submarine that was the motive force in the Cadogan West murder."

"Good heavens!" If Mycroft Holmes was involved in the matter, than perforce British Intelligence must be, as well. Holmes was right—these were deep waters indeed. "Are you suggesting young Wiggins was somehow involved in an espionage plot?"

"Or attempting to foil one." Holmes shook his head. "No data as yet. It is a capital mistake…"

"…to theorize without data." I smiled. "Yes, yes. 'One cannot make bricks without clay.' Very well, then, Holmes, where shall we dig for your data? Should we attempt to see Wiggins?"

"Not without more than we have. No, I think in this case a flank attack is warranted. We shall consult Mycroft first, at the Diogenes Club. If we move swiftly and are fortunate with our cab we shall be just in time for the lunch seating. After that we shall be better armed for a visit with Wiggins."

❋ ❋ ❋

The Diogenes Club was, as I have chronicled in the past, an eccentric establishment even in a city that was home to more than its share of such. It was designed for unsocial, misanthropic men who loathed human society, yet still craved the luxuries offered by the better gentlemen's clubs: fine dining, brandy and cigars, a library of the best current newspapers and magazines. A 'club for the un-clubbable,' Holmes had referred to it, and the description had stuck with me over the years. The amenities of the Diogenes, and it must be admitted they were all quite first-class, were offered in an eerie, dreamlike silence—for speaking even in a whisper was forbidden throughout the establishment save in the Stranger's Room just off the front stairs on the first floor, and even there the insulated walls and thick carpeting prevented sound from traveling well. Eye contact with anyone else on the premises was frowned upon save with the staff, who used merely a raised or lowered eyebrow, and the occasional hand signal, to conduct the majority of their business with members.

Mycroft Holmes, who abhorred the social impositions usually required of men that moved in Whitehall's corridors of power, managed to eschew the majority of such things by virtue of sheer willpower. His refusal to participate in the normal political rituals common to the men of his station, coupled with the necessity his great intellect had become to Her Majesty's operations, had led to a curious state of affairs where the mountain routinely journeyed to Mohammed, as it were. Mycroft Holmes did a great deal of government business out of the Stranger's Room at the Diogenes, for not only was this one of the few places Mycroft could be persuaded to socialize at all, but as it turned out the bizarre and misanthropic principles that guided the establishment were also quite ideal for a meeting place to discuss the clandestine operations that occupied so much of Mycroft's government duties. In the four or five times during our association that Sherlock Holmes wished to consult his brother on a case—I must pause at this juncture to explain that the brothers Holmes were not overly troubled by the conventions of filial duty and saw one another, generally, only upon those occasions when Holmes' criminal cases intersected with Mycroft's matters of state—we usually sought him at the Diogenes.

When we arrived we found Mycroft just tucking a large white napkin into his collar, in cheerful anticipation. He gestured to the waiter that we were to join him and Holmes and I tiptoed like wraiths across the lushly-appointed dining hall. At one point my shoe squeaked and I was the recipient of several furious glares from other diners. I blushed like a schoolboy and prayed fervently that I should not need to cough before our lunch was safely concluded.

The food in the club dining room *was* excellent, once one became accustomed to the ghastly silence of the place. Lunch was a hearty lamb stew, well-spiced but not unduly so. Judging from the beatific expression upon the face of Mycroft Holmes it was the high point of his day and I rather enjoyed it myself, as I did the crisp salad and pale ale that accompanied it. Holmes, for his part, wolfed his portion without appearing to taste it, but that was his way. "Food is fuel for the engine, Watson, nothing more," was his usual response when I encouraged him to be venturesome in his culinary choices. Today he was eager to get to the business at hand, but experience had taught us that Mycroft was more likely to be forthcoming if he had eaten well.

When our meal was concluded, Mycroft rose and beckoned us to follow. We padded after him to the Stranger's Room, where he settled himself into his favorite of the well-upholstered leather chairs scattered about the room. "Well, Sherlock, let's have it. It is the matter of young Hornby's death, of course. Do you have pertinent information for me? You must be aware the culprit is already in custody."

Neither Holmes nor myself questioned how Mycroft could have known this when we had passed the last hour in utter silence. He was, after all, Mycroft.

Holmes shook his head. "I had rather hoped for the reverse," he said. "I think you must have relevant information for me, since I am engaged to find the real killer. You have the wrong man in custody."

"Really." Mycroft looked mildly amused. For a second, no more, I thought I glimpsed the indulgent older brother he must have been to Holmes when they were boys. "Please elucidate."

"I cannot demonstrate a chain of logic you would accept," Holmes admitted. "I require more facts. I had hoped you could furnish them. Surely it does not compromise government secrets to tell me of matters not directly connected to the manufacture of this submarine. To begin with, have you any reason to suspect espionage? Was the glass-works building itself burgled or the submarine compromised in any other way?"

Mycroft was not at all disturbed that his brother spoke so casually about a submarine that was still one of Her Majesty's most closely-guarded secrets. "No, not that we can detect. But that does not rule out espionage." He rubbed his jaw. "I am inclined to think it was a private dispute of some kind. Possibly thieves falling out or, more likely, a master thief disposing of his helpers once their usefulness had ended, only to realize he had been premature and fleeing before finishing the job. I think this young Wiggins was probably in line to be executed along with his friend Hornby, but something intervened. However, the police have marked him as the killer and his conviction and eventual execution are foregone conclusions as far as the Yard is concerned, so there is no need for his master to attempt his life in jail. My colleagues are content to let the wheels of justice grind slowly on in that direction, since the youth cannot be persuaded to talk. It is hoped that as the pressure mounts and his date with the hangman's noose draws closer, the lad will crack and lead us to the rest of the conspirators."

Holmes was quick to pounce on a possible lead. "Have you formed any conclusions regarding the identity of these conspirators?"

"No conclusions," Mycroft admitted. "Merely surmise. But we continued to investigate Hugo Oberstein's spy network after the Cadogan

"I cannot demonstrate a chain of logic you would accept, I require more facts."

West matter was resolved. And though it will not satisfy a police-court or even my colleagues in the Department, I may tell you in confidence that evidence has led me to believe Oberstein was part of some larger organization. This shadow network of spies and saboteurs would be my first priority in any investigation. Hence our interest in this Wiggins, for he may well provide us with a solid lead."

"You are convinced he was partnered with the dead man on some nefarious enterprise?" Holmes looked dissatisfied.

"Certainly." Mycroft ticked points off on his fingers. "Consider. The two men were temporary employees, they had only sought work at the one warehouse rather than up and down the entire waterfront, they had expressed a preference for the night shift, and they had agreed to come at a lower wage than is customary. These are all indicators of one thing—they did not want the job for its own sake, they wanted the job for access it provided to some other goal. Ergo, it follows that they planned a theft. Yet they ignored the expensive furs they were hired to guard, eschewing this obvious burglary target for the glass-blowing concern a few doors down. Obviously then they knew the clandestine purpose to which the glass-works had been converted, which proves espionage. The body was found, with the killer standing over it, by the dockside wharf entrance, suggesting a rendezvous with a boat. It is not a great feat to deduce a confederate who abandoned the two, and the only motive for murder must be to silence witnesses. This Wiggins must still fear his former employer, else why would he stand mute?" He flipped his hand outward in dismissal. "I have had agents in to see this young man and he will not admit anything, not even to knowing the dead man. In fact he will not speak at all, not even to his wife. But there was no other possible target for thieves in the area save the fur warehouse and they clearly were not interested in that."

"You are certain there was no alternate target for any theft?" Holmes knew the answer even as he asked it, but he did anyway.

Once again Mycroft let the indulgent expression flicker across his face. "Of course I am. It was my department that initially chose the site. There is the furrier, a pawnbroker, a failed veterinary concern that is now vacant, and a tea wholesaler. And of course the glass-works itself, which does a small amount of legitimate business in the neighborhood."

"The vacant veterinary…"

"Is not actually vacant," Mycroft added, with what I thought was the slightest amount of smugness to his tone. "It is where my agents are headquartered. It provides a good vantage point where we can keep an eye on the neighborhood in general and the glass manufactory in particular. It is in fact why the police arrived so quickly. My men summoned them as they went to investigate suspicious noises they heard, doubtless foiling the theft."

"But the dock is not visible from there," Holmes put in quickly. "Else you would have had the lot of them, master and henchmen both."

"I suspect it is why they chose the water for the approach," Mycroft admitted. "Had I been on the premises I certainly would have taken steps to insure against this, but I rarely venture forth to oversee such things directly. But the matter has been remedied. We have a man watching from the roof at night now."

"Nevertheless no one *saw* Wiggins, Hornby, or the killer as they arrived. It does provide possibilities for an alternate theory." Now Holmes was the one who looked slightly smug. "Allow me to suggest a new perspective, Mycroft. Consider the same scenario on the assumption that young Wiggins is innocent. Does no new interpretation of these facts occur to you?"

"With that basic assumption? The facts in no way support…"

"I know," Holmes said, with some asperity. "Hence my involvement. There is no need to consult either one of us when a hypothesis is obvious. But I suspect your customary indolence—now, be honest, brother mine, that is the word that best describes your habits—has led you to accept a theory of the case that is in error. Try formulating a fresh one with the assumption I suggest."

"Very well." Mycroft's eyes closed briefly and he looked almost asleep. I knew better, though. His mental capacity was the antithesis of his physical being—agile, restless, and capable of racing at the speed of a thoroughbred stallion. Mycroft was, even more than his younger brother, entirely devoted to the mind and I often suspected that his gross physical laziness was because he begrudged any energy not given to his mental processes.

His eyes flickered open. "Sherlock, it is perfectly obvious to me that you have an emotional investment in this young man Wiggins, but I fear it is clouding your judgment. The only way your scenario makes sense is if the young man was on the scene trying to prevent a crime, but there is no way he could have been aware of one if he and Hornby were innocents. The glass-works is too far away from the furrier that employed them. Let us say that Hornby was a thief and Wiggins pursued him. Why then would he stand mute when captured and not offer an explanation? Why would Hornby have made it a point to enlist Wiggins in the first place? For we have ascertained that it was he that sought the young man out to join him at the guard job. Why would Wiggins not name the true attacker? Where is the weapon? It won't do."

"All good questions." Holmes looked grim. "But they have answers. We must find them. Because I will never believe that the young man I trained could have fallen so far in a mere three years. Your business is politics, Mycroft, where perhaps human convictions are more malleable. But in my field I have found that a man's character is not so flexible a thing." He stood. "Come, Watson, we must try to persuade Wiggins to come clean with us. Mycroft, you are not keeping the lad isolated, are you? We shall not need special credentials to get in?"

"We have left his incarceration to the Yard," Mycroft said. "We prefer to keep my department out of the matter, officially, as long as it is feasible to do so." He paused. "I wish you good luck, Sherlock, truly, but I fear that this time you will not find success. Three years is more than enough time to turn a man if the matter is desperate."

Holmes merely shook his head—a noncommittal gesture that I was not certain meant disagreement or acknowledgement of Mycroft's words and rose to go. I followed him out.

❋❋❋

Holmes' expression remained grim as we emerged out on to the steps leading up to the Diogenes entrance. "Mycroft's objections are sound," he admitted. "Still, though, I cannot credit that someone clever enough to plan such an assault on the glass-works in the first place would then panic to the extent that he would murder his assistants before achieving his objective. Yet Mycroft said that the glass-works was not breached. It chafes me that I cannot arrive at an alternative theory that—here, now, what's this?"

Three rough-looking fellows faced us on the street. The one in the center licked his lips and smiled. "Couple of nosey parkers need to be taught a lesson, looks like to me," he said. "We're here to tell you to mind your own business."

"I hardly think I need any lesson from your sort," Holmes said with a thin smile. "Though perhaps if you were more specific? I have interests in many matters."

"You need to lay off the Hornby killing," growled the ruffian. "You got lots of other matters, that's all very well then. See to them and leave this be." He stepped forward and thrust out a hand to shove Holmes in the chest. I did not have my revolver, but I carried my heavy walking stick with the steel knob at the top and I gripped it more strongly as I saw the fellow closest to me tense in the shoulders. Sure enough, he raised his fist to swing at me and I flicked out my stick to clout him on the jaw. He staggered back and the other two turned from Holmes to me.

"We're not finished yet," Holmes said. And then he leaped and whirled his leg around in the most astounding kick, which landed with an ugly thud upon the skull of the roughneck closest to him. Holmes spun in mid-air to land catlike upon the cobblestones. He sprang at once to his feet again and his hands lashed out in a series of chopping motions almost faster than my eyes could follow. In moments his two assailants lay groaning in the street.

In my astonishment, though, I had forgotten the man who meant to attack me, and suddenly there was a sharp blow on the back of my own skull to remind me. I fell to my knees with an oath.

But Holmes was there; scooping up my steel-headed stick from where it had fallen, and he spun it and lashed out at the man standing over me before the ruffian could pursue his advantage. I tried to rise but could not. My vision was blurred and I was barely holding on to consciousness. I had a vague sense of the three roughs taking to their heels as I heard a police-whistle, and then I saw red spill over my eyes to the cobblestones. "Watson!" came Holmes' voice. "Here! You, cabby, give me a hand with my friend…"

But then all was black and I heard no more.

Consciousness returned slowly. At first I was aware of nothing but a throbbing ache at the back of my skull that seemed to pulse with each beat of my heart. Then there was the feeling of icy dampness at my brow. I gradually realized that I was lying in bed, and someone was wiping my forehead with a wet cloth. I opened my eyes.

"Easy there, Doctor." A young man's voice. My vision blurred for a moment. "Lie still, please, and let's have another look at your eyes. Mr. Holmes tells me you were assaulted with a paving-stone."

"My fault, Watson, entirely." Holmes' voice, now. "I had assumed you were aware of him. Had I thought to warn you as he turned…"

"Please, Mr. Holmes, stand back now." The young man's voice was deferential, yet firm. "You must let me apply the skills for which you summoned me."

I blinked and saw the young man leaning over me. I knew him from somewhere but it took me another moment or two to recognize him. "Dr. Trevelyan!"

"Yes." Percy Trevelyan smiled. "Mr. Holmes sent a policeman to summon me even as you were being brought here. It was somewhat startling to find an anxious young officer on my doorstep telling me to accompany him to Baker Street at once, but of course I was glad to come. I have not forgotten the assistance you both rendered to me in the past. But come now, Doctor, you must hold still that I may examine your eyes." He brought a lamp closer, then moved it away. "Good. Your pupils are reacting to the light as they should. I do not believe there is any serious injury, though it certainly bled copiously as scalp wounds do. You were fortunate, Doctor, since from what Mr. Holmes tells me I have no doubt it was intended as a killing blow. No, lie still," he added in a firmer voice as I struggled to sit upright. "There is still danger of concussion."

"Doctor's orders. No more street brawling for you, Watson." Holmes' voice was laced with humor, though I fancy I saw relief in his expression as he stepped forward. He turned to Trevelyan. "Our gratitude, Doctor. I am so used to having Watson on hand here that at first I was at a loss to think of another medical man to consult; you were only other London practitioner I could recall. We were fortunate to find you still at Brook Street after all these years."

"I was glad to be of service, though really it looked much worse than it was. Once I had cleaned and dressed the wound I saw that it did not even require stitches. Change that bandage upon the morrow and clean it again and he should be fine. I see you have a complete chemical laboratory in the sitting-room. Perhaps you have something that can serve as an antiseptic should the wound require further attention?" Trevelyan managed to hide his medical distaste for such an unsanitary arrangement, and for my part my head ached too profoundly to laugh. Holmes' chemical experiments were a constant source of tension in our lodgings, particularly when they created odors so foul that I was forced to vacate the premises, or, in one memorable instance, an explosion that resulted in Holmes being forced to replace the entire sideboard as well as two of our velvet-upholstered reading chairs.

"I have sufficient supplies in my own medical bag, Trevelyan," I said, weakly. "You'll find it in the bottom of the wardrobe there behind you.

Best to leave Holmes' concoctions out of it."

"Ah, of course. Very well, then, gentlemen. I'll be on my way. You must notify me if there is any change for the worse." Trevelyan nodded at us both and departed.

Now that the doctor was no longer present to forbid it, I struggled to sit up. "Holmes, how long have I been unconscious? Have you…"

"Please, Watson, do not distress yourself. It has only been a few hours. Trevelyan took utmost care with your injuries. I was somewhat concerned when you did not waken as he cleaned your wound, but he said it would be best to let you sleep and wake naturally." Holmes scowled in self-reproach. "I misjudged our assailants. I thought a clear demonstration of superiority would stampede them. I did not think they would lash out so savagely, or else we would have retreated into the Diogenes."

"I should be ashamed to retreat from such common ruffians. Especially the kind of coward that attacks from the rear." It was my turn to scowl. "The fault was entirely mine. I should have been more cautious, Holmes, but I allowed myself to become distracted. Tell me, what was that style of combat you employed against those men? I have never seen the like. You almost seemed to levitate at one point."

"Ah, that." Holmes looked pleased. He could be as vain as a schoolgirl sometimes. "During my enforced absence after the death of Professor Moriarty, you will recall that I traveled across Tibet and Asia under the guise of the Norwegian explorer Sigerson. I have always been a student of the Asian fighting styles—it was the Japanese *baritsu* that saved me during my struggle with Professor Moriarty at the edge of the Reichenbach Falls. As Sigerson, I chanced to encounter an order of Chinese monks during my journey out of Tibet and into China, shortly after I departed Lhasa. They call themselves 'Shao-Lin.' These monks employ a style of unarmed combat known as *gung fu*, and one of them was kind enough to demonstrate a few of its more basic moves to Mr. Sigerson. I assure you that what you saw was the rankest sort of amateur performance; the discipline of *gung fu* is a lifetime undertaking according to the Shao-Lin, and requires mental and spiritual training that begins in childhood along with daily practice of its physical skills. Nevertheless, I possess enough knowledge to be at least somewhat dangerous." One of his rare smiles flickered across my friend's face. "Any of my monk friends would make short work of me, I fear, but fortunately my half-remembered improvisation of *gung fu* was sufficient to the matter at hand today. There are some interesting weapons that are used by the monks as well; a lethal pair of chained clubs called

nunchaku, and tiny edged throwing-blades known as *shuriken.* I cannot
show them to you at the moment since mine currently reside at the bolt-
hole I was using when I first returned to London. But one of these days I
shall retrieve them and add them to my files here."

I knew that Holmes maintained several secret apartments hidden
throughout London—bases where he could at necessity conceal himself from pursuit or don one of the disguises he occasionally used in the
course of his investigations. I had yet to see any of these myself though
I knew he had one in Brixton, and another near Whitehall, and a third
somewhere not far from the docks. There were probably others. I asked
him, "But have you spent all day here then? Have you not at least been to
see Wiggins?"

"I am on my way there now. No, no, old friend, you heard the doctor's
prescription," Holmes added. "You remain in bed. I assure you that I can
manage. I think I may have to disappear for a few days in any case. Our
movements are obviously under observation."

"Because of the attack on us." Reluctantly, I did not renew my effort to
stand; I had become somewhat dizzied from the attempt. Nevertheless it
frustrated me to see Holmes preparing to depart without me.

"Yes. That, coupled with Mycroft's surmises regarding Hugo Oberstein
and the network he once commanded, have led me to suspect that we are
once again dealing with the Hierarchy."

I suppressed a gasp. The Hierarchy was the organization that had
formed from the remnants of Professor Moriarty's criminal empire.
Holmes had already dealt them a blow with his disposal of Colonel
Sebastian Moran some months previously, but he had said at the time that
we were not finished with them. Now it appeared this sinister cabal had
set their sights on the Bruce-Partington submarine. "Holmes, this is intol-
erable. Can we not have Scotland Yard detain the men that are watching
us?"

"And charge them with what? Loitering?" Holmes shook his head. "It
would accomplish nothing. They would be replaced within the hour. As
it is I am aware of them and can elude them when I choose to. It is your
welfare that concerns me. I hesitate to leave you here unprotected."

"Bosh!" I sat up straight, ignoring the intensified throb of pain this action caused. "I am perfectly able to defend myself, even with a headache.
If I am not capable of dashing about London's underworld, I certainly can
remain in bed in relative safety as long as my service revolver is handy." I
gestured at the dresser. "It's in the top drawer there, along with a fresh box

"It is your welfare that concerns me. I hesitate to leave you here unprotected."

of cartridges. Fetch it here so I have it on the night-stand, that's all I need. You can just trot along to your interview with Wiggins."

Holmes took no offense at the sharpness of my reply. "Good old Watson. No one doubts your courage, certainly not I," he said gently, and my anger evaporated. "But you have often cautioned me about the perils of ignoring physical needs when hot upon the trail. Please try to remember your own advice to me over the years regarding the taking of foolish chances with one's health." At my crestfallen expression, he hastened to add, "I promise you, I shall not make any decisive move without you. But this is strictly investigatory, information-gathering. I shall have to adopt a disguise, probably, to shake the watchers off my trail, and if I am to penetrate to the criminal circles frequented by the Hierarchy I will do better alone. When the trap is set to close, though, I will have you by my side, never fear."

At last I nodded, mollified. "Very well. But young Wiggins is my friend also, Holmes, and I want to be included in this matter."

Holmes nodded and departed. I fell back into my pillows, cursing the circumstance that left me injured. From this day on, I vowed, I would not take my eyes off an assailant, not for a moment.

Three days passed with no word from Holmes. My injury was healing well, and by the evening of the third day I was chafing at my enforced inaction. I was certain I was physically recovered enough to be of aid to Holmes... and it was not unthinkable that some agent of the Hierarchy had got the better of him. Despite his mental and physical prowess, he was not superhuman. I was almost certain he was not going armed, since he routinely left that to me and he was such a creature of habit that I feared he had not considered doing so, even though I was unable to accompany him. I had an irrational conviction that Holmes was putting himself in some sort of danger that could have been prevented were I at his side, and I was troubled with visions of Holmes being held in captivity in some terrible rat-infested dungeon. My face twitched in a rueful smile as I recalled the many times Holmes had chided me for my failures of imagination. How I wished for such a failure now!

There was a pounding at the front door that I could hear even at the top of the stairs. Certain it was news of Holmes, I called out, "I shall attend to it, Mrs. Hudson," and moved quickly to the entrance to our home.

Just as I reached the foyer the door burst open and I beheld Davy Styles, bleeding from a cut on his cheek. "They've taken Mr. Sherlock," he wheezed. "Two of them, with knives. Grabbed him right off the street and bundled him into a black carriage before I could move, and then they were off like lightning! I didn't know where else to go, Doctor. I don't even know where to begin to look for him!"

So my imagined fears turned out to be real, it seemed. The time for in-action had clearly passed. The trouble was, without Holmes to advise me, I had no clue what that action should be.

✻ ✻ ✻

I decided to begin with the obvious. "Come in and sit down, Styles, and let me see to your face. I'll get my medical bag."

As I tended to the cut on his cheek with a bottle of antiseptic and a bit of sticking-plaster, he told me the tale of Holmes' misadventure. "He'd asked me to meet him at the wharf, Doctor, and he was in disguise as a river scavenger, with his face all blacked-up and wearing a long pea-coat and a scarf. It took me right back to the old days with the Irregulars, it did. 'Styles,' says he, 'I'm hot on the trail of the Hire—hire—uh...'"

"Hierarchy," I supplied.

"Yeah, that was it. Hierarchy. 'I'm hot on the trail of the Hierarchy and I need you to have Watson come meet me...' And then there's a clatter of hooves and this carriage comes racing up to us, Mr. Sherlock shoves me into an alleyway and I went sprawling. When I come out I see these blokes in hoods shoving poor Mr. Sherlock into the carriage at knifepoint and off they go."

"Meet him," I mused. "Meet him where, Styles?"

Davy Styles goggled at me. "Why, I was assuming you knew, Doctor. Have you no idea where Mr. Sherlock meant for you to go?"

I shook my head. "I can guess, but you know how Holmes feels about guesswork. I must think." Privately I wondered how much good that would do; it was Holmes that was the thinker. Nevertheless, the burden had fallen to me and I must not fail my friend. "Tell me more of what you were doing for Holmes, Davy. How did you come to meet him there? What was your errand?" I had a flash of inspiration. "I need a report, Davy, just as you would give to Mr. Sherlock. Leave nothing out."

As I had hoped, my invocation of his past experience as an agent of Sherlock Holmes squared Davy's shoulders and settled him down. "Yes sir, right you are. Well, he got in touch with me night before last, said there was a gentleman he wanted some information on. Sailing man, dark blue jacket and white mutton-chop whiskers, been seen lurking about the street where the glass-works was. Well, I still know my way around the streets and I'd asked around some, found out he was at a pub in the next street most evenings, place called The Angel's Wing. Though there haven't been any angels ever found at *that* address," he added with a grimace. "It's a vile little place. I ain't no gentleman myself, first to admit it, but even I have standards. Naught but villains and their whores at that thieves' den."

"Did this bewhiskered gentleman have a name?"

"Hadn't got it yet, Doctor." Styles looked abashed. "I'd thought to dare The Angel's Wing tonight myself and see if I could winkle a name out of someone, perhaps even get a few words with the gent himself. On the sly, you know, the way we used to do for Mr. Sherlock when we was younger."

I nodded. It seemed a sound strategy. "We shall do as you planned, Styles, except I shall accompany you."

Styles looked appalled. "But—begging your pardon, Doctor, no one would mistake you for anything but a gentleman. And this Angel's Wing... well, sir, they don't cater to no gentlemen, see. Chances are a dozen of them would be on you with clubs or worse for whatever's in your wallet, and then fight over it like wild dogs."

I smiled. "I'm an old campaigner, lad. I'll have my revolver, and I can dress the part a little. I have not Holmes' skill at disguise but I think I can improvise suitable clothing, at least. But before that, I want to try something else." At Styles' bewildered expression, I explained, "Holmes had originally planned to visit Wiggins in jail. I think we should start our inquiry there also. If Wiggins did indeed speak to Holmes, I have hopes he can be persuaded to speak to us as well. He might even know the name of this whiskered seaman Holmes was seeking. Then we'll be off to The Angel's Wing."

✱✱✱

It was no trouble to get Styles and myself admitted to see Wiggins. Inspector Lestrade knew me of old and arrangements were promptly made to have an officer conduct us to the cell where Wiggins was being held pending trial. The jail was damp and dark, a forbidding stone edifice. I shuddered to think of the eager lad I remembered condemned to such a foul dungeon, and I hoped that his spirit would not be crushed in such a place.

The officer led us to a barred door set close in to the stone wall. Wiggins was sprawled on a cot; taller, thinner and exceedingly pale, but otherwise much as I remembered him. He was dressed in ragged street clothes, not yet forced to wear a striped convict's uniform. But I knew if we could not find Holmes he would be wearing one soon enough.

The officer nodded at him, then at me. "It'll not be necessary to go in to the cell, will it, Doctor?"

"No." I shouldered past him and stood before the bars. "Wiggins! It is Dr. Watson. You must remember me, surely."

Wiggins looked up. For a moment he smiled and would have spoken, and then abruptly he closed his mouth and merely nodded at the three of us standing in the corridor.

"Wiggins," I pressed on, "Mr. Holmes was here, was he not?"

Another nod.

"Lad, you must tell me what you told him! He's disappeared. I must find him. Locating Holmes is the only way we can help you. Time is of the essence!" I waited.

Wiggins shook his head. Finally he whispered, "I cannot speak of it. I must not."

"But it is I, Wiggins, your old friend Doctor Watson! And Holmes, your wife Fanny, your old friend Styles…we are all trying to help you!" I was growing agitated. "But you must help us in return, you must tell…"

"I *cannot!*" For a moment it looked as though the youth might actually begin to weep. "I can say nothing! For God's sake, Doctor, do not ask me!"

I was at a loss. I had not Holmes' gift for reading people, and I could think of no lever to use that I had not already tried. If invoking his wife's name had not the power to loosen his tongue… yet I was not ready to give up. "Wiggins, lad, we are helpless. Can you be so determined to leave Fanny a widow? Do you not trust Mr. Holmes' abilities? Give us something, some trail to follow, something we can work with! A name! Anything!"

Wiggins licked his lips. His expression was terrified. Finally he said, "Daggett."

"What?" I leaned forward, all eagerness.

"Find Jeremiah Daggett." He turned his back to us. "I can say no more."

Further expostulations were met only with silence. At last I nodded to the officer and we left Wiggins to himself.

Out on the street, I turned to Styles. "At least we have a name. Jeremiah Daggett. He must almost certainly be your whiskered seafarer. Let us return to Baker Street and don some more appropriate clothing, and then we'll be off to this Angel's Wing of yours. I may not be Sherlock Holmes but I daresay we still have a good chance of getting something out of this Daggett. If he balks, we shall see if a revolver persuades him to talk to us. It's a place to start."

Styles nodded, grinning. "Just like the old days, Doctor! The game's afoot!"

Even as worried about Holmes as I was, this still caused me to smile.

Upon the return of Styles and myself to Baker Street, I asked Mrs. Hudson to provide the lad with tea and a few slices of cold mutton while I excused myself to Holmes' bedroom. I knew Holmes kept a trunk of miscellaneous clothing there that he utilized in his various disguises. We were not of a size, by any means—I was an inch or two shorter than he, and much broader in the shoulder—but Holmes' impersonations often required him to assume different sizes of appearance. I was certain that a diligent search would turn up something adequate. All I needed was enough of an ensemble that would allow me to pass for a typical patron of a seedy establishment such as The Angel's Wing had been described to be. I soon found a striped sailor's jersey and a battered tweed cap. This, coupled with an old pair of black trousers and a worn woolen jacket of my own, would serve as sufficient camouflage.

When I emerged into the sitting-room in this garb Styles looked up, startled, then nodded in approval. "Aye, that's the ticket, Doctor. You still look a little too tidy about the face—most of the roughs we'll be seeing aren't so regular in their shaving habits. But it's certainly better than a silk hat and tie. At least you won't be such a tempting target. Shall we be off then?"

I was soon to see the efficacy of my disguise proved when we attempted to hail a cab. The first two passed right by us despite my bellowing. Fortunately, the third one to pass us was driven by a fellow who knew Holmes and I of old and, once he had amused himself sufficiently with a few gibes regarding my clothing, was more than willing to drive Styles and myself to the Angel's Wing. As a precaution I bade him to let us off at the corner of the next street and we preceded the rest of the way on foot.

It was early in the evening but the atmosphere of the pub was already quite boisterous, and the air was thick with tobacco-smoke. I let Styles guide us to a table in the back and when the barmaid arrived he ordered us a couple of ales.

"Look around, Styles," I said quietly when the girl had departed. "See anyone fitting the description of this Daggett?"

"No, but the air's so blasted thick in here. Let me stir around a little. You stay here, Doctor," he added as he rose. "I'll shout if there's trouble, never fear."

The barmaid brought our ales. I took a sip of mine, mostly for appearances' sake. It was thin and bitter. I reflected that the last time I had been in an establishment comparable to this one was when I had been in Kandahar, about to join the Fifth Northumberland Fusiliers as company medic back during the Afghan war, almost fifteen years ago ago. Then the floor had been covered with dirt instead of sawdust, and most of the patrons had been off-duty soldiers such as myself, but apart from that, the noise and smoke and roughness of the furnishings were nearly identical. Even the ale tasted as poor as the ones I remembered imbibing back then. It was I who had changed. Now I felt absurdly out of place, despite my disguise. I was certain my awkwardness must be as visible as a lighthouse beacon to everyone around me, and hunkered down a little.

Then I saw something that drove these dark musings instantly from my mind. It was one of the roughs who had assaulted us outside the Diogenes Club; the same fellow who had attacked me from behind. He was standing at the bar, exchanging words with the barkeep. I stood and carried my mug over to the bar, trying to move surreptitiously, in hopes of overhearing something useful.

"So it's Daggett then, is it?" The ruffian's laugh was hoarse, and I could tell he was somewhat the worse for drink. "Well, we'll be ready, never fear." Then, cursed luck, he turned and saw me. A glitter of recognition flared in his eyes and I knew the game was up.

"Well, now," he said thickly, with a grin that revealed jagged and discolored teeth. "Back for more, are we? Good you left your nice clothes at home this time, since you'll be getting mussed."

He began to raise his fists and the barkeep leaned forward. "'Ere now, Clyde, you take that outside now. I don't want no fights in here this early."

"I'm not looking for a fight," I said. "I only want information."

"Well too bad mate," the ruffian answered. "Because..."

I did not wait for him to finish. Before he could get another word out I whipped out my revolver and cracked him smartly across the jaw with the barrel. As I had hoped, several of his already-fragile teeth broke completely and he howled in pain and rage. There are few nerves in the body more sensitive than those housed in the teeth and I knew he would be in terrible, blinding pain. It is shameful for a medical man to admit such a thing but I felt no sympathy, only gratification at exacting a mild vengeance for the paving-stone injury he had dealt me a few days previously. I stepped forward and jammed the revolver barrel into his middle. "Outside."

He looked at me with hatred but made no argument, and I escorted him out into the street. Styles emerged from the saloon entrance behind me. "What's all this Doctor?"

"A man with answers, perhaps. He mentioned Daggett. And he was one of the men that attacked Holmes and myself." I gestured at him with my revolver to step to the alley adjoining the Angel's Wing, where we could conduct our business in relative privacy. "Now, fellow—Clyde, is it? Tell me who you work for and where we may find Sherlock Holmes."

Clyde wiped blood from his mouth and uttered an obscenity.

Without taking my eyes off him, I said, "Styles. Find us a cab. He'll talk to us—if not here, then at the Yard." I addressed Clyde directly. "Despite your cowardly attack upon my person I have little interest in you, or in handing you to the police. I seek Sherlock Holmes. You can tell me what you know or we shall hand you to the police and it's out of my hands. It's your choice."

Clyde glared at me with loathing and, I was pleased to note, some semblance of fear. "All I know is a man hired us to scare you and your friend away from Hornby. Then today I got word we was to look for a man named Daggett. We was going to meet at an address by the docks, a place your friend Holmes owned."

One of Holmes' bolt-holes, surely. But that made no sense. "Why there?"

"I can answer that, Doctor," Styles interrupted. "It was where Mr. Sherlock kept his files on the Hierarchy. He feared they would not be safe in Baker Street."

I nodded. It was a reasonable assumption, especially since our address was widely known. Holmes would have sought to avoid any possibility of harm coming to myself or Mrs. Hudson should the Hierarchy attempt a raid of some sort on our lodgings to gain custody of whatever evidence Holmes had amassed against them. "Tell me the address," I said to our captive.

"I don't know it," Clyde said, his tone surly and martyred. "You and your friend queered the pitch. The man I was supposed to meet's probably in the wind by now."

"You must know something," I pressed. "I remind you that I have more than enough to send you to prison already, just for your murderous attack on Holmes and me. Do you want to spend the next five years breaking rocks at Dartmoor?"

"I tell you I don't know nothing!"

His tone was defiant. I could see him tensing for some sort of action—whether to fight or flee, I was not sure. At the first twitch of his shoulder I struck him with my fist, another sharp blow to the jaw that doubtless reawakened the throbbing nerve pain in the broken teeth. He sank to the cobblestones, moaning.

"I'm though playing with you, my man." I put as much threatening menace as I could into my voice. "Tell me what I want to know or I promise it will go hard with you."

I had not the knack for such threats that Holmes did, but it sufficed for the unfortunate Clyde. "All right," he muttered. "Just... for the love of God stop hitting my face, you've broke my bleeding jaw."

"Hardly. If that was the case you would be incapable of speech." I raised my fist. "However, I can arrange to..."

"No!" Clyde held up his hands in surrender. "Somewhere down by the waterfront. Blackfriars Bridge. I swear that's all I know!"

The fight had gone out of him. His sincerity was evident. I nodded and gestured toward the street. He slowly rose to his feet and, when I nodded again, he broke into a run.

"Best be on our way, Doctor," Styles said. "He'll be back once he's got some liquid courage in him, probably with friends. You sure we shouldn't have handed him to the Yarders?"

"Holmes probably would have done so," I admitted. "But we are in a hurry. Come, let us see what we can find at Blackfriars. This Daggett must be there—since Clyde will not be keeping his appointment, we shall keep it for him."

Again we had some difficulty with getting a cab. I wished I'd had the presence of mind to have retained our earlier driver, but there was no help for it. I was becoming keenly aware of the handicap I labored under, trying to investigate without Holmes to lead; he always seemed to think of these little things before they became problems. But eventually we found a driver who was willing to take a chance on us despite our appearance, and were on our way.

I had instructed our cabby to take us to the northern end of the bridge, since the row of warehouses along the shore between there and Southwark seemed to me to be the most likely location for Holmes to have chosen for this particular hideout. The southern shore was too heavily traveled and the railyard adjoining Waterloo was clearly out of the question. Once I had dismissed the hansom and we were standing there on Upper Thames

"Come, let us see what we can find at Blackfriars."

Street, though, the hopelessness of the task I had set for us became apparent. There was little light, and one darkened warehouse looked much like the next. There were dozens of possibilities. Would we have to search them all? I had assumed Styles and I would have found some sign of Daggett and the Hierarchy upon our arrival but we had the fog-shrouded streets to ourselves. Again I felt the frustration at... well, at not being Sherlock Holmes, for I was forced to admit that was truly the problem.

Very well, then, what would Holmes have done?

Styles hesitantly plucked at my sleeve. "Doctor..."

"Hush, lad. Give me a moment to think." I scowled and tried to picture in my mind's eye what Sherlock Holmes' actions would be upon disembarking from the cab. He would *observe*, I realized. He would note locations, telltale signs of use, the names of...

And then I saw it. A sign hung over a shabby and weathered storefront: SIGERSON IMPORT AND EXPORT LTD.

"While in Tibet," I murmured, "under the name of *Sigerson*." It was exactly the sort of joke that would appeal to Holmes—amusing to him, incomprehensible to anyone else. Heaven knew I had been the victim of enough of them in the past.

Styles looked baffled. "Doctor?"

I clapped him on the shoulder. "That one there, Styles." I pointed.

Together we crossed the street and examined the façade. "It's locked and the windows are boarded up," I said. "Perhaps the back?"

Styles flashed me a wolfish grin. "Ah, Doctor, despite the clothes you're still thinking like a gentleman. Lock's no problem. Give us a moment. Can you strike a match? I need a little light is all." I did so. He produced a pair of metal pins from his pocket and bent over the door latch. In moments the door was open and we entered.

Once inside, the darkness enveloped us. I struck another match and saw the room was largely empty, merely a couple of rows of vacant shelves and some crates. Then as the match went out I saw a faint glimmer of light flickering under the rear door. Slowly, as silently as possible, we advanced towards the faint glow, endeavoring not to give any sign of our presence. Styles stumbled against me once in the dark but fortunately recovered himself before he crashed into a crate and betrayed our approach. I braced myself as we reached the door, not sure what we would find. Then I reached for the knob and flung it open.

It was a small study, strangely incongruous in that setting. One wall was lined with books, the other piled with boxes of papers. I recognized

Holmes' penchant for accumulating documents. In the middle of the room a gray-whiskered man in a dark pea-coat was standing over a desk, endeavoring to read a bundle of papers by the light of a small dark-lantern.

"Daggett!" I said sharply. "Do not move. Stand up slowly and raise your hands."

The figure at the desk straightened slowly and turned to face the two of us. "I am afraid, Watson, that in order to follow your instructions I have no choice but to move, at least a little. Try not to do anything impetuous."

"Good God, Holmes!" I burst out, torn between amazement and relief. "*You* are Jeremiah Daggett?"

"An occasionally useful alias," Holmes chuckled as he removed his whiskers. "I confess, though, I am surprised to see you—*Watson!* Beware!"

A mighty shove propelled me forward to land sprawled on the floor at Holmes' feet. I rolled upright and froze in shock as I saw Styles holding a revolver aimed at both of us. I realized the gun was my own—he had deftly plucked it from my jacket a few moments ago, doubtless when he had stumbled against me. I recalled bleakly that most of the Irregulars had been above-average at picking not just locks but pockets, as well.

"I appreciate your assistance, Doctor Watson." Styles was smiling broadly. "I'd never have located Mister Sherlock without your help, especially after you ruined poor Clyde for us." He gestured with the revolver. "I'll take the Hierarchy papers now, Holmes, and no funny business."

I struggled to my feet, still trying to comprehend the scene before me. "Styles? But—how...? What are you...?"

"He killed Hornby, Watson." Holmes' voice was calm. "On the orders of the Hierarchy. I had already begun to suspect such was the case when we were attacked at the Diogenes, for no one else could have alerted the Hierarchy so quickly that I had taken an interest in the case."

"No one smarter than Mister Sherlock," Styles said, with a half-grin. "That's what we always said."

"But—*why*, Holmes?" I could not make sense of it. "Surely Wiggins could not be..."

"No, no." Holmes looked grim. "Wiggins and Hornby were both innocents in the matter, unwitting dupes of the Hierarchy. I overlooked the most obvious clue of all—the link between Hornby, Wiggins, and Styles here is *their prior association with me*. For it was Styles that recruited them both. Isn't that so, Styles? What did you tell them when you ordered them to take the warehouse job? That it was a secret mission for Mr. Holmes? Like old times?"

"Aye." Styles was openly amused now. "'Twasn't difficult. Both the lads have fond memories of the old days; it was easy to get them on board. Getting the old gang back together."

"But something went wrong, obviously."

Styles scowled. "I almost had them, but then Hornby twigged to what we was trying to do at the glass-works. He was already getting bothered because I had kept them away from Baker Street, see. My story was that we couldn't be seen talking to you, but Hornby wasn't having it. Said Mister Sherlock would never have asked us to do such a thing as we was rigging, getting ready to go down there under the dock. He swung on me and I had to put him down, and Mark saw me do it as he was coming round the corner. I'd have done for him too but then we heard the whistles, I knew the coppers were coming, so while Mark was bending over Jim trying to see if he was alive I jumped back in the boat and told him I would slit Fanny's throat if he let out so much as a peep. He knew I meant it, too. Wasn't no chore to stay close to Fan, we've known each other since we was kids." He snorted. "Fouled things a bit when she insisted on coming to you, but there was no way out of it."

"Your masters were quick to recover," Holmes said. "Their original goal was just the submarine, but my involvement must have changed matters."

Styles looked pleased. "We knew about your secret lodgings throughout London," he said. "The Hierarchy's been anxious to see what-all you've got on them. It was me what told them about the other two. I'd been through the one at Whitehall, and what I found there impressed my bosses enough that they asked for more. So that was me new job, tracking them down."

"Of course. The Hierarchy does not tolerate failure—you had to give them something when your attempt on the glass-works ended in failure. *Quid pro quo.*" Holmes nodded. "I saw yesterday that my Whitehall apartments had been burgled. It confirmed my suspicions regarding your involvement, since only you and Wiggins knew of those rooms apart from myself, and Wiggins was incarcerated. I then retreated to this little bolt-hole as a base of operations, since I was certain no one knew of this one, not even Watson." He glanced at me with a somewhat apologetic expression. "It seemed safest, old fellow. I confess to some surprise that you found me here, despite my precautions."

"Ah, you underestimated your old pal, Mister Sherlock," Styles said, laughing. "He might not be a deductive genius but the doctor's a bright enough fellow, and so loyal! I knew with the right prodding he'd lead me

straight to you and your hidden lair. Fed him a story about kidnapers and
cut my cheek, that's all it took and he was off like a hound. Even tonight,
after he messed me up with my man Clyde before I could talk to him, he
sussed out which one of these buildings was yours, all on his own."

My face grew hot with shame and anger to hear how I had been used.
"But what's it all about, Styles?" I demanded. "For God's sake, Holmes
was good to you, to all of the boys. And Wiggins and Hornby were your
friends! How could you..."

"Good to us!" Styles spat. "Table scraps! Biscuits from the housekeeper! Leftover mutton and a shilling if we did well! That was life in the
Irregulars, Doctor! Maybe you forgot but we was still on the streets while
you and Mister Sherlock were living high and mighty! Someone comes
along with an offer for real money; of course I'm taking it! The wonder is
that Wiggins and Hornby wouldn't—the more fools they. Well, they've
reaped what they sowed, haven't they, and here I sit. You all are done for,
it's me what holds the whip hand now. You'll be joining old Jim as food for
the worms soon enough." His smile was a reptilian thing, an expression of
gloating triumph. "And we haven't forgotten the submarine, either. By the
time we're done here tonight that'll be history as well."

I could feel tension rising in the little room. Styles was enjoying his
victory but I knew that he was growing impatient with Holmes' delaying
tactics, and I was conscious of Holmes steeling himself for some sort of
desperate effort. I braced myself, determined to aid however I might—it
had stung, hearing Styles explain how I had aided him in his betrayal, and
I swore I would even the account somehow.

Then Holmes exploded into motion. He shoved me to one side and I
saw his hand flash forward, hurling something at Styles. The gun went off
even as Holmes and I went to the floor in a heap. Holmes was back on his
feet immediately, clutching his shoulder with a grimace. He flung himself
towards Styles.

Styles lay on the floor, choking. I saw a star-shaped blade lodged in his
neck.

"*Shuriken*," Holmes said with a thin smile. "He took my *nunchaku*
sticks earlier when he broke into the Whitehall rooms—I think that must
have been what he used to kill Hornby—but he left me my throwing-stars.
Damn it," he added. "I was trying for his gun arm." He scooped up my revolver from where it had fallen and knelt by the fallen youth. "Styles!" he
snapped. "It cannot matter now, you have seconds at most. What did your
men do tonight at the glass-works? What was your plan?" He turned and

glared helplessly at me. "Watson! You must…"

I shook my head. "The artery, Holmes," I said, and pointed at the pool of blood surrounding Styles' body. "He is beyond my aid, or that of any physician. With the vessel severed so close to the brain, he was already gone before he hit the floor. But what could he…"

"Sabotage, Watson!" Holmes stood, wincing, and I became aware that there was a red stain spreading from his shoulder where he gripped it. "No, never mind me, there's no time," he said as I moved forward to examine the bullet wound. "Styles said it was planned for tonight…I should have realized that the Hierarchy would not have abandoned their scheme against the Bruce-Partington vessel. Styles' failure would not have been allowed to stand. The intent was never theft, but sabotage. They must have planted a bomb. For all we know the damage has already been done! We must go!"

There was no arguing with him, though he did consent to let me tear some strips from the lining of my disreputable jacket to bind his wounded arm as we emerged on to the street. "No cab at this hour," Holmes sighed. "We must run for it. It's not far." He took off and I had no choice but to follow as best I could.

Holmes knew the streets of London better than any man alive. I trusted his choice of route absolutely, though I could never have duplicated the twists and turns he took as we sprinted down along the Thames. We cut through loading-yards, squeezed through fences, and leap-frogged over stacked crates along the wharf. In twenty minutes we were in front of the glass-works building. Holmes skidded to a halt and I could see his face was white and drawn. "I am nearly done up," he panted. "This bullet wound has cost me. It will have to be you, old friend."

"Of course!" I was nettled that he could think otherwise. "Just tell me what to do."

"The riverside entrance," he said. "Under the dock where they load the boats. Mycroft's men watch from the roof, the only approach is below. If these villains made another attempt, and they must have, then any bomb will be there. Can your leg manage the climb?"

"Never mind my leg," I growled, and moved around the building to the wharf facing the Thames. There was a wooden ladderway on one side of the dock, slick with dew and algae. I descended a few steps and peered under the boards. I could see a silhouetted package tied to a piling. I swung awkwardly out from the ladder and clung to a support beam to get a closer look. My stomach lurched when I saw bundled sticks of dynamite, and even over the slosh of the Thames below me, I could discern the sound of clockwork ticking.

Dare I tamper with it? To do nothing would guarantee an explosion. I resolved to take the chance. If I could simply remove the hellish thing without disturbing the triggering mechanism.

Carefully, I reached out and felt around the deadly parcel. It appeared merely to be tied to the piling with a twist of rope. My hand fumbled with the knots, which were hard and slippery with river-water. I wished I had thought to carry a pocket-knife as my fingers tore at the knotted hemp. Then, miraculously, one of the knots loosened and I tugged at a loop with my finger, and the parcel slipped free. For a sickening moment I felt it falling and then the bundle was in my hand. Without letting myself think about the insane chance I was taking, I heaved myself back over to the ladder one-handed and, once I was clear of the dock supports, flung the bundle out into the middle of the Thames.

It exploded on impact. I do not know if it was because of my clumsy handling or if the timer had merely reached its prearranged hour. The concussion was deafening and for a moment it was bright as noonday.

It took me a moment, hanging limp with reaction, before I heard Holmes calling my name. "Watson! *Watson!*"

"I am here, Holmes," I managed. Several hands reached for me and it was a blessed relief to accept their help as I was hoisted back to the dock.

✳ ✳ ✳

Several days later, Wiggins and his bride were sitting with Holmes and myself in Baker Street. Mrs. Hudson had made much of the couple, insisting on providing a luncheon that was extravagant even for our housekeeper's hearty standard. "No, really, I couldn't eat another bite," Wiggins protested as she offered dessert.

"You must be starving after your prison ordeal," Fanny said. "Eat up."

"The only ordeal was my fear for you," Wiggins said softly. "That snake Styles—I dared say nothing. My only desperate hope was that Dr. Watson would recognize the name of Daggett."

I shook my head ruefully. "Alas, lad, Holmes rarely takes me into his confidence at the beginning of a case. I did not even know of his secret rooms until recently. As it was, we were fortunate that Styles did not realize Holmes had already been to see you in his Daggett disguise. He might have taken action then. As it was, he only had heard of a bewhiskered man making inquiries along the waterfront. Had he made the connection with the name Holmes was using he might well have made good on his threats against Fanny."

"On the contrary, I think he would not have hurt Mrs. Wiggins, despite his threats." This was Holmes. He reached for his clay pipe and tapped a pinch of tobacco into the bowl. At our expressions of surprise, he chuckled and added, "Oh, Davy Styles was more than capable of any number of heinous crimes, make no mistake. But you must consider his motives. He knew he was taking a risk by involving his boyhood friends in his criminal endeavor, even if only as his unwitting dupes. Why do it? Why take the chance? Because he had designs on you, Mrs. Wiggins. I could see a tenderness in his expression when he spoke to you here that was evident nowhere else. Clearly he considered himself in a place to supplant your husband once Wiggins had been disposed of."

Wiggins scowled. "I knew he had a soft eye for Fan, but... God! I feel such a fool. How could I have not seen it? How did I fall for the lies he told at all?"

I flushed a little. "I too was his dupe, lad," I said. "He deceived us all. Except Holmes."

"Oh, I was deceived briefly as well," Holmes said, smiling. "Certainly I noticed that Styles was overly solicitous of your bride, Wiggins, but that was all. It did not strike me as sinister. There are many husbands whose wives are the envy of their friends. But it did suggest a motive once I realized that Styles was the one who had informed on us to the Hierarchy."

"Poor Davy." Fanny Wiggins shook her head, and I thought I detected moistness in her eyes. "I cannot conceive how he could have turned so sharply from the good boy he was—when we were all kids together. How a heart so black could stay hidden...I thought I knew him."

She looked so bleak that I felt we should speak no further of it. In an effort to change the subject to something more cheerful, I said, "What are your plans now, then?"

Wiggins brightened. "America! Mr. Mycroft's arranged for us to go on a steamer to New York the day after tomorrow. He assures me there's a job for me there," he added.

I raised an eyebrow. "Not too dangerous, I hope." I knew the sort of employment that Mycroft usually offered to the young men he sent abroad.

Wiggins patted Fanny's hand. "Just dangerous enough, perhaps," he said. "After all, I was trained by the best. I think I shall be glad to put that training to use again."

"It is as well you are leaving the country," Holmes said. "The irony is that I had no particular designs on the Hierarchy after we disposed of Colonel Moran. Styles sold them a phantom in an effort to excuse his first failed attempt at planting the bomb; my files were not terribly extensive and mostly concerned Moran's activities of a year ago. But the situation has changed, for clearly now they have declared open hostilities." He stood and strode to scowl out the window, his brow as clouded as the fog that swirled in the street below. "We have won this battle, but I fear that the war has just begun."

"Then let them come," I said. "We shall be ready."

Wiggins looked at me, and nodded. The resolve was as apparent in his face as it must have been in my own, for after a moment even Fanny nodded as well.

"So say we all," she said, and took her husband's hand.

The End

Afterword: Sherlockian Specialties

Those of us who attempt to follow Arthur Conan Doyle in telling tales of the Great Detective usually end up staking out a particular area of the Holmesian canon. Carole Nelson Douglas writes about *the* woman, Irene Adler; John Gardner and Kim Newman both chronicle the criminal career of Professor Moriarty; Laurie King writes about a married Holmes in the post-World War I years.

Me, I like telling stories of the time right after the Return, roughly 1895. That gives you all the Moriarty history to play with, and a Holmes that's at his peak, but he's been through some seriously rough stuff. And of course Watson's suffered the loss of his wife. They're both still game, still fighting the good fight, but a little weathered. It gives them depth.

The other thing I seem to gravitate towards doing is "postscript" stories—sequel adventures that bounce off a Doyle original in some way. My first one in *Consulting Detective* volume six was following up "The Adventure of the Empty House," and the one in volume seven was a direct sequel to "A Case of Identity." This one, obviously, is a follow-up to "The Bruce-Partington Plans," in which Doyle filled in more about what Mycroft Holmes actually was doing for the British government and made it clear that if Mycroft wasn't actually running the Secret Service, he was pretty high up in that organization.

I also like checking in with characters we haven't seen in a while. Arthur Conan Doyle had a habit of creating great ideas and then just walking away from them. Two of these concepts are the Diogenes Club and the Baker Street Irregulars, and it was a pleasure to revisit these institutions and put a bit of my own spin on them. And it occurred to me that since I needed a doctor character other than Watson then I should try to make use of one from the original Holmes canon, so I drafted Percy Trevelyan from "The Resident Patient."

Other notes—there's an adage in writing that you should reward readers for knowing things, but don't punish them for *not* knowing things. In that spirit I try not to go overboard with in-jokes and Easter Eggs in these stories, they are designed to be self-contained; but readers who are familiar with Philip Jose Farmer's Wold Newton Universe will doubtless recognize the Hierarchy. The full name of this sinister organization is the Technological Hierarchy for the Removal of Undesirables and the Subjugation of Humanity... or THRUSH, as the United Network Command for Law and Enforcement usually refers to it. It was UNCLE writer David McDaniel who first suggested in his novel *The Dagger Affair* back in 1967 that the Hierarchy was formed from the remnants of the Moriarty criminal empire, and there have been several of us who've run with that idea since then. So I always like to acknowledge Mr. McDaniel's ingenuity in creating the initial hypothesis when the subject comes up. Likewise, though Doyle could not have explicitly stated this was the case, it is my feeling that the battle between Sherlock Holmes and the Hierarchy was a sort of ongoing Cold War that was a background to his entire later career, with occasional skirmishes occurring from the time of "The Adventure of the Empty House" until it climaxed with Holmes' capture of the German spy Von Bork in "His Last Bow." Holmes scholars will recall that this last case involved Holmes spending a year or so in America under the cover identity of Altamont, and doubtless he had the assistance of Wiggins and other operatives in Mycroft's employ during that time. As far as I'm concerned Von Bork's spy network was THRUSH, no question.

Likewise, though I would never say so explicitly in a story, I completely subscribe to Holmes biographer William Baring-Gould's theory that Rex Stout's Nero Wolfe is a direct descendant of Sherlock Holmes, and therefore any resemblance between Wolfe and my version of Mycroft Holmes may be taken as wholly intentional. If there had been a branch of the Diogenes Club in New York during the fifties, I am convinced that Wolfe would have abandoned his orchids and taken up permanent residence there. I also toyed with the idea that, once in America, Wiggins and his wife took the name Goodwin in an effort to conceal themselves from agents of the Hierarchy. I talked myself out of putting it in the story, but in my head, that's what happened: it's just too perfect that the genius detective Nero Wolfe is descended from genius detective Sherlock Holmes, and Wolfe's exuberant young aide Archie Goodwin is descended from exuberant young Wiggins.

As for the story itself, apart from the notion of seeing what eventually happened to Wiggins and the "ragged band of street Arabs" we call the Irregulars, I wanted to play with the idea of Dr. Watson struggling to handle a case *without* Holmes. What would happen if Watson was forced on his own to solve a case? It's a tough line to walk, because in my head Watson's not the bumbling comedy relief he is often depicted to be on film—he's smart and tough, a man of action. But convention requires that Holmes still has to be the one to solve the mystery, so the challenge is to make Watson mistaken without showing him as just being stupid. My usual answer for this is that Watson is too honest and forthright a fellow to be good at subterfuge, which is how villains get the better of him.

That's mostly what I was thinking of when I wrote this one. I am grateful to other Holmesian scholars in addition to Mr. Baring-Gould—in particular, Michael Harrison's *In the Footsteps of Sherlock Holmes* and Jack Tracy's *Encyclopedia Sherlockiana* were invaluable, as well as Charles Viney's *The Authentic World of Sherlock Holmes*. And as always, I appreciate the input from the usual crew of beta readers: Sena Meilleur, Anne Hawley, Tiffany Tomcal, Ed Bosnar, Lorinda Adams, Brekke Ferguson, John Trumbull, and Jessica Stephens.

Finally, I could not do any of this without the support of my wife Julie, who listens to my rants about plot and character and the proper structure of mystery fiction without complaint and even claims to find them endearing. Fellas, when you find a lady who not only tolerates your eccentric hobby but insists that it's cute and fun, trust me, you *marry* her.

❋ ❋ ❋

GREG HATCHER - is a writer and schoolteacher from Burien, Washington. He has been published in various places since 1992 and is a three-time winner of the Higher Goals Award for Children's Writing. Currently he writes a weekly column on comics and pop culture for Comic Book Resources.com, as one of the rotating features on the Comics Should Be Good! blog. Pulp and adventure fiction remains his first love, though, and writing stories for Airship 27's various anthologies is one of his favorite gigs. In addition to writing, he also teaches the Cartooning and Young Authors classes as part of an after-school arts program for grades 7 through 12. He lives in an apartment just south of downtown with his wife Julie, their cat Maggie, and ten thousand books and comics... including at least eighty that feature Sherlock Holmes in some fashion.

Sherlock Holmes

in

"The Problem of the Theatrical Thefts"

By
Aaron Smith

nspector Lestrade was red in the face, disheveled in dress, and appeared exhausted as he paced back and forth across the Baker Street flat I shared with Sherlock Holmes. He had just burst in unexpectedly after rudely rushing up the stairs past the startled Mrs. Hudson, and, upon entering the room, shouted, "Holmes! Show your face, Holmes, for we don't know where else to turn!"

"Holmes is not here," I said as I emerged from the bedroom. It was still early in the day and I had rather lazily slept until half past eight, having only now risen and dressed. Lestrade, on the other hand, had been up all night, and was in such a state that I did not need Holmes' skills to tell me so.

"Well, where is he?" the inspector demanded.

"Investigating something, I suppose," I said. "I do not actively participate in all Holmes' cases, and he often does not tell me the details until the matter is concluded."

"When do you expect him back?"

"Inspector Lestrade, will you please calm yourself and tell me why you have come here? I do not know when Holmes will return, but I am genuinely curious if I can be of assistance."

"This is making us look like bloody idiots!" Lestrade shouted. "As if all of us at Scotland Yard are amateurs or buffoons!"

The door burst open for the second time in several minutes. This time, it was Sherlock Holmes who entered. He was dressed in a black suit and his face was the ghastly, sickening yellow-white pallor of death.

"You look terrible, Holmes!" Lestrade spat, temporarily forgetting whatever had him in such a state.

"All an illusion, I assure you, Inspector," Holmes said. He wiped the back of his hand across his cheek and held it up to show the makeup that had been transferred in the motion. "I spent most of last night as a dead man, waiting and listening until a rather unscrupulous undertaker decided I would be the next corpse to be sliced open and filled with stolen goods to be smuggled into Belgium in a container no customs official would dare open. That man is now in the custody of the constabulary and

I am free to cleanse my flesh of this foul greasepaint."

"You've had more success than I, Holmes," Lestrade said as he finally dropped the leather case he had brought with him and sat down.

"That much is apparent," Holmes observed, "from your haggard state, and the fact that your tiredness is not due to any makeup, but to pure exhaustion. Watson, pour this man a drink and we will listen to what worries him so."

"Holmes," I said, "you have been awake for many hours. Perhaps you should …"

"Rest, Watson? I think not! A case has been satisfactorily concluded and now it seems the good inspector here has brought me something new to think about. I feel perhaps as joyful as a child on Christmas."

Lestrade took a swallow of the brandy I had served him and, breathing normally for the first time since his frantic entrance, began to relate his reason for visiting us that morning.

"Burglaries!" the inspector shouted. "Surely you've noticed the reports in the papers! Four wealthy families robbed over the past year by some scoundrel who's entered their homes, made off with jewels and other valuables, and left not a clue."

"Then there has been another, I gather," Holmes said. "Yes, I have followed the story and recall there being three victimized households."

"The latest was this past night," Lestrade explained. "A Mr. and Mrs. Greythorne returned to their residence after an evening at the theatre to find the rear entrance to their home left open and several belongings, including the wife's jewels, missing. Police were summoned immediately but little evidence was found. Mr. Greythorne swears he locked all the doors before leaving. He also states that no person other than he, his wife, or their son, who is stationed in Africa, possesses a key to the house. They have no resident servants, and the cook, cleaning lady, and driver are only admitted when one of the spouses is home.

"My superiors at the Yard have begun to resort to threats of demotion now that the other inspectors and I have failed to make much progress concerning this rash of robberies."

"You believe," Holmes asked, "that all four intrusions and thefts were perpetrated by the same criminal?"

"It would seem so," Lestrade answered. "All the locks seem to have been expertly picked, for no damage was done to the doors and no windows were broken. And all the robbed homes are in the same general area, all in Westminster."

"Was any evidence found at the other three sites?" Holmes asked.

"Only the fact," Lestrade said, "that property was missing."

"The other victims: who were they?"

"A solicitor called George Salmon and his wife; a highly-decorated old soldier named Colonel Clemens, who is a widower; and Sir Roger Monroe, some sort of government clerk who is married and has three children."

"Houses or flats?"

"All have houses, with Salmon possessing the largest."

"Servants quartered within?"

"Colonel Clemens has a manservant who accompanies him everywhere; the Monroes have a governess, but she was with them at the time of the burglary, for the children had gone to the theatre with the parents; and the Salmons do not employ servants, for Mr. Salmon has some eccentric ideas which are against hiring household help."

"Lestrade, you just said that the Monroe family had gone to the theatre that evening, just as the Greythornes had done last night. What of Clemens and Salmon? Where were they while their homes were entered and emptied of certain valuables?"

"They also were at the theatre."

"I do not recall the full details of what newspaper accounts of these burglaries I have read," Holmes admitted. "How much time has passed between each incident and the next?"

"At least two months each time," Lestrade said.

"Did each of the robbery victims attend the same theatre on the nights in question?"

"No, it was the Savoy Theatre for the Monroes and their children, and the Lyceum on the other three occasions."

"I see," said Sherlock Holmes. "Have you any other information you believe pertinent to this matter, Inspector?"

"I've brought you all my notes, Holmes," Lestrade said, leaning forward to open the case that sat between his feet. He pulled out a thick sheaf of papers, handed them to Holmes. "Read these, or burn them, or do whatever you like with them, Holmes, for I've wasted too many hours sifting through them and finding not a clue! All I want is to wash my hands of this case and move on to the next."

"Allow me time to peruse these notes," Holmes said. "As for you, Inspector, I suggest your next journey be to your bed. An exhausted policeman is of no use at all. Refresh your mind and body and perhaps soon you will be able to look upon this case with eyes that see what they did not detect before."

"Thank you, Holmes," Lestrade said, and left.

"And what of some sleep for you, Holmes," I said. "Your statement of a moment ago applies to consulting detectives as well."

"I rested well enough in my casket, Watson," Holmes insisted. "I am sure you have real patients to attend to. You will find it a pleasant morning for house calls. I have reading to do."

When I returned to Baker Street many hours later, I had to step over a wasteland of scattered papers. It looked as though Holmes had tossed the entire bundle into the air in frustration, something he was wont to do when irritated by a case. As for Holmes, he had fallen asleep in his chair with his chin resting on his chest. A bit of smoke still sailed skyward from the pipe that sat in the ashtray on the table beside the chair, leading me to believe the detective had succumbed to tiredness only moments before my arrival.

"Useless rubbish," Holmes muttered as he opened his eyes. "All that is of use in that pile of paper is the first page, which summarizes what little Lestrade and his cronies have learned of the burglaries. I have discovered nothing! Had the inspector told me only the dates of the crimes, he would have done as much service to the investigation as all these scribbled sheets have done."

"Then we are at a dead end?" I asked.

"A temporary blockade," Holmes assured me, "which we will burst through, Watson, with force if need be."

With that, Holmes busied himself refilling and lighting his pipe.

"What can I do to help?" I offered.

"Is it late in the day?" Holmes asked. "Run to the library and find the newspapers from the days after the nights of the robberies, Watson, if you would be so kind."

"I would be happy to," I said, and hurriedly donned my coat again as I rushed from the flat.

Holmes took the stack of newspapers from me when I returned to Baker Street for the second time that day. He divided them into two piles of equal height, handed one bunch to me, and began paging through his portion. I sat and began my own reading.

It was my habit to take notes when combing through papers for information, a method Holmes did not need, as his memory was like a sponge and capable of soaking up vast quantities of data with ease. On this occasion, however, I found little to write down, as the newspaper articles gave accounts of which residences had been burglarized and at what times, but little else that Lestrade had not related to us during his visit.

"It is all the same information," I complained after a while. "The Monroe family attended Gilbert and Sullivan's *Princess Ida* at the Savoy Theatre and had their home robbed. Colonel Clemens went to *King Lear* at the Lyceum and his residence was broken into while he attended the play. And, I should guess, your papers say the same of the other victims."

"Indeed," said Holmes. "Mr. and Mrs. Salmon at a performance of *Macbeth*, and the Greythornes at *Henry VIII*."

"Then what is our next avenue of investigation?" I asked. I glanced toward the window, saw that night had fallen. "It is perhaps too late now, but I suppose we should go and interview some of the victims tomorrow."

"Perhaps," Holmes said. "For the moment, we continue our reading."

"I have already gone through three different articles on each of two burglaries in my stack," I protested. "There is no more to read."

"Watson, the plays the victims attended will be written about in other sections of the papers, will they not?"

"Well, yes. I am certain some mention of such prominent families will be made in the society columns, and there are sure to be critics' reviews of the performances."

"Then carry on, Watson," Holmes said, and dropped his gaze back to the pages.

An hour passed. Holmes was correct in his guess that those who had been robbed were mentioned as having attended the plays, at least in some of the articles, though I failed to see how that might impact our investigation in any way. I then turned my attention to the critical articles concerning the productions. I found nothing of promise in that task either and was about to announce to Holmes that I wished to retire for the evening, but I first casually commented, "I am rather enjoying the articles of this critic called Vincent Savage. His opinions are laced with a smart sarcasm. Although I'm sure the actors and directors do not find the tendency as amusing as I do."

"Honesty, however brutal, is, I suppose, essential in a man of his profession," Holmes replied. "I was just having a look at one of his reviews myself, wherein he expresses his dislike of the actress portraying Lady Macbeth."

"Yes," I added, "he had some rather biting comments about the performers in Lear and Ida as well."

"You are more versed in the arts than I, Watson," Holmes said. "Is it common for a critic to write on such very different sorts of plays as Shakespeare and comic operas?"

"Well, from what I gather," I replied, "Vincent Savage is the official critic of the Times."

"Let me see those papers, Watson," said Holmes, and he stood long enough to take them from my hand.

He returned to his chair and ferociously searched the pages, reading rapidly, and then commanded, with a voice that was almost a shout, "See what my index has to say on this Savage, if you would!"

Holmes had long been in the habit of keeping notes on interesting people of all categories, from the richest men in the world to the lowliest of common criminals, and his files included, of course, all manner of celebrities. Holmes found this method easier than memorizing the details of the lives of those whose existence might never have bearing on his cases.

I stood and found the volumes for the letter S, and in one of them located a small biography of the man in question, from which I read aloud.

"Vincent Alexander Savage, born in Liverpool, 1850. Theatre critic for the Times of London. Previous occupations include schoolteacher, magician's assistant, and actor. Resides in London."

"Ha!" Holmes let out a single laugh, clapped his hands together loudly once, and flung a handful of newspaper ceiling-ward to flutter back to the floor like the feathers of a bird that has just been shot from the sky.

"What, Holmes?" I asked, failing to see what had him suddenly so excited, for his mind worked in ways I could not always easily follow, and connected one fact with another with such blinding speed that a man of average intellect would often be left far behind him in the race for the resolution of a mystery.

"Three vital pieces of information, Watson," the detective explained in the fast manner of speaking he used when trying to clarify his logic. "First, the victims of the burglaries were well known enough in society to be recognized upon arrival at the theatres. Second, Vincent Savage once worked as the assistant to a magician. Part of a stage magician's set of skills—and this certainly might be learned by the magician's aides as well—is the abil-

"Ha!"

ity to pick locks. If you recall from the police reports, the locks of the burgled homes were not forced or damaged, but expertly made to yield to the thief. And, third, you may not have noticed that Vincent Savage, in his remarks on each of the four plays, displays what I perceive as an oddity. Concerning *Princess Ida*, his commentary focuses on the first and third acts while almost completely ignoring the second. And, when writing about the Shakespearean productions, he concentrates on the opening scenes and the conclusions, but pays little attention to the middle portions of the plays, each of which is five acts long."

"Holmes," I said, shocked at my friend's leap to such suspicions, "are you suggesting that Savage recognizes the theatregoers and knows where they live, leaves the theatre for the middle section of each play, uses his skills to enter the empty homes and steal their belongings, and returns to view the end of the show?"

"That, Watson, is precisely what I am suggesting! What better alibi could our thief have than to be seen at the play and have his opinions of it published in the following day's newspaper?"

"But," I protested, "as Vincent Savage is a critic of some fame, would his departure for a portion of the performance not be noticed?"

"There are possibilities," Holmes assured me. "It is late. In the morning, we will speak with Lestrade and find a way to confirm what I suspect."

✲✲✲

Inspector Lestrade had his doubts about Holmes' theory, but agreed to accompany us to the offices of the Times of London. The presence of the police, we had found in the past, could help to convince others of the importance of cooperating in our investigations.

Holmes, Lestrade, and I sat sipping tea with the editor-in-chief of the city's most prominent newspaper. We informed him of our suspicions and swore him to secrecy on the matter.

"Outrageous accusations!" he argued. "Vincent Savage has long been a valuable member of our staff! If I give you the information you have come here to request, I put my paper at risk of a major embarrassment."

"And if you don't," Lestrade countered, "I'll just have one of my men follow Savage wherever he goes. Why not spare Scotland Yard the trouble? All I want to know is where and when Savage's next assignment will take place."

The editor sighed and began to search through some papers on his desk.

"Here it is," he said after several moments. "There is a new production of *Dr. Jekyll and Mr. Hyde*, a play by Thomas Russell Sullivan, based on the rather grotesque novel by Stevenson, which is to open tomorrow night at the Adelphi Theatre. It originally ran with Richard Mansfield in the title role, but this new version features relatively unknown actors and so is considered a risky endeavor. I expect Savage will tear it to shreds, though I must admit his negative reviews seem to be much more thoroughly enjoyed by our readers."

"Where does Savage live?" Holmes asked, interrupting the editor.

"A flat in the middle of the theatre district," the editor answered. "Quite the convenient location."

"Yes, in several ways," Holmes said.

"Write the address for us," Lestrade requested.

"If I must," the editor mumbled, scratching a name and number with a pencil and handing the note to the inspector.

"Thank you for the information, sir," Lestrade said. He stood and walked out of the office, with Holmes and I following close behind.

The next evening, Holmes, Lestrade, and I stood in the balcony of the Adelphi with the theatre's manager. We looked down as the audience entered and found their seats. It looked to be nearly a full house.

"I'll admit to a case of nerves, gentlemen," said the manager. "Knowing that Savage, aptly named as he is, will be here tonight makes me perspire. A few sentences from that man can fill the seats or have people avoiding a show like it's the plague. I expect he'll be here any moment now. He always seems to choose a seat right in the middle rows, not too close to or too far from the stage."

"Better to blend in with the crowd," Holmes muttered, "and hide his true work in plain sight."

"Ah," the manager said, "there he is now. The man in the bowler hat and long brown coat."

From his pocket, Sherlock Holmes produced a small pair of opera glasses, through which he looked down at the man our ally had just specified.

Holmes passed the glasses to Lestrade and then to me. I peered through the lenses and studied the features of Vincent Savage. He was tall and solidly built, with a full head of brown hair revealed as he removed his hat.

His face bore a thick beard, and he wore spectacles with round rims of a golden-colored metal. He scurried through the gathering crowd, shaking hands with several men, clapping one on the back as if they were old friends, and kissed the hand of a lovely young lady. Savage was obviously a true celebrity of the theatre world.

As I watched, it occurred to me that if our suspicions were true, the fact that this man, with his strange double life, now attended a production of the Jekyll and Hyde story was poetically appropriate. I turned to remark upon this to Sherlock Holmes, only to find that he had vanished from the balcony.

"Where has Holmes—" I began to ask, but I saw his lean figure bounding down the steps from the balcony to enter the main section of the theatre floor. He hurried by Savage, raising his hand as he passed. Looking through the glasses again, I saw what Holmes had done. A thin line of white now marked the back of Savage's coat, right at the point where the collar folds down. Chalk!

Savage, unaware of Holmes' mark, finally took a seat in the center of one of the middle rows of the theatre, just as the manager had predicted. Holmes returned to the balcony and instructed Lestrade, "Inspector, it is time for you to go. If my theory is wrong, there will be nothing for you to do here. If I am correct, you know where you must be."

"Indeed," Lestrade agreed, "though I wish I could grab the scoundrel before he commits the act!"

"That would be a great risk," Holmes explained. "We might not have sufficient evidence at that point, and, also, Savage is not a stupid man and might easily notice if he is followed when he sneaks out of the theatre, assuming he does at all and I have not foolishly brought us here on a blunder."

"Well, I, for one, am beginning to think you're right about this business, Holmes," the inspector said.

"Time will soon tell, Lestrade," Holmes said. "Now go."

As soon as Lestrade had departed, the theatre went dark and the play began. Even in the much dimmer light, Holmes, through his opera glasses, kept watch on Savage, occasionally whispering a bit of information to me. "He is taking notes with a pencil." "He shakes his head often, as if he does not approve of the direction."

When the first act ended and an intermission began, Savage rose from his seat and excused himself as he brushed past those who remained in the row.

"Shall I follow him, Holmes?" I asked.

"Leave him, Watson. He will incriminate himself without any interference from us."

Perhaps five minutes had passed when Savage came back into view and took his seat again.

"There he is, Holmes," I said.

"No," responded Holmes, and handed the opera glasses to me.

I look down at the man in the brown coat. The back of his head looked the same, with its thick dark hair, and the beard could be seen each time the head turned slightly to the left or the right, but one detail prevented the picture from being identical to what we had seen before the intermission.

"The mark of chalk has gone from his coat," I whispered.

"Indeed it has, Watson," Holmes said as I gave the glasses back to him and noticed the satisfied expression on his face. "Before the final curtain of this play, the imposter below will grow quite agitated, I predict."

Holmes was correct. As the play progressed, the man in the brown coat began shifting in his seat, glancing back and forth as if waiting impatiently.

We took turns observing through the opera glasses. The man who was not Vincent Savage scribbled with his pencil, but the motions of his hand were different. At one point, he snapped his pencil in half and shoved the pieces into his pocket.

When the play reached its end, Holmes put the glasses away and said, "Come, Watson, let us fetch the accomplice before he flees!"

We caught him just outside the theatre. Holmes grabbed him by the coat, whirled him around, and shoved him against a wall.

The resemblance to Vincent Savage was remarkable, though not exact.

"Let go of me!" he shouted.

"Not tonight, friend," Holmes said. "Watson here is armed, so attempting to run would be unwise. You are clearly not the critic Savage. I suggest you tell us your true name before your trouble multiplies further."

"Jacob Grimes," he said, hanging his head.

"Why do you impersonate Vincent Savage?" Holmes asked.

"Because he pays me for it."

"For what reason?"

"So he can sneak off and see his mistress and still be seen at work watching plays so they don't get caught. And he always comes back for the end, until tonight. He never returned and I didn't know what to do, and I came outside and you grabbed me! He must have lost count of the time."

"Do you truly believe that is where he is, Grimes? You have no knowledge of the true reason Savage must leave for the middle portion of the plays he analyses?"

"Eh?"

"It seems not!"

"I don't know what you're talking about!"

"If you tell me the truth of how this arrangement came to begin, Grimes, perhaps I can see that you end up in far less trouble than your partner, Savage. Speak the truth!"

"I was down on my luck, out of work, had no place to stay," Grimes explained. "Then one day I'm walking about and this fellow comes up to me, says I look a lot like he does, and he's right; I do see the resemblance. And he offers me a job. Says he's been seein' this lady and her husband doesn't know for sure but maybe he's beginning to suspect. Now this fellow's got the perfect scheme to cover his reputation and he tells me he'll pay me quite well if I'll become him for an hour or so one evening every so often. And it sounds like easy money, so I agree. He makes me watch him walk and sit and all that, so I can imitate him, and he makes me grow this beard—damn thing itches something awful when the weather's warm—and wear clothes that match his and gets every detail to fit, right down to these spectacles, except the lenses don't do nothin' on mine, cause my sight is perfect and Vincent is nearsighted, you see. So I start doing him this favor and he pays me and I'm not on the street no more, and he gets to see his lady friend—or whatever it is he's been doin' when I'm in the theatre."

"I see," said Holmes.

At that moment, a constable rushed over, shouting, "Mr. Holmes, Dr. Watson!"

"Yes," I said to the young policeman.

"Inspector Lestrade wants the both of you at the home of Vincent Savage straight away."

"Constable," Holmes barked, "take this man into custody, but do not officially arrest him yet, for I believe he is as much a victim as those whose homes have been robbed, and merely a pawn in this charade."

✱✱✱

Holmes and I were admitted to the flat of Vincent Savage by the sergeant who now guarded the door. Inside, Savage sat in a chair while two constables stood behind him. The critic looked dejected. Lestrade, his face aglow with a grin, gestured at the large heap of jewels, silver, coins, and other valuables that lay on the carpeted floor.

"Sure enough," the inspector said, "he came sneaking home with a big sack of stolen goods, just as you predicted, Holmes. He was ready to drop it and scurry back to catch the end of the show, but I was here awaiting his arrival. I don't know yet whose home he entered and robbed tonight, but I expect to know as soon as the burglary is reported."

"Excellent work, Lestrade," Holmes said. He then turned to Savage. "Why? You had attained a position as a noted critic with a wide readership and steady work, so what would possess you to concoct a scheme wherein an imposter would take your place to allow you a narrow span of time in which to rob innocents of their prized possessions?"

Vincent Savage shot a sneer of contempt at Holmes. "I did it because I could. There need be no deeper reason. It was a thrill."

Sherlock Holmes waved his hand in a dismissive gesture and walked from the flat. I followed.

✳ ✳ ✳

To my surprise, a visitor awaited me, specifically, and not both of us, upon our return to our Baker Street flat. "A gentleman upstairs to see you, Dr. Watson," said Mrs. Hudson as we entered. While it was typical for clients to call on Holmes at any time of the day or night, I certainly expected no guest at such a late hour.

I entered our rooms to find the editor-in-chief of the Times pacing back and forth.

"I am relieved to see you, Doctor," he said. "I have a favor to ask, for which you will be compensated, of course."

"Are you having medical difficulties?"

"No, not at all. With Savage, blasted scoundrel that he's turned out to be, in the custody of Scotland Yard, tomorrow's edition is going to be missing its review of tonight's opening."

"Most unfortunate," I said.

"Yes, but perhaps you can help," said the editor. "You were, after all, in attendance at the Adelphi ... and you do have some experience with the written word, having chronicled the cases of Sherlock Holmes ..."

"Are you suggesting that I …"

"Yes, I most certainly am, Dr. Watson. I realize the deadline will be a tight one, but a short collection of your thoughts on the production will suffice. And I do not expect you to be as mean-spirited as Savage often was. Just be honest, Doctor, and you cannot go wrong. Will you help me?"

"I suppose I can try," I said, sighing at the realization that I would have little or no sleep that night.

Across the room, Sherlock Holmes laughed.

The End

Sleep Writing

The story you've just finished reading came to me in a dream, with a completeness that's never come out of one of my nighttime hallucinations before! My writing has been inspired by dreams before, but usually in small ways, where visions that come to me while asleep provide concepts, short scenes, or hints of stories I might someday tell. For example, it was a dream that inspired me to write the Allan Quatermain story that eventually made its way into an Airship 27 anthology, but all it told me was that I should look into borrowing that great character from his creator, H. Rider Haggard. It didn't tell me what the story was about, but left me to do all the work myself!

A few years before that, the entire first chapter of my very first novel, *Gods and Galaxies*, came to me in a dream, but I then had to figure out the rest of the story.

On another occasion, I woke with the phrase, "Real robots don't wear pants," in my mind and quickly scribbled it in the notebook I always keep beside the bed (which is something I suggest all writers do, as you never know when a dream will give you a gift). Years later, that phrase turned out to be the perfect title for a short story I was asked to write for an anthology. That story hasn't been released at the time I'm writing this essay, but it very well might be when this book sees print.

And I have many other notes jotted down in various files due to bits and scraps of dreams that may or may not make it into one of my stories eventually. But none of those dream inspirations compares to what happened with "The Problem of the Theatrical Thefts." I woke up one morning with the entire plot of the story in my head. I dreamt it all! I knew the nature of the crimes, who had committed them, and how Holmes figured out who the guilty man was!

It was so easy; it almost felt like I had cheated! But...that doesn't mean I didn't have to do any work at all! I still had to write the story, which means I had to choose the right words to tell the tale, had to make sure there were no inconsistencies in logic (because dreams are notorious for those!), had to come up with the characters' names (if they had names in the dream, they faded too quickly for me to recall), and had to do a bit of research regarding the names and locations of theatres and what plays might have been performed in London at the time of Holmes' adventures.

And, truthfully, I'm glad I did have to do some homework, because that's when I learned that a stage production of *Dr. Jekyll and Mr. Hyde* had been performed in London in the 1890s, and that play fit the theme perfectly, as Dr. Watson remarks in the story.

Overall, I have to say this was the easiest to write of all my Holmes stories, thanks to the fact that I literally wrote it in my sleep! That's a great way to get a head start!

❋ ❋ ❋

AARON SMITH - will never pass up a chance to visit the 221 B. Baker Street of his mind to write another Sherlock Holmes story. His previous Holmes mysteries have appeared in volumes 1, 3, 4, 5, 7, 8, and 9 of this series.

Smith's other works include the Moments After Midnight series of vampire novels (*100,000 Midnights* and *Across the Midnight Sea*), the Richard Monroe spy novels (*Nobody Dies for Free* and *Under the Radar*), the zombie horror novel *Chicago Fell First*, and short stories in multiple genres in many anthologies and magazines.

More information about Aaron Smith and his work can be found on his blog at www.godsandgalaxies.blogspot.com He invites readers to follow him on Twitter as @AaronSmith377

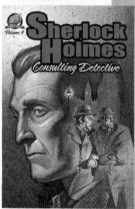

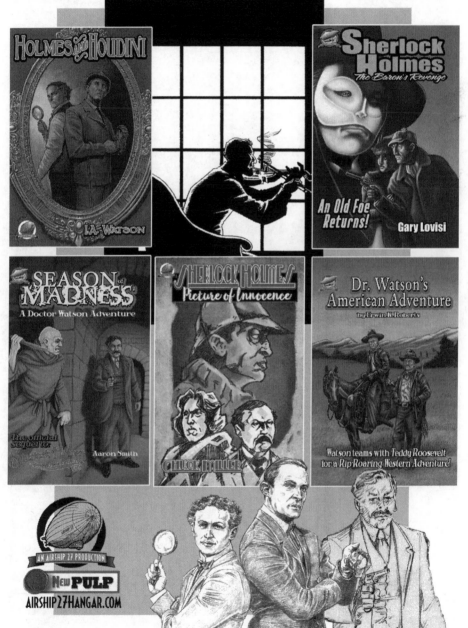

BIRTH OF A LEGEND

In 1190, two years after wresting the crown from his father, Henry II, Richard the Lionhearted departed France for the Holy Lands and the Third Crusade. He left behind regents, Hugh, Bishop of Durham and his chancellor, William de Longchamp. But his younger brother, Prince John, lusted after the crown and saw Richard's absence as a golden opportunity to seize control. John began a program of heavy taxation that threatened to destroy the social-economic stability of England.

While the royals conspired against each other, it was the people of the land who suffered. Working under inhumane laws, they became no more than indentured slaves to the landed gentry. Amidst this age of turmoil and pain, there arose a man with the courage to challenge the aristocracy and fight for the weak and helpless. He was an outlaw named Robin of Loxley and how he became the champion of the people is a timeworn legend that has entertained readers young and old.

Now I.A. Watson brings his own vivid imagination to the saga, setting it against the backdrop of history but maintaining the iconic elements that have endeared the tale of Robin Hood to readers throughout the ages. With beautiful covers by fan-favorite artist Mike Manley and interior illustrations by Rob Davis, this is a fresh and rousing retelling of an old legend, imbuing it with a modern sensibility readers will applaud.

Airship 27 Productions is extremely proud to present —

Robin Hood

KING OF SHERWOOD · ARROW OF JUSTICE · FREEDOM'S OUTLAW · FORBIDDEN LEGEND

PULP FICTION FOR A NEW GENERATION

AVAILABILITY INFORMATION AT: WWW.AIRSHIP27HANGAR.COM

Made in the USA
Middletown, DE
27 October 2017